DANGEROUS DREAMING

The Witch of Appalachia

Book II

FRANCESCA C. QUARTO

DANGEROUS DREAMING

By Francesca Quarto

© 2015 Dangerous Dreaming

Swartz Creek, MI 48473

Cover design by Clarissa Yeo

Tell-Tale Publishing Group, LLC
5714 Peri St
Swartz Creek, MI 48737

New Adult Paranormal

Dedication

For my Patrick, who lovingly put the "courage" back into "encourage" and helped me take the first step of the thousand on this Magical journey.

Chapter 1

The wind howled in the blackness of the woods surrounding my house. There was something scratching against the roof that sounded eerily like a long-clawed creature trying to tear its way through. I tried to suppress an irrational fear gnawing at my sleep deprived mind. I am a Wizard after all.

That fact didn't keep me from nearly jumping out of my flannel PJs when my cell phone sprang to life like an angry wasp. I shuffled through the mess on the bedside table until I uncovered its flashing yellow face.

"Hello," I answered, with a note of concern in my voice. It can't be good news when you get a call at three in the morning, and I wasn't looking forward to whatever the person who needed to wake me in the middle of the night had to say.

"Cathleen, it's me, Joanie."

"Joanie! What's wrong? Are you OK?"

"I am for now, but I need your help, sweetie. I couldn't call you sooner because it has to do with my Wicca sisters. You know how private they are. But things have gotten really scary. I need your help, Cathleen."

“Joanie? What's wrong? Why are you calling at this hour?”

Alert to the concern in my friend's voice, I slid my feet into the warmth of my faux sheep wool lined slippers, and struggled into my ratty but comfortable fleece robe.

On stepping over him, my dog Ollie gave me an accusatory look for thoughtlessly getting out of bed before he was ready. I left him to resume his nocturnal pursuits and padded my way downstairs.

With the push of a button, program-override soon coaxed the aroma of morning elixir to waft enticingly in the chill air.   While I struggled to wake up, Joanie continued her story.

"Cathleen, you know I'm not prone to jumping to conclusions. Something is wrong here, and I don't feel safe."

"Joanie, I'm putting you on speaker so I can clear my head with a cup of coffee, but go ahead, I'm listening. Just slow down a bit so I don't miss anything important." With that I poured a cup of coffee before the pot had a chance to fill and got the cream out of the frig.

"I got here from Pittsburg a few days ago with one of my coven sisters. She worked with me at Community East Hospital up until a year ago. Anyway, we arrived at the compound in Utah which is actually situated close to one of our holiest power sites."

I took a seat at the kitchen table. "That's the Valley of the Gods you told me about, right?" I said quickly, to curtail any off-track information overload.

"Yeah," she answered.   "Anyway, my friend--I'll use her Wiccan name, Jemma-- was pretty tired from our long trip, so she went directly to the room she'd been assigned by our coven leader, Wynn.   That's when I was told by Luna, another sister, of the three missing coven members." She finally took a breath after this torrent of words and continued in a subdued voice.

"Cathleen," Joanie said, with the all solemnity of a high priestess. "You understand that these are their *sacred* Wiccan names and normally I couldn't use them, but I feel it's important you know them before you come out here."

"Whoa!" I said loudly as I spilled coffee onto my only clean placemat. "What did you just say? Come out there?"

"Sweetie, we've been best friends, sisters really, for over half our lives. I know two things right now for certain; you're a mage with magic and I need you here to use it. There is something terrible happening to our coven members. Maybe even now, unless they're dead. They are disappearing, Cathleen, vanishing in the night. No matter what we do with our prayers and spells, they are disappearing without a trace."

I could hear the desperation in her voice. My sister-save began to nudge my resolve.

"Has anyone else disappeared since the first three, Joanie?"

"No, but there are only 9 of us left in the house and quite honestly, we're all pretty anxious."

"But you have your own Magic spells and chants, how can my brand of Magic be any more useful than yours?"

I heard her sigh and then, "Cathleen, ours isn't the kind of Magic that can ward off the Demons that you've dealt with. We are like the "pacifists" in a war; we want peace through natural means. Remember what I told you our credo was in essence? Harm none."

"Yeah, you've got that karma thing going. Tell it to me again." I took a gulp of Java.

"That's the Three Fold Law. Basically, whatever a person does, whatever energies they extend into the world will return to them threefold; three times over in this life or the next life."

"So I guess you Wicca girls can't harm whatever has begun to harm you. Pretty screwed up if you ask me," I said with some disgust in my voice, for what I saw as a weakness in their belief system.

"I'm not asking that you believe, Cathleen, just that you come out here and help us before any others of us are taken," Joanie said, a bit exasperated. I couldn't really say no to her request for help. No way was I going to let my dearest friend become the next victim in this mystery. Besides, I've always loved solving mysteries using my Magic. I had to act fast and I told her I'd need a day to get my ticket and board Ollie with the vet.

"Uh, I sorta already took care of that. Your ticket is waiting for you at the Pittsburgh Airport. And I hope you don't mind, but I've called your friend, Jason, too. He's coming by at one this afternoon to pick Ollie up to take him to your Vet's. He said he'd be happy to help out."

"Did you pack my suitcase while I was sleeping too?" My chuckle took the sting from my sarcasm. We really had been friends a long time.

"No, but pack jeans and T-shirts. Oh, and a jacket as it gets nippy here after dark."

"I wish you had called me right away, Joanie," I said, while I refilled my cup. "Tell me the sequence of events as best as you remember them."

"In hindsight I wish that too. The first girl disappeared three nights after the first of our group arrived. Luna told me they had all gone to their rooms for private meditation and figured Alana, just went on to bed since she never came back to the gathering area."

"When did they realize she was missing?"

"They weren't really alarmed until later the next evening, as many of us use this opportunity to meditate on our own in the natural setting of The Valley."

"So how soon before the second member went missing?" I asked before taking a sip of coffee. I heard the wind picking up and hunkered deeper into my robe.

"The next night," she answered. "They had just finished the last group sharing and discussing Alana's absence. Rain and Wynn went out for a *Celestial Bodies Reading.*"

"Didn't they stay together after what happened to Alana?" I asked, frowning into the phone.

"Wynn left Rain sitting on a small bench near the back door to the kitchen. She went inside to get their sweaters, hanging inside the door, so she was only gone a minute. When she got back, Rain was gone."

"And the third girl?" I asked, trying hard to make mental notes.

"That was Maud. She disappeared the night before Jemma and I arrived. They told me she said she was going to stay overnight in the Valley of the Gods and would return to the compound by breakfast the next day. They tried to dissuade her, but she said it was a perfect opportunity to commune so intimately with the forces of nature, and she wasn't afraid. That was two days ago."

"It's hard for me to believe that your coven leader, Wynn, didn't alert the authorities, Joanie. With three missing girls, what stopped her?"

"Cathleen," she replied after some hesitation "there are things going on here besides the missing girls. I suspect some kind of power struggle or something like that. We were thirteen in our coven until Ursa had a falling out with Wynn over the direction our coven should follow."

I was standing in front of my sink and looking out at a bleak February pre-dawn when I was hit with a deep chill that had nothing to do with the weather. I sensed what my friend would say next.

Joanie whispered her next words into the phone as if she was afraid they'd be heard by unseen ears. "Ursa was adamant that our Wiccan powers could be strengthened if we followed her lead, but then Wynn uncovered the truth behind her bragging. Ursa's been involved in the Dark Arts."

I could hear the concern and fear my friend was feeling in the stricken tone of her voice. "Don't worry, Joanie," I said, trying to reassure her. "When I get out there, we'll get to the bottom of this.

Meantime, have your group stay together as much as possible and do not go out at night unless you do the same. Whatever happened to those girls is going to happen again unless you stay together for protection. And by the way," I added, "where are you, exactly?"

"We're just outside The Valley of the Gods in a place inherited by Wynn years back, though she'd only been here a couple times until our coven started coming here a few years ago. It's extremely remote. I'll be picking you up at the airport, so don't worry about getting lost, sweetie."

I thought for a moment and then asked, "Joanie, what about the Tribal Police in the area? I know they have legal authority in any suspected criminal issues. Don't you think you should have made them aware of the missing girls?"

"We're not sure how to make contact with them and quite frankly, I don't know how helpful they'd be to a bunch of Goddess loving Wiccans," she said, with that practicality I'd come to expect from her.

"Hm. You might be right, but when I get out there, I'm going to check in with them myself so that they'll be aware of our presence."

"Oh, they know we're here, trust me. We've heard their dirt bikes and motorcycles during the day."

"What? No horses?" I asked.

"This is the 21st century, Cathleen. These aren't John Wayne's Indians."

She had a point. I stopped thinking about Indians in full-feathered head dress riding on the backs of Harleys long enough to ask, "By the way Joanie, before I get there I want you to try to figure out what all the girls in your coven have in common…you know, some kind of thread that ties your lives together."

Without hesitating, she answered, "That's easy. We're all nurses, Cathleen; we went to the same Nursing School and now work in hospitals and clinics around the Pittsburgh area."

"Hm," I responded.

Chapter 2

I was stuffing three pair of jeans and several non-descript T-shirts into my suitcase when the sound of Jason's SUV crunching the snow under its heavy tread broke into my thoughts. I'd already packed a carry-on with my laptop so I could do some research on the area I would be exploring around the Wicca compound. I hoped I could shoulder all I had crammed into this bag without causing myself permanent injury.

Jason Tate has been the Sheriff of Iron Mountain, my home in the Appalachian Mountains, for nearly six years. I've been his girlfriend for almost two of those years. This is an old coal mining town founded in the early 1800's. It once enjoyed a roaring economy reflected in some of the elegant old mansions and public brick buildings scattered around the area. My own house is one of these relics from a flamboyant past, when coal was called "King" and miners faced death in the dark every day of their shortened, hard scrabble lives.

Jason and I have found a kindred spirit in one another as well as the person we'd most trust in the entire world to have our back. We have found that our deepening friendship over the past three years has taken a turn of the heart and are in the negotiating process of a shared future. We've been through lots together and amazingly, he's totally accepting of the fact that I'm a trained Celtic Mage, a seasoned Wizard in the Irish tradition of Magic.

Of course this enlightenment came about after some lively adventures together as co-detectives on some pretty hairy cases. Jason is no slouch in the Magic department either. Though not a Wizard like me, he has a finely honed, near-Magical instinct about people. He can pick up on the most obscure ticks in a person's demeanor, or translate a quick glance, or shift in body language as if he was reading a form of police hieroglyphics. He always says he can "smell a lie a mile off." The scent of an untruth is not something I had been trained to recognize, so I also rely on Jason's finely tuned instincts for my own preservation.

When he was just a boy, Jason had "waking dreams," as he called them, where he could see future events like illness within his family. He was so terrified of this strange gift that he blocked any visions after he turned ten by the sheer strength of his will. In a way, relying solely on his perceptions of others, he has become the perfect lawman.

My Magic has always seemed a natural part of our relationship. He understands it's only used for protection, healing and putting down the occasional werewolf or fiend that unwisely crosses into our mortal realm from the Dark.

He told me once he saw me as a kind of guardian, or champion. I sounded like a female Terminator. It wasn't very romantic, but I enjoyed the compliment to my skills. In reality, my Magic has earned me a place as a sworn member of the *Guild of the Green Wizards* and the status of *Protector* in the service of the *Green Mother*.

Since I was now called away to perform some serious Magic, it was good that Jason was taking on the job of making sure Ollie was doing well at the Vet's during my absence. I tend to agonize over the mental state of my 15 year old dog-friend, though I suspect any separation anxiety would be experienced on my part alone.

As always, Jason took some of my breath away, while I used what was left to make some smart wisecrack to ease the urge to throw myself into his arms. "Jason! Are you here to tell me it'll be spring in two more months?" He was up to his one good eye and a black eye patch over the bad one in a scarf, his heavy brown wool Sheriff's coat buttoned up to his chin fending off the bitter winds of February in Appalachia. His boots were made for hard mountain terrain and snow that could cover an idling car in less than twenty minutes.

I think he said "Mornin' Cathleen," but with his muffler wrapped so snuggly, it could have been "Let me in, Cathleen." I opened the front door as wide as I thought safe to keep the swirling snow at bay.

As I took the scarf he'd unwound I said, "I really appreciate your help getting Ollie settled in at Doc Sawyer's, Jason." He was stamping around on my once decorative hall rug. The effects of three winters and hundreds of washings had decidedly turned it into mash up of murky grays.

Before he said anything else, he grabbed me into one of his wonderful hugs and kissed the top of my head, giving my curls a quick tussle. "I'm happy I could help you out, Cathleen. I'd keep Ollie myself, but I think he'll be happier with Doc and his staff. I'd be gone all day, and they like to spoil him," he said, stopping my heart for the millionth time with his crooked grin.

I took his chilly hand after a brief kiss on the lips as if to seal our bargain and led the way into my cozy sunflower-yellow kitchen. I painted it that color to capture my fond memories of the farm house I grew up in, among the foothills of the Allegheny Mountains.

My dad, Liam, a highly ranked Celtic Mage in the *Guild*, taught me most of what I know about Magic before he found out he couldn't swim in the Allegheny River. My mom moved back to their mother country, Ireland, soon after dad was lost under the swirls of that muddy river. She told me she wanted to live out her days there, without her one love and without Magic I supposed, though she herself is a Wizard of extraordinary talent and repute in the exclusive Magical community.

Opening cabinets I said, "Grab a mug and some coffee, Jason, while I get Ollie ready for his big adventure." I called over my shoulder as I left, "There are some muffins in the cupboard too if you want to try them. I'll be a minute."

I heard a mumbled response as he obviously had wrapped his mouth around one of my crumble top muffins. Baking seems to be good for my spirits and I do it often, keeping the local constabulary in goodies during their long shifts of patrolling our rugged mountain roads. Jason has named me a *Kitchen Witch.*

Ollie was still stretched out on his rug, his head snuggly nestled under the bed skirt. He must have figured he was hiding from any further intrusions. He couldn't see me. I couldn't see him. If only my Magic would work as simply.

I knelt beside him and said, "Ollie, you are going to visit Doc Sawyer at the Vet clinic for a few days." He poked his head back out from under his camouflage and looked at me with a knowing glint in his eyes. I firmly believe dogs understand us better than cats as any cat I've ever been owned by always looked at me like a poor relation with her hand out for crumbs of affection. Not so with Ollie. He clearly wanted to please me and if that meant going to the Vet's for boarding, he was ready to pack his rug and my favorite old slipper for company.

After throwing a few last minute items into my bulging suite case, I hauled it and my carry-on downstairs with Ollie close on my heels. Jason was polishing off his second muffin and sipping his coffee while he lounged with his long legs stretched out in front of him. He looked very at home and I noted he actually always occupied that same chair whenever he visited which was pretty much daily. I bagged up the rest of the muffins and handed them to him to take to his office. He smiled and leaned down from his six-foot-four vantage point and placed a gentle kiss on my smiling mouth, caressing my cheek with his free hand. My morning was looking brighter by the minute.

I packed all the special foods my elderly companion would need at the Vet's and lots of treats which I knew they would shower on him. They loved his visits, but I wasn't too keen on leaving him now that he was so old. I told myself he'd be in good hands and made Jason promise he'd visit the clinic often to make sure Ollie got lots of special attention during his stay.

I followed Jason in my car, which thankfully he'd warmed up for me before loading Ollie into the back seat. I planned to leave for Pittsburgh International right away. My ticket was for a red-eye.

Once we got Ollie settled in, I slipped out and found Jason waiting by our running vehicles. He asked about my flight plans and said earnestly, "Cathleen, call and let me know when you get into the airport, or at least when you arrive at the Wiccan Retreat House." I told him it would be pretty early our time, but he assured me he still wanted to hear from me. Then we stood looking at one another waiting for one of us to speak and break the spell of sad goodbyes.

Jason took me in a tight embrace and said, "You have a safe trip Magic Lady and take care of yourself. I know you can handle the bad guys, but I still wish I could be there as back up." He brushed some snow off my shoulders and looked self-conscious with his feelings. I smiled up at him as he finished with, "Remember to call when you get the time to check in from time to time so I know you're OK."

I was touched by his obvious concern, but before I got too teary I noticed the eye patch over his left eye. "Hey, you've got on a different patch," I said.

"Matches my boots," he said succinctly. Guess I shouldn't have ruined the moment.

We gave each other tight hugs wishing our bulky clothes weren't in the way and a decidedly long kiss. I practically ran back to my car before the idea of staying took as firm a grip on my resolve as Jason's arms.

I saw Jason watching my departure in my rear view and almost fogged up my windows with my panting breaths. My heart began to slowly find its rhythm as I enjoyed the warmth that now flooded through me like a really good cup of hot chocolate.

I knew we'd be talking often if I could manage it.

Chapter 3

My drive down the mountain roads was made safer with the new snow tires Jason insisted I buy before the start of our long snowy season.

I got to listen to my radio station for a good part of my drive down as I'd also spent money on better equipment to boost our signal at WISH Radio; the station I purchased four years ago when I came into my inheritance. "Might as well enjoy your money," like my dad always said after he borrowed some from my birthday stash. I enjoyed his philosophy of living life to the maximum degree, especially since he could never really afford many luxuries. Now that I had the means to buy all the luxuries I wanted, I found I didn't really have much use for most of them. Guess he paid me back in full, enriching me with his love of life and teaching me the craft of a Celtic Wizard.

After a thankfully uneventful flight from Pittsburgh, we landed at an airport with the romantic sounding name of La Plata. I dared to look at my watch and discovered it was close to five A.M. I had only dozed sporadically on the flight in. I knew there would be a three to four hour drive ahead to reach the Wiccan compound from the airport. I needed to stay awake so I could make some headway on solving the mystery facing me at the end of this journey, so I drank more coffee before landing and called the cream breakfast.

I had just grabbed my suitcase off the carousel and was preparing to lug it over to the nearest bench so I could unload my carry-on bag before my shoulder was permanently deformed. This was just an old duffle bag of my dad's that I'd stuffed with a small purse, my all-important tablet computer, sunscreen, ball cap, Google Maps, research of the area I did during the flight and my makeup bag. I never trust my face to the airlines.

I heard my name being called excitedly by someone near the exit doors who from the look of her could just as easily been telling fortunes at a fair. "Cathleen!" *Is that Joanie?* I thought, squinting in her direction. And it wasn't.

Coming toward me, her sandals making delicate slapping sounds as she honed in on me was a girl about my age, wearing a long, flowing dress in all the colors of a restless sea. Her arms were deeply tanned and I thought to myself that she must enjoy the outdoors as she looked trim and fit. Her hair was plaited into a single, waist length braid and so black it was almost blue. She approached me with her arms wide and an even wider smile. Her hug seemed as natural to receive as it felt to return and I liked her instantly.

"Cathleen! It is so wonderful to finally meet you!" she nearly shouted at me. I'm Jemma, Joanie's friend. She's waiting out front. Can I grab your bag?" I was smiling back at this very energetic young woman and probably due to jet lag thought *Are we all going to fit on her broom?* Luckily, I resisted that particular breech of manners and answered, "That would be great Jemma, and it's very nice to meet you too."

As promised, Joanie's muscle car, a used El Camino she'd purchased recently from an old boyfriend was sitting at the curb by Pick-Up. She jumped out the minute she saw us emerge from the terminal. Our laughter and hugs and kissed cheeks were a wonderful reminder of our long friendship and just how much we both missed living in the same city.

After piling into the Camino, three across, no seat belt for me as the middle passenger, Joanie put her foot down hard on the gas pedal and we shot off into traffic. Because of the hour, there was little competition for road space and we sailed along quickly, leaving the harsh lights of the airport and entering the softer light of a slowly emerging sunrise.

Our first hour of driving, I felt like one of the red-noses in a clown car, buzzing with noises and laughter and the occasional squeal when memories were happily tweaked. By the start of our second hour on the highway, we had settled down and started to talk business. Magic business.

I felt I should be the first to start discussing the topic we all wanted to avoid. I began with, "So girls, now that I' m here, I want to try to understand a few things about your coven and some of the undercurrents that you may have detected before the disappearances."   Jemma shot Joanie a quick glance and Joanie gave me a sidelong glance before saying, "Cathleen, there is so much to go over with you, but we thought we'd wait until you had time to rest and then we'd start."

"Look, ladies," I answered seriously, "My time here is limited as I do have a radio station to run. Let's take advantage of our quiet time as we drive with no distractions and no interruptions." I looked from Joanie to Jemma.

"Sounds good to me," Joanie replied, looking almost relieved to begin. "I can give you a better over-view of the coven, as Jemma only came into our circle three years ago. I've been a member since it was formed."

"As I recall," I said, "That was after your eighteenth birthday." Joanie is not quite two years older than I am, but she always seems so mature and settled. Guess it's the nursing profession that formed her stability.

She began with a quick rundown of the members in the coven so I could get acquainted with their names and a bit of background.

"Of course you already know our coven leader is Wynn, which by the way means *holy* or *blessed*. She's a marvel, Cathleen," she almost gushed. Jemma was quick to agree to that accolade and Joanie continued, "I was mentored by Wynn and brought into the coven she was forming. It's been almost ten years ago now."

I recalled how wound up Joanie had been about her discovery of Wicca. "It's Magic that *I* can do, Cathleen!" She was almost vibrating with her excitement when she told me of this new *love*. It never occurred to me that my best friend was probably feeling left out of the most important part of my life. She sat passively by as an observer, whenever I did any kind of Magic. Wicca was Joanie's door into the world of spiritual freedom she'd never experienced until then. Wynn was her guide and guardian. I felt just the tiniest twinge of jealousy at losing my place as guiding light to my best friend, but when I saw her eyes shining with the birth of a seminal discovery, I couldn't be anything but happy for her.

Joanie's voice brought me back to our current conversation. "I recruited Skye who worked with me when I first got out of Nursing School and of course, Jemma, as you already know."

"Who recruited the rest of them, Joanie?"

"The rest of the sisters were mostly recruited by Wynn. They are Maud, Rain, Alana, the newest member, Luna, she's the girl who told me about the disappearance of Maud and Rain. The other sisters are Morning Bird, Niamh, Aileen and Aeron."

Jemma had been counting on her fingers and blurted out, "You forgot one."

"Oh, yeah, that would be our ousted sister, Ursa," Joanie responded. I could hear the sneer in her voice as her hands gripped the steering wheel a little tighter.

"What happened with Ursa, Joanie?" I asked. Joanie is one of the sweetest and kindest human beings I know. She is very tolerant and slow to anger, so it was difficult to fathom her answer in light of her disposition.

"I mentioned her to you when I called you, remember? Ursa tried to corrupt our coven." She answered with real anger in her voice. "She tried to destroy Wynn's leadership, by luring the rest of us to the use of the Black Arts. In short, she's an instrument of evil and a Sister of the Dark".

"Wow!" I said, rather stunned with the vitriolic description. "Joanie, how long has Ursa been out of your coven?"

"Unfortunately, not long enough. Not before she was able to plant her seeds of deception and mistrust among the other sisters."

"She was still part of the coven until just before we arrived at the compound," Jemma added in a soft voice. "They didn't send her away until after the first night."

"We missed the fireworks. I heard about them from Luna," Joanie said in a calmer tone. "They were in a group Circle of Sharing when Ursa began to challenge Wynn's leadership again, saying she was weak and preventing the coven from using the powerful Magic she could teach them."

Nothing more was said while I tried to digest the information about Ursa and the rebellion against the coven's leadership that she was clearly fomenting. In the silence we all seemed riveted to the expanse of highway we were now passing over. Studying the passing scene I recognized the shallow, dry river channels that pock-mocked the red terrain, reminders of ancient water ways.

The breath of a new day had marked itself like a pastel fog on a landscape awash in muted colors. Deep bruised purples, warm blush reds and silvery lapis lazuli blues splashed lavishly over the rocky terrain. I dreamily recalled the paintings I so admired by

Georgia O'Keefe of her beloved Southwest and tried to imagine the peace she must have found among her cattle skulls and terra cotta adobe buildings. The desert flowed by like an ancient ocean of color, studded with the tall masts of stately crimson ships.

Even as I daydreamed, lulled by the motion of the car and the sound of the road, I felt a pang of unease, realizing that there was no peace at the coven's compound. "Joanie," I said softly so as not to disturb the quiet that now brought heaviness to the atmosphere like a humid night. "Could you give me a thumb-nail study on Wicca, just so I have a better grasp on the structure and motives behind the Wiccans in general? That may help me understand your coven in a sense that reflects Wicca rather than my own interpretation of what I've heard or read."

Although I'd known Joanie was a confirmed follower of the Wiccan beliefs and rites, I never really studied it and even in our early teens, when she first began to delve into Wicca, thought it might be a passing fade for her. So now it would be helpful to see Wicca through her eyes and understand its philosophy.

I saw Jemma's head nod toward the window as she continued the nap she'd started about fifty miles back. We were all tired and though we had only about an hour or so of driving ahead of us, the trip was taking a toll on our energies. I knew some of this was because of the emotional state the two women were in.

"I think you want to know the history so you can judge how my coven has, or hasn't kept to those core beliefs. Am I right?" she asked. As usual, Joanie had a keen insight into the mind of a nosy Mage.

Being a Magic user didn't help me hide my skepticism about a group of women coming together in perfect harmony *anywhere!* Let's face it, females of all ages and backgrounds, form clicks and special bonds as a natural means of self-preservation. It must have something to do with eliminating the competition by staking a claim on their loyalty.

Joanie squirmed around in her seat for a minute, making sure she was comfortable for what I feared was going to be a lengthy history lesson in Wicca and a good lesson to me not to ask so many darn questions.

Chapter 4

Joanie's dialogue began with, "The word Wicca is derived from an old Anglo-Saxon word *wicce* which means *one who practiced sorcery*. Originally it was applied to both sexes, especially if they were versed in herb usage. It wasn't until after the Crusades that Wicca was mostly for women."

She paused long enough to merge onto an even more remote highway and then resumed her dissertation.

"Wicca has roots in a diverse set of religious practices from Paganism, Hebrew Mysticism and Greek folklore. But actually, I've learned that myths and legends from a variety of cultures have had a profound impact on Wiccan beliefs."

I stopped her with another comment "Joanie, I didn't know Wicca was considered a form of religion."

"Yeah," she answered slipping out of her teacher mode momentarily. "Actually, a Federal Appeals Court ruled that it was a legal form of religion in 1986 and therefore, it's actually protected by the U.S. Constitution."

"Geez! Why am I just learning this stuff? You could have explained all of this to me years ago," I said.

She gave me a quick look "Now that would have been an interesting conversation. Hey Cathleen, I'm studying to be a witch while I go to nursing school. Not exactly confidence building for a medical professional."

We were still chuckling quietly when I noticed a sign reading Moki Dugway. "Hey, Joanie I remember that name, "Moki Dugway" from my internet search on the area. Are we taking that road?"

"Yeah and It's a *very* scary section of highway 261, with a series of switch-backs that will curl your already curly hair!" She added, "We only have another 40 minutes and we'll be at the compound. The Valley of the Gods is connected with 261 on its western end, but we need to go further south. We'll be closer to Mexican Hat."

I smiled at the quaint name, but remembered that I lived in a town called Iron Mountain so Mexican Hat wasn't too farfetched. Since we had only limited time left, I asked her to give me some more insights into her Wiccan practices.

"Well," she said, getting back into her lecturing character. "Did you know that Wicca celebrates many holidays similar to other religions?" Before I could respond in the negative she launched into details I would soon forget. "For example, Yule or Winter Solstice as you may know it and Christmas are closely timed in our celebration. We have Pagan New Year and we celebrate what we call Second Harvest, which is very much like Thanksgiving."

I was watching the strange red rock formations that seemed to march across the landscape as Joanie picked up her speed. I was thinking of how my own Celtic Magic roots were so similar to Wicca. "I know your ceremonies involve nature and the seasons just as my own Magic does, Joanie. I wonder if Ursa subverted nature in some way when she turned to the dark."

"I don't know about that, but Ursa never seemed fully comfortable with accepting Wynn's position as coven leader, always questioning her knowledge of Magic. She even questioned our ceremonies, saying they lacked mystical remedies, whatever that is. She used to complain that our coven could make significant changes in the real world, rather than *passively sitting by, studying the night skies like a flock of turkeys,* as she put it."

We drove on in silence, listening to the tires humming a lonely song as they ate up the miles along the narrow highway. I caught glimpses of an almost primeval landscape as we flew past like intruders from another world. Just us and the occasional hawk, or vulture, I noticed riding the wind currents, swooping down and up again like Alpine skiers, high above the flat-topped spires of plum and burnished red rock.

I had read in the research I did while flying here, that Navaho legend held that the sky-piercing sandstone pillars were once warriors, turned now to stone, sentinels over this fifty square miles of rock, shallow, parched river beds and stunning buttes.

I was nodding off with the monotonous sounds of the road, when Jemma stirred and said, "Hey, what did I miss? Boy my head is buzzing. I must have dozed off and slept funny." She was rubbing her eyes and trying to stretch her long legs and back in the confines of our crowded front seat when Joanie answered.

"You've only missed the whole trip and our deep conversations about life and the universe."

I laughed at that and added, "I was getting some instruction on Wicca, but I know Joanie has only begun her lecture. Am I right?"

"We'll be arriving in a bit girls, and I can finish my *lecture* on a long, much needed walk, Cathleen. See that sign ahead? We're nearly there and I hope they have the coffee on! Right now, let's pray to the *Goddess* that we make it down into The Valley in one piece. Here we go."

The sign we passed simply said, *The Valley of the Gods* with an accompanying warning sign reading *Dangerous Switchbacks 5 MPH.* "Hmm," I said, to no one in particular.

"Joanie," I asked, "Would you like me to drive? I'm really pretty good behind the wheel."

"No sweetie. You just sit back and enjoy!" From where I sat, I seriously doubted this was going to be anything like enjoyable!

We drove through some of the most beautiful country and the views from the road were nothing short of spectacular. But this part of our journey was going to be a white knuckle experience for all of us as Joanie squeezed the life out of the steering wheel and Jemma and I held onto the dusty dash board. No one spoke. We were instructed by new warning signs every few feet about the switchback ahead and to *Stay 5 MPH!* One sign even added, *No Kidding.* I didn't know whether to laugh or cry. So I compromised and just quietly cringed as we crept along over a gravel road that I was sure a long vanished indigenous people had carved out millennia ago.

The lanes were very narrow and at one point actually looked like only one car could possibly drive it safely. The *Goddess* must have heard our silent prayers because the only other car was so far below us we were able to find a wide shoulder and used it to safely pull over.

I was beginning to believe this road was really an old goat path, just as the other car came abreast of us. All four occupants vigorously waved their thanks out their windows as they proceed back up the narrow way we had just vacated. They looked like a car full of Kabuki Actors. Their faces were all stark white and frozen in terror. We probably looked as petrified and we had a long way to go.

Taking advantage of our momentary safety, we all got out of the car for a quick respite from the drive and also to have a clear vantage point to see the Valley below. A magnificent land spread out beneath us, like an artful mosaic, filled with gorgeous color patterns and fantastic rock formations that pressed themselves into the raw beauty of the land they sprang from with the weight of eons.

From our lofty perch on this over-look, we were afforded a panoramic view of the Valley of the Gods and Monument Valley adjacent to it, both holy sites according to my companions.

As I scanned the distance for signs of life in what seemed a trackless no-man's-land, I directed my friends to a thin column rising like a dark gray pillar, joking that it was a smoke signal from a local Indian reporting our progress.

Joanie answered seriously as she looked from me to Jemma, "It looks like it's from our compound and it's too hot for the fireplace to be in use."

Without comment, we hurried back to the car and piled in. With no oncoming traffic Joanie made a careful maneuver back onto the curvy road and we resumed our cautious descent into the Valley of the Gods and all the mysteries it held in its beauty and dangers.

Chapter 5

Nudging the El Camino down toward the floor of the valley as fast as she dared, Joanie headed for the thick pillar of smoke. I hoped they were just having a Wicca Barbeque, but not even I could convince myself it was a possibility.

Joanie had told me the Wicca compound was situated in a remote area where it was wise not to attempt an approach with anything less than an off-road vehicle. Her car only qualified by virtue of its squat, battered body. Joanie didn't believe in coddling her vehicles and drove the El Camino like a Ram truck pushing back at any dirt hillock or occasional large rock like a small bulldozer.

We came to a dirt trail that Jemma seriously identified as the road to the compound. After ten body-jolting, teeth-rattling minutes we came to a stop in front of a low adobe building the color of the surrounding desert sand with a large swath of what appeared to be cow or horse dung smeared across the front wall. Not a very cool first impression as the dark brown stucco looked like a two year old had smeared the contents of his potty chair across the front of the building. When we piled out of the over-heated car, I realized that it *smelled* like manure too and I had little doubt this wasn't the latest in south-west home design.

I looked over at Joanie when she joined Jemma and me after we exited the panting car. Her hand was covering her mouth as was Jemma's. I had enough sense to have my hand covering my own very sensitive nose. "Is that some kind of Wicca ceremony gone terribly wrong?" I asked anybody who cared to answer.

"This is just beyond anything I thought she was capable of," Joanie said, her voice muffled by her hand. Jemma still hadn't spoken, but had lowered her own hand, her mouth moving in what I assumed was some kind of silent incantation. We moved toward a rough wooden door that gave a sorrowful squeal when Joanie opened it wide.

My eyes adjusted quickly to the dim room and I noted a precisely executed circle on an expanse of the wooden floor a few feet to our left. Lying in the center of the circle was an attractive, white haired woman. Joanie breathed out one word, "Wynn."

On the wall opposite the prone figure, a fire was burning with an unnatural intensity and temperature behind the fireplace screen. Its flames were a fierce blood red, not a peaceful yellow, or crisp orange bouncing among their jagged tongues and terrible heat. I looked over at the still woman and knew we were in for some trouble.

As short as I am, I felt like I needed to crouch upon entering further into the low ceilinged room. I moved quickly, but was saying a quiet ward to protect us from any unwanted attention of whomever, or whatever was at work here. I could see that Wynn was still breathing although it seemed shallow like her lungs were freezing up. Her eyes were wide open, but glassy as if someone had taken her real ones and popped these stony baby blues in place. She was lying on her back with her arms thrown wide from her body; her long dark blue dress was twisted around her legs into a perfect binding. *Hm,* I thought, *this looks like an old fashioned churning spell.*

I had used something similar in the past to stir up snow, or create an unnatural wind screen that would give me an edge in hiding, or running, depending on how I was doing in a fight. They say, "Everything is fair in love and war," and I am a big believer in *that* motto!

Joanie, with Jemma following close behind, moved toward their friend when I cried out, "Stop! Don't move an inch until I can sort this out." With that I knelt down, grateful to the wooden floor and pressed my palms down until I felt the *Green Mother* respond to my call.

There is only one way to describe the *Green Mother* to the uninitiated. She is the Mother of all the Earth, the Power of all the waters, the strength of every rock, the life in every growing thing. In short, She touches our lives with Her bounty. Of course, there is Her other side. She punishes those who should husband Her many gifts when they exploit, or corrupt, or abuse the life of this realm. Her memory is long and her mercy given sparingly.

I stayed kneeling until I felt completely recharged and only then did I stand and holding my hand up to keep the girls where they were, did I approach the circle. Wynn's breathing was steady, but upon closer look I confirmed she was only taking a small amount of air into her lungs. I reinforced my ward with a calming element from the *Mother* so I didn't rouse her too quickly because I was certain she was put into this sleeping state with Magic.

I stepped over the curved line which I noted was drawn in a deep red ochre color. In fact it seemed sticky looking, like it hadn't dried completely. I would investigate that as soon as I revived Wynn and questioned her. One of the things I needed to establish was the whereabouts of the other coven members. I sensed no other life in the thick silence that clung to the walls like the padding in a cell.

Feeling the energy surging through me I took a quick glance at Joanie and her petrified looking friend, Jemma, who I noticed had closed her eyes as if she couldn't watch what was happening to her leader.

The girls had remained planted where I had halted them. I wasn't sure what state we'd find Wynn's mind in and it could prove dangerous to them. I wouldn't know until I determined the spell used just how friendly Wynn was going to be when she woke.

Chanting softly I moved closer to the prostrate figure in blue and knelt by her side. It was obvious she couldn't have escaped whatever was thrown at her as her own dress was used to bind her from movement. I reached out my hand and carefully placed it on her wrist. Her pulse was weak and her color was like watered milk. When I leaned in closer to her face, her breath felt cold as it touched my skin. This, together with the stone-dead eyes and stiff limbs made me draw back as if avoiding the fangs of a serpent.

"Joanie," I said in as calm a voice as I could manage, "Wynn has been put into a Zombie state, but she hasn't been animated. Not yet." Joanie looked back at me in complete horror as Jemma stood stark still like a robot with a dead battery, eyes still firmly shut against the truth I guessed.

"I don't understand, Cathleen. We don't ever call on the Dark Arts. They are against all we hold holy and sacred."

Joanie was close to a fuller explanation, but before she could launch into a litany of all they held holy and sacred, I stood up and said, "I need you both to go outside while I sort this out."

Joanie started to state her objections when I held my hand up again, starting to feel like a traffic cop. "I know you girls want to help, but believe me, you will only be in my way and I need total concentration to read this spell and try to break it without harming Wynn or myself."

They turned as one, and Joanie steered Jemma out by her elbow. Very quietly, they left the house, leaving the door slightly ajar. *Ah well, I might need some help cleaning up the mess later* I thought, as I prepared to deal with my first Zombie defrosting!

Chapter 6

My father was a very accomplished Wizard. He learned from the best Celtic Magic Users in the *Green Guild.* His whole clan, reaching back beyond the Dark Times trained from early youth, in the mystical arts of the Druids and other practitioners of Magic. I broke the male mold after all those hundreds of years when my father took me into his apprenticeship instead of choosing from among my second or third male cousins in Ireland. He knew there would be no O'Brien boy fathered by him and I suspect he had visions of his own passing into the *Green Mother's* arms sooner rather than later in his life. As it was, he was only in his early fifties when he was filled with the waters of the Alleghany River. Having Magic doesn't mean you are an immortal being, though dad often lived as if he thought he was.

Through all my years of being tutored in the chants, spells, wards and special prayers to the *Mother,* my dad only shared one spell–breaker for those beings trapped in a Zombie state. It was buried somewhere in my subconscious and I had to access it by going into my own kind of suspended animation. It was a risk I was willing to take, knowing I could revive easily as long as there was no outside disturbance.

Wynn's eyes still held the, *I'm out to lunch,* look as she continued to stare unblinking at the roughly timbered ceiling of the room. I stood flat footed, my feet slightly apart to help maintain my balance when I went under my spell. My chanting was not of the lilting, skipping along the meadows kind, but dark and heavy like thick running sludge moving down a drain.

I felt my father's presence as I reconstructed the mystic puzzle that was all spells. Mid-way through the casting, my legs felt like sturdy wood stumps. My arms became leaden and heavy.

Suddenly, just as I was about to say the last of the incantation, Jemma burst into the room with a wide Demonic grin twisting her sweet mouth. Incredibly, she was clutching what looked like an ancient Highland Dirk, its bizarre history known to me from my Father, a great collector of ancient weaponry.

This was a highly deadly weapon used effectively by the Scottish Highlanders who enjoyed a reputation as being a warlike people. This particular Dirk had Magic on it as I saw the blade radiating some muted glow of energy. It would slice through anything it touched.

Seeing this ancient tool of death in Jemma's delicate hand as she began to slowly advance toward me, gave me a brief moment of alarm and then I pitched forward and was sprawled across Wynn's legs. *Wow*! I *didn't expect that!* I lay there like a felled tree and because I couldn't see her, I had to find her with my skin sensors. Not that it would make much difference since I was unable to move. That was probably just as well because I wasn't in the way of the heavy clay pot being smashed against the back of Jemma's head by Joanie.

I felt the threat vanish under the shards of fired clay and resumed my chant as if some possessed women hadn't just threatened to hack me into Irish kabobs.

There was no sound, except the dragging of an inert object out of the room and back outside. Why the heck Jemma turned into a would-be assassin would have to be a mystery for later solving.

Quickly freeing myself, I stood over Wynn's body and resumed the casting. This particular spell breaker was intricate and full of what dad always referred to as, "wayward words," meaning those words that just sprang out of nowhere and retreated back into the subconscious of the spell breaker.

As I watched closely I sensed Wynn's breathing crank up to normal along with her body temperature. *Yes!* I thought as my confidence was restored and my Magic justified. Wynn moved her arms and then blinked up at me, and screamed.

I normally don't have that effect on people, but then I've never attempted to introduce myself to a newly freed Zombie. She came around slowly as I told her who I was and assuring her that she was out of danger. I helped to untwist her long skirt from around her legs. She swayed slightly until she grabbed my arm

She wasn't much taller than my own five-foot-four, but she had a wiry strength in her arms that surprised me as she clutched my upper arm in her hand and said, "Cathleen, you are as wonderful as Joanie told us. I don't know how to thank you for saving me from the dark forces. I knew I was dying and there was nothing I could do to help myself or the others." Her voice trembled slightly.

"Hold on Wynn, let's get you seated and maybe get some tea going so we can find out what's happening here. I'll go outside and bring Joanie and Jemma back in." We both gingerly left the rusty red circle, carefully avoiding any contact with it. *I'll have to study what elements were used to draw that,* I was thinking as we stepped out and onto the dark wood of the floor.

I left Wynn sitting quietly in an old over-stuffed chair and watched her a moment while she closed her eyes and leaning back, rocking back and forth, seemingly trying to calm herself.

Joanie was sitting down too, but she had planted herself on an unconscious Jemma's narrow back. When I looked at her questioningly she simply said, "It was more effective than ropes, and I couldn't leave her long enough to find any."

"Okay then," I said, let's get her back inside. Hopefully, she won't remember turning into a pretty psychopath!"

Jemma hung between us like wet wash on the line, but we managed to bring her inside without injuring her, or ourselves. Wynn looked up from her chair and moved her head from side to side as if denying the young Wiccan being dragged into the room could be possessed of an evil force. When we finally deposited her on a throw rug near the fireplace, I noticed Joanie's head was bleeding near her left ear. "Joanie, you're bleeding!"

"It's nothing to worry over, sweetie. While I was watching you in the circle with Wynn, Jemma disappeared around the side of the house so I went to look for her. Fortunately, as I poked my head out and turned to see where she'd gotten to, she only managed to graze me with a log from the wood pile. I fell down to act like she'd succeeded in getting me out of the way. I knew it was Jemma who hit me and that just didn't make any sense, but I figured she wasn't right in the head as she kept saying, *I will kill her*, over and over."

"You were smart to play dead, Joanie," I said. "There's definitely something wrong with Jemma, but right now let's get that cut cleaned out." Joanie had always loved watching when Magic was involved and this time her curiosity was rewarded with a lump that could have proved more serious.

We never found any rope to tie Jemma up until we could determine what had possessed her, literally, so she couldn't do any more mischief. I decided to use Magic to make her legs like over-cooked noodles and her head like a pumpkin on Halloween, lit up but empty! She wasn't going anywhere. We put her on the dark burgundy couch that was so lumpy it could have been stuffed with straw and small boulders.

After Joanie went into nursing mode to make sure Jemma wasn't suffering a concussion after getting clobbered with the pot, we left my would-be attacker sleeping as we went into the kitchen. She looked sweet and harmless and I was hoping she'd stay that way.

The three of us sat at the kitchen table just off the front room. I had a clear view of the sleeping would-be assassin as we talked over three steaming cups of chamomile tea.

"I still don't understand what happened to me, or why Jemma tried to attack you, Cathleen," Wynn was saying, with the far off look of a person coming out of a coma and trying to make sense of the changed face in the mirror.

"You were magically attacked by Ursa, that's what happened to you, Wynn, and probably what happened to Jemma too!" Joanie said, with a scowl of determination on her freckled Irish face. I looked at her and fully realized how close I had come to possibly losing her and that she had saved my life when I was in that circle.

Joanie Dolan was a flaming red-headed *Irish lass*, as my dad often referred to her with true affection. Her glow-in-the dark white skin took to sun freckles like kittens to milk. She wouldn't be considered beautiful until you knew her and saw the love and loyalty she always showed friends, except when she was throwing flower pots at them. "Wynn," Joanie was saying, "you know how much Ursa hates you and this coven. You can't possibly have any doubts that she's behind your attack and our missing sisters' disappearances--not to mention Jemma's crazy behavior."

Wynn seemed to cave into herself as she hunched forward. "I feel so weak and depleted of any emotion right now." Her eyes still held some faraway, haunted look and I could see she was making an enormous effort to try to snap out of her mental fog.

I looked at her and said, "Wynn, let's just take a few minutes and sip our tea. You don't need to work on any mysteries until you feel up to it and then we'll all work together to get to the bottom of all of this." She smiled as if it hurt and nodded her head without speaking. We sat there until the tea was finished and the quiet gave us all time to regroup our energies.

I was tired from my Zombie-busting spell and my nerves were pretty frayed after I was nearly done in by the weapon wielding Jemma. I thought *Death by Dirk, who would believe it? It did have an imaginative ring to it though.*

I stood up after drinking two cups of tea, hoping that wasn't a bad idea considering what I planned. I said, "Let's take a walk, ladies and Wynn, if you can, please let me know what's happened here since Joanie left to pick me up. Also, what you think might have happened to the rest of your coven."

She seemed recovered enough by then and it was still early in the day, so we had plenty of sun light to brighten the mood. "What about Jemma, Cathleen?" Joanie asked.

"She'll keep until we get back here. Right now, I've put her into a deep, restful sleep and hopefully she'll remember what came over her before she turned into a case-study."

Wynn grabbed a battered straw hat the size of a small planet and stuffed her long silvery hair under it. I was tempted to ask if long flowing hair was one of the prerequisites to becoming a Wicca follower. No wonder Wicca was mostly women now.

We passed a sagging wooden shed so primitive in its haphazard construction it might have been built by some long gone desert dweller. Joanie stopped and called out "Wait a sec," and retrieved a long walking stick from just inside its partially open door. "Made this myself," she said proudly. I smiled at her sense of pride in the accomplishment and had to admit that there was no way I could find the right branch, strip it naked, and whittle and sand it to such smooth perfection. She had also been carving Celtic Runes along its sleek sides, but said that was still a work in progress. I was duly impressed. It's good to find out you still have things to learn, even about best friends.

"Joanie, will you cast a spell on your walking stick?" I asked. "You might consider using it as a weapon someday." Joanie looked over at Wynn who was between us and with her head down, seemed to be watching for signs of life on the desert floor.

"You don't understand Wicca, Cathleen," Wynn said as she slowly turned her head up to face me. "We are living in harmony with all of nature and while Wicca Magic is an important part of our religion, harming others is not. Would you mind if I shared a few insights that might help you to understand our Wiccan beliefs? Perhaps it might help you to solve this terrible mystery facing us today."

"Of course," I said, knowing that saving my own butt if I ran into a Demon on my turf was going to take precedence over shaking hands with it.

She spoke in hushed tones as if afraid to disturb the lizards, scorpions and snakes that I was certain lurked under every rock and scraggy bush poised to strike at the unwary traveler. I refocused on Wynn as she continued.

"Wicca should be looked at as a spiritual pathway, a conduit to a fuller life in harmony with all of nature and all the creations in the universe, human and non-human alike. While Magic is at the heart of our Wiccan beliefs, it is always used to bring us closer to the power of nature, while at the same time giving us a more intimate knowledge of those powers.

If you think about it, Cathleen, every kind of spiritual practice, be it your own Celtic, or ours, is a form of Magic, because it forces us to enter a sphere of understanding that we don't naturally inhabit."

I was starting to get a clearer picture, but I wasn't prepared to give up on my protective chants and spells and trust in the innate goodness of others. In any case, Wynn seemed to tire out after that bit of schooling and looking down, resumed her reading of the ground, bringing an end to conversation.

Suddenly she stopped and Joanie and I had to turn around to face her. She said, "We are not as powerful as Nature, Cathleen, and if we try to subvert the elements to our own will we will pay dearly. I fear whatever happened to our coven sisters has something to do with a perversion of one of our fundamental rituals. Dream Sculpting. It isn't a skill well known beyond our Wiccan circles, but dreams are the key to our understanding of Nature on a more intimate basis and also of seeing ourselves in the spiritual light we need to grow."

While the haunting strings of some new age music started playing in my head while Wynn explained the use of dreams, I realized that I needed some answers to save the girls of this coven. I turned off the star gazer concert in my brain, probably brought on by lack of sleep as well as Wynn's hushed tones. I'd need to be wide awake to succeed and I suspected, to survive.

Chapter 7

I wasn't sure I had heard Wynn correctly. Did she say *Dream Sculpting*? I had a mental picture of someone with a stone chisel whacking away at my head as I lay sleeping. "What exactly is that?"

"If you don't mind, Cathleen, I think I'd like to go back and get another cup of tea while I explain our practice. And we really should check on Jemma too."

With that rather evasive answer we retraced our steps over the unyielding ground and returned to the squat adobe house. If Wynn had noticed the dung smeared on the front of the building she didn't mention it out loud. When we opened the door I spied Jemma still sleeping like a baby. It was obvious she hadn't stirred a raven-colored hair while we were gone and I was relieved to see her smooth, even breathing that indicated that she was still very relaxed.

We quietly moved past her into the kitchen where Joanie put the kettle on. I took the rinsed cups from the rack and got out the tea bags from the cupboard where I saw them stored earlier. All in all this was a very peaceful, domestic scene with friends, but I began to sense a buildup of tension and turned to Wynn.

She sat with her head pressed back against the kitchen wall with her eyes closed as if dozing. Was she experiencing some residual effects from being in her frozen state? I turned back to fixing the tea, but felt a definite shiver run down my spine when I was looking at the coven leader. She seemed more closed down than at rest. *Hmm* I mused over my cup.

When the water came to a boil and Joanie poured it over the bags in each cup. Wynn opened her eyes at the sound and came back from wherever Wiccan Leaders go when they step away from the real world.

"Guess I'll start by telling you that our Magic is very intertwined with our dreams, Cathleen." Joanie sat quietly sipping the soothing tea and looking at Wynn like she was the last Prophet. Wynn continued, "We have always recognized the power of dreams to sort out problems or challenges we've been facing, or as a way to pass into other realms, or alternate realities. But perhaps more importantly, dreams can be prophetic and help us to see what lies ahead so we can choose a clear, safe path."

I looked at her a moment before asking "Do you think someone is perverting the dream experiences of your coven members?"

"Not just someone, Cathleen, but a very strong sorceress and former coven member, Ursa. She has turned her face away from the light of the *Goddess* and toward the darkness. She knows this coven's strengths and weaknesses and can use them against us. I am convinced now, that our coven sisters have been lured away by Ursa through the subtlety of their dreams. She is re-sculpting them to reflect her messages of hate and Black Magic, tempting them in their dream state to join her in the Dark Arts."

While she related her fears and suspicions to me, I felt like there was more she could tell me, things she was shielding from my understanding, but just then I felt our little Dirk Deranged friend stir in the front room.

"Jemma's waking up," I said. "Let's make sure she's ok.

We left our tea cooling on the table and went in to find Jemma rubbing her eyes and looking around at us as if we had just disembarked from a space ship.

"What happened to me? Why am I on the sofa? Did I fall asleep in the car?"

Joanie leaned forward and brushed Jemma's long dark hair gently away from her eyes saying, "Jemma, do you remember *anything* after we arrived here and found Wynn lying in the circle?"

Jemma just moved her head slowly from side to side as if the process of speech was just too difficult. "I sort of remember dozing off in the car and when we got here I felt kind of strange, like there were ants walking around in my brain. I know that sounds weird, but my head felt like it was invaded by bugs! I sort of remember being in the house, but nothing else."

I looked over at Wynn who sat facing Jemma at the end of the coach. "Jemma, can you remember if you were dreaming before you woke up in the car?"

"I was dreaming about you, Wynn!" she said excitedly. "I almost forgot. You were lying on the floor and were surrounded by blood. It was awful." Jemma put her head down into her hands and shuddered. Joanie rubbed her back and spoke soothingly to her. I knew Joanie was using a calming charm on her friend and was relieved as an agitated Jemma was unpredictable at the moment.

I stood a small distance away so I could better judge her reactions and to be sure the spell I was weaving would work without distracting her. I was protecting all of us from as of yet, some unseen visitors. I had felt their presence before we entered the room to check on Jemma and wanted to be sure they were not dangerous. I felt a peculiar heat that seemed to encircle the couch where Jemma sat with her legs pulled up to her chest. She appeared unaware of the change in temperature and Joanie and

Wynn didn't acknowledge it either. With Wynn perched at the end of the coach that seemed rather odd to me.

It took me a second to realize that the heat source was definitely coming from life forms. They had placed themselves around Jemma and I suspected they were somehow acting as her protector as she slept. I didn't sense any inherent danger, but I didn't know if that would change.

"Joanie," I said quietly so as not to alarm anyone. "How about we all go back into the kitchen and get Jemma some tea and finish our own. A tea biscuit would go nicely with that if we have any." Joanie helped Jemma regain her footing on what appeared rather wobbly legs. Sleeping that deeply hadn't seemed to have rested her as much as it should have. *Hmm* I thought.

As is often the case when dealing with an unknown entity, sorcerers, witches, wizards, always have an arsenal on hand to defend against the unexpected. As one of the elite class of Celtic Magic users, my own carefully honed weapons are hidden deep in my subconscious so I must clear my mind of the " here and now" and go back to the "there and then". Not an easy concept to grasp, and not an easy trick of mind control to perform.

As the three coven members settled around the much-scarred, round oak table, I filled the tea kettle once more and put it on to heat. While I fussed about with these chores, I kept my inner eye on the entities that had followed us into the kitchen and arrayed themselves around the room. I began to relive the long-forgotten spell I needed to enhance our protection. I knew now that these little guys as I started to think of them, were barely holding out against a greater force, and that couldn't be good.

Joanie looked over at me as she was putting small cookies onto a plate. "Everything OK, Cathleen? You look kind of concerned."

"I'm just thinking about our situation, Joanie, kind of reviewing all the information so far." I answered with what I hoped was a convincing smile. Her frown told me she wasn't buying it, but she put the cookies on the table without asking anything else.

For the uninitiated, the *inner eye* or *guiding eye* as some call it is often employed by gifted and trained Magic users as an ideal way to discern what the human eye can't. Intuition some might call it, but it's much more than that. Sometimes we humans just don't have the imagination to even suspect there might be other beings occupying our earth, or even closer still, our personal spaces. The very *thought* of other life forms sometimes terrifies and astounds people, so often claims that they exist are ignored, discarded, or the believers are just plain attacked as nuts. Such are our mortal limitations.

The beings I saw with my inner vision could only be perceived as blurred shapes and while non-threatening at the moment, they were becoming restless and agitated as they moved in a tighter and tighter circle to enclose the table and the seated Wiccans. It was a circle I wasn't standing in at the moment.

As nonchalantly as I could I said, "Wynn, do you think you could say a brief prayer to your *Goddess* of the kitchen or whatever?" Wynn shot me a quizzical look and must have read my concern as she started a sweetly sung song of praise and thanksgiving to a Wiccan Deity and added a prayer to banish negative or harmful influences. By the time she had finished I had moved into the circle created around them and had accessed my own shot of sorcery.

As I sat down in the remaining chair I looked at each of my companions and said "Ladies, would you do me a favor and hold hands?" Without hesitating, they each took their partner's hands and looked at me expectantly.

"What's going on, Cathleen?" Joanie asked.

"First off," I said, "We have a circle of good friends who seem to have attached themselves to the spell I cast for protection earlier, before we left Jemma to sleep off her crazies. They're very dedicated to our protection and mean us no harm."

"And second?" Joanie asked, her eyebrows rising like red warning signs.

"That would be the dangerous entity that is trying to attack us through our protective circle."

Chapter 8

I closed my eyes to focus my inner sight more keenly. I was able to clearly see the tiny Faeries buzzing around us now, occasionally turning their backs to our group and shouting some kind of Faerie spell in the direction of the entrance to the front room and the newly empty red circle.

The couch looked empty, but as I scoured the rest of the room with my enhanced sight, I caught the shimmering presence of an enormous *urus arctos horribilis*, a grizzly bear. Its massive head was swinging to and fro like the pendulum on a really grotesque Grandfather clock. *So, there you are Ursa!* I said to myself.

She must have felt my mental touch while I probed the area for other power users, as she stretched herself to an impossibly gigantic height. I knew she wouldn't be contained for long by the Magic of our Faerie guardians, not because they were so tiny, but because they had limitations on this plane.

I called out an old Celtic greeting to our protective ring of friends and asked them to open the circle so that I could attack the evil threat standing just feet away now. Within a breath the circle dissolved in front of my chair. I joined Joanie's hand with Jemma's keeping the circle of flesh unbroken and stood up to face the evil force that was projecting itself in the form of a bear.

Ursa's varmint persona moved quickly to confront my measly human self, but I had raised my hands in front of me to hurl a blast of *Green Fire* directly at this furry avatar. The *Fire* is a gift from the *Green Mother* who lavishes its magically imbued heat upon all living things. If it touches the un-living such as this powerful projection created by Ursa's evil, this same fire will consume and destroy the negative life completely, down to its last atom of energy.

The bear's mouth was opened in a blood curdling growl exposing long brownish teeth, coated with blackened flesh of some unfortunate other-world beast. Its thick purplish tongue was dangling from an impossibly tooth filled jaw, when the *Green Fire* hit it squarely in its torso, dispersing all its fierceness into atomized dust.

Joanie, Jemma and Wynn were still clutching one another's hands and seemed stunned by my witchery. Sometimes that happens even among fellow Magic users. I humbly admit my Magic is quite impressive when the *Mother* is so inclined to offer that sort of power up to a good cause. And saving my life and my friends seemed to be sufficient.

I turned back to the Faeries and thanked them in glowing words in the old language. I bowed my head in respect to each as they took their leave by coming close to my face and winking out, letting me count their number, 33, a lucky Faerie number indeed.

My friends had unclenched their numbing hands by then and watched me closely as I stood seemingly nodding and smiling at thin air since they couldn't see the Faerie Troop with their human vision alone. After the last one departed this realm of life for their own, I knelt down, flattened my palms on the wood and thanked the *Mother* for sending the little Troopers. They held off the threat until I was able to identify it, saving our lives with their ancient and unique brand of Magic.

My father had shared many stories of the Faeries and their Magic over long days and nights of training as his Apprentice. There were tales of bravery and cunning as impressive as any from the world of mortals. According to him the "little peepers" as some named them, are mysterious to all, but totally loyal to the

Green Mother. There are many tales surrounding their kind, not least among them the story of their great wealth. No matter how their story is told, however, all know they are fearless in the face of Demons and conjured beasts. They stand firmly on their tiny-booted feet against dark creatures and those who create them. They are truly the *Mother's* champions.

By the time I had finished my fare-thee–wells and thanking the *Mother*, the three women were standing by their chairs looking expectantly at me. "Let's finish our conversation with Jemma on a walk toward The Valley of the Gods," I said, hoping they'd all agree. "Maybe we'll find some needed respite from the smell of bad Magic," I concluded.

We all grabbed some outerwear and Joanie took the blanket off the couch that we had used to cover Jemma saying, 'It might get colder than we expect on this walk. Better to be prepared." *What a Girl Scout* I thought, smiling to myself.

By now it was close to three o'clock. Time always felt like it was caught in swamp mud when I was involved in Magic and I hadn't realized how late it had gotten. We left the house unlocked, "Just in case our lost sisters return," Wynn had said solemnly. We all nodded our agreement.

I still had to unpack my stuff from Joanie's car, but knew that it would have to wait until after dinner, whenever that was. I wasn't sure if my Wiccan friends had specific ceremonies they followed at meal times, but my stomach was beginning to remind me I hadn't filled it since my coffee and cream breakfast and the cups of tea I was drinking like an English Lady. Jason would have given me one of his, "If you don't eat right you'll weaken your Magic," lectures. I secretly enjoyed these as he was pretty funny when he went all mother-hen on me. It was nice to feel he cared and I tried to let him know the feeling was reciprocated.

I was anxious to call and check in with him later as I'd only gotten in a quick call from the airport as Joanie loaded my bags into her car. The sound of his voice triggered a longing for him that sort of surprised me, even as I smiled to myself. We'd been together nearly every day for two years and I hadn't realized how much a part of my heart as well as my life he really had become.

The air outside the house had the clean smell of Cedar Mesa sandstone with an undertone of salty rock from eons of formation. The sky was still a dazzling bright blue, with a line of clouds scudding along the base of the horizon, a portent of cooler weather.

Jemma had not spoken more than a few necessary words since we left the compound so I decided it was time to open a friendly interview. "Jemma, how are you feeling? Any problems with our walking?" She shook her head "no". *Geez, not even a monosyllable* I thought. *What's up with that?* I noticed Joanie was watching Jemma from under her long reddish brown lashes, like she didn't want her to know she was under observation. She caught my eye and gave a slight shrug.

Suddenly Jemma blurted out, "I'm afraid to sleep!" She had stopped and grabbed for Wynn's hands. Wynn looked over at me as I was studying Jemma's terrified face.

Joanie quickly reassured the terrified woman with, "We would never let anything hurt you Jemma, even if that means we stay up all night to guard you."

"It's not that I'm afraid I'll be hurt, Joanie. It's that I know if I sleep, Ursa can take me while I dream. She did that to all the others. She's forming her own coven of Dark Witches and she wants me to become like the others. She'll call to me like she did to them, and I'll go." She had said all of this in a flood of words, as if fearing she didn't have much time to explain herself.

I looked directly at Wynn and raised my eyebrows in an unasked question. She responded to my unvoiced question. "Dream Sculpting."

It took a few minutes and lots of soothing whispered chants to calm Jemma down, but once we did, we were able to continue walking. I took the opportunity to say, "It's time to explain more fully what you mean by Dream Sculpting, Wynn."

She took a deep breath of air into her lungs as if she was about to sprint off, but instead she began, "Wiccans have always used dreams and dreaming as a doorway to enter our spiritual self. We call it Dream Sculpting. Our members believe that Magic is a part of nature, not supernatural, but a part of the superior power found in the natural world around us. Our Magic is rooted in nature just as yours is, but without the possibility of injuring, or harming others." She gave me a quick look to see my response, but when I didn't blink she went on. "We Wiccans believe that our human, *Goddess*-guided intelligence makes us responsible to husband our natural resources and protect our environment. I think I can sum up our philosophy by saying that Wiccans strive to control any evil forces within ourselves so that we can live our lives with honor and without harm to what is natural to our world. That includes a peaceful attitude toward others of course."

She took a second before resuming. "What Ursa is doing is taking our dream state when we are most open and vulnerable and twisting our natural inclinations toward harmony until it becomes chaos incarnate as you saw in Jemma." The girl in question snapped out of her trance-like amble at the sound of her name.

"I swear to you, Wynn," she said firmly. "I didn't want to do any harm to Cathleen. It was like, I had no control over my body. I don't even remember deciding to hurt her."

"I know, Jemma," Wynn responded in a motherly way. "None of us think you meant Cathleen any harm, but we must be realistic. If Ursa can pervert our will and control our actions while we sleep, imprinting her evil on us, we are all in danger."

Diabolical body snatching was how I interpreted Wynn's explanation. We all mulled this truth over in our own ways as we continued toward the Valley of the Gods spreading out before us like a prehistoric diorama, muted tones of coral, lavender, bluish grays and the ever present, ochre reds. That last color jarred my memory. The circle drawn around Wynn when we discovered her was the same red tone only it had a tacky look to it. That was something I'd need to investigate when we returned to the house, especially in light of Jemma's comment about seeing Wynn surrounded by blood.

Joanie had taken her hat off to fan herself in the last heat of the day and looked like her face had bloomed with more freckles if that was possible. "Wynn," I said turning to her as she stooped to gather some unusual mauve colored stones and slipped them into the pocket of her sweater. "Would you mind if I walked ahead a bit with Joanie? I just want to ask her some questions about Ursa and I don't want Jemma to be upset by them."

I said the last while looking directly at Jemma to gauge her reaction to hearing Ursa's name and all I could sense seemed oddly like a discomfort at not being aware of what information I might be gleaning from my friend. She shot me a look of concern and looked away quickly when she caught me watching her. I made a mental note to myself that all might not be mended in our Jemma's lovely head.

Wynn and Jemma took a separate path moving toward a large outcropping of rust colored rock. "We'll just be working around over there," she called back over her shoulder. "I want to gather

more stones. We'll watch where you are and join you in a while."
With that they left us as we made our way deeper into the Valley
of the Gods and I was hoping, toward answers to questions that
nagged at me since our arrival and encounter with a possessed
Wiccan and a demonic spirit Bear.

"What's troubling you, Cathleen?" As always, Joanie was
direct.

"I need some answers, Joanie, and I didn't want the others to
hear yours," I said.

"OK. Shoot," she said, while chasing a lizard from our path
with her walking stick.

I began, "How long have you known Jemma and who brought
her into this coven to begin with?"

"I've known her, let's see…" she mentally calculated, and
answered, "a year and a half almost. We met at the hospital and it
was …" She took in a sharp breath before saying, "*Ursa*, who
brought her to our Circle. Oh by the *Goddess*, why didn't I think
about that before? We all worked together at the hospital until
Ursa left for a clinic in the downtown area of the city. Or at least
that's what she told us." She said this with alarm and a hint of
anger in her voice.

"You shouldn't be angry with yourself, Joanie." I was looking
back at the two small figures bobbing on the dessert floor quite a
distance off now. "I believe that Jemma is what might be called *a
ringer* in your coven. She was likely used by Ursa like her puppet
and was unknowingly filled with whatever darkness Ursa stuffed
into her before she brought her to Wynn and introduced her as a
fellow Wiccan."

"You mean Ursa created an acceptable Jemma and an evil
Jemma to do her bidding?" She asked me.

"That's my theory, Joanie and I think her attempt to kill me was triggered because Ursa knew I would undo some of her Magic. Ursa wants to destroy your coven, Joanie, but Jemma is only a tool."

"What should we do with her, Cathleen?" she asked with obvious concern in her voice.

"Well, we can't exactly keep her tied up, but I do believe I can keep her spell-bound while we try to unravel some of the knots holding this threat together. I want to keep things as normal looking as possible so we don't tip our hand through Jemma. When she sleeps, she likely slips under Ursa's control and is dredged for information. I don't think the poor girl has had a free night of peaceful dreaming since she ran into that *she bear*.

"I do feel kind of sorry for her, Cathleen, but she's a spy in our coven "she stated firmly.

"Remember the old strategy in war and politics, Joanie? "Keep your friends close and your enemies closer" Well, our enemy will be under constant observation and we'll be ready for any attack from the outside because of that."

There was one other item that needed to be addressed on this little stroll of ours, "Joanie, how long was Ursa a member of your coven before the blow up with Wynn?"

"She was in our circle for just a bit longer than Jemma. When I knew Jemma through our work at the hospital, I didn't know she had an interest in Wicca. Ursa claimed to have met Jemma at a Celebration of the Winter Solstice which occurred right before Ursa showed up in our group."

"And how did she come to know of your coven?"

"She told us she had heard marvelous things about Wynn and how she was leading our circle with a deeper understanding of Wicca Spirituality. She sounded very eloquent actually and we were very impressed by her sincerity and knowledge of our customs and beliefs. Just think Cathleen, a whole coven being so taken in by one evil person." *Remember Hitler* I thought, but kept that to myself.

We walked toward a particularly beautiful rock formation and I stopped just to breath in the dry, sweet air. My trip here took on many aspects of danger, intrigue and spiritual corruption, but I could still enjoy the breath-taking views and the marvelous bounty spread under our feet. Without thinking I literally threw myself down on the still warm gritty skin of the desert and with outstretched arms, thanked the *Green Mother* for her wondrous earth.

Of course, Joanie was beside herself with stark fear etched on her freckled face and fell to her knees beside my prone body yelling in my ear, "Cathleen, are you hurt? What's wrong?" I sat up and apologized for my impulsive joy and assured my friend I was not only fine, but very strong as the *Green Mother* had filled my heart. "Oh thank the Goddess, sweetie. You had me scared there for a moment and from the way they're running in our direction, I guess you gave them a fright too!"

Sure enough Wynn and Jemma were beating a dusty path in our direction. Guess that would teach me to go all "hippie" on folks. Even Wiccans find spontaneous joy too much to go unchallenged.

When we were reunited with the two rock pickers, we decided to go further into the Valley as a group. Staying together seemed paramount on everyone's mind and with the sun heading for its daily rest in the firmament I agreed.

The others wanted to hold an impromptu ceremony to honor the start of a new day. It seems the Wiccan day begins at sundown on the previous day so now I would have to face tomorrow sooner than I wanted. I needed some alone time to process our situation and the prospect of sleep, although alluring about now, only held concern for the coven members.

The girls were all busily erecting some sort of make shift shrine. Wynn used Joanie's walking stick to draw a jagged circle in the sand and sprinkled with fine rock and stones. As the sun kissed the earth goodnight, we all gathered inside the newly drawn prayer space. "They want you here," Wynn told me, "for your purity of heart," which made me feel pretty good until I looked into her eyes and thought I saw a fleeting hint of sarcasm there. I smiled and she smiled back, while I wondered why I had such a strange thought.

The breeze had picked up a bit and the desert was beginning to live up to its reputation for chilly nights. I shivered in my jeans and T Shirt as my light jacket didn't seem to cut the wind. Or was that cold air just the cooling down of the Valley in the absence of its solar guardian?

I noticed the others seemed totally comfortable with the change in temperature and they were dressed in similar light jackets. I was holding hands with Joanie and Jemma when I distinctly felt another presence among us, and it wasn't friendly. The chill I had felt earlier began to deepen into my bones.

My skin felt prickly and the hairs on my arms stirred with expectation. That's when I realized that Jemma had tightened her grip until my fingers started to go numb. "Jemma," I said softly, leaning slightly toward her without looking at her. "You're holding my hand too tightly." Joanie looked over at us, opened her mouth and let out a scream that could start an avalanche.

I focused my strength on what was left of my pulverized left hand and yanked it out of Jemma's crushing grip. Her eyes went from gentle brown, to seething black pits where I could see coiled, writhing snakes hissing back at me. The whole monster possession got even scarier when Jemma's head spun around twice on her shoulders before it stopped, with her facing me. I was very impressed by the gyrating head. Ursa was flexing her Magical Muscles for my benefit.

I guessed the malevolent gaze that Jemma was trying to sear through my own quite stable head, was supposed to disarm me somehow. *Boy, did Ursa underestimate my Magic, which was actually probably a good thing.* I raised my arms and shouted *Deluma Nocturna* to throw a *Deep Sleep Mantle* over the possessed girl from head to toe. Fortunately for me the *Mother* did not take kindly to people trying to subvert Her energies for their own evil purposes. Jemma collapsed just inside the circle, not moving a muscle let alone spinning her head.

We gathered around and looked down on her like some insect we had just netted for future study. Joanie said stiffly "I guess that answers the question of whether Jemma is completely free of Ursa's control."

With that matter-of-fact observation, I took a minute to be certain the *Deep Sleep Mantle* was firmly in place and then fashioning a sling of sorts with jackets and the blanket, we pulled together to haul Jemma's inert body back to the relative safety of the compound.

The sounds of the desert under the influence of a rising moon were a mixture of hoots and howls, rustling and slithering and my super-sensitive ears were taking it all in like twin radar dishes. I could hear the quiet breathing of the sleeping Jemma as she gently swung back and forth with the movements of our feet and arms.

I decided not to float Jemma on a stream of cool night wind as both Joanie and Wynn seemed to need the activity of helping their friend. In spite of the distance we had to travel, it was better that they were focusing on their burden rather than the peril we were all in.

We didn't speak at all, probably to conserve our energies as we hauled Jemma's dead weight. But there was definitely something else going on, something that kept us silent like the shadows we followed, leaving our mute stain upon the ancient red earth.

Chapter 9

As small as she was it was not an easy task getting Jemma back to the house and her bed. We all had aching arms and scuffed hands. After she was secured by the *Holding Charm* I placed on her, I made sure her sleep would be undisturbed by intruding spirits. Kneeling beside her bed I prepared for my Magic. It isn't simple to block unwanted wizardry, but I recalled my father's admonition one night when we were talking about the Black Arts, or as he called it, "The Blight on the Flower of Magic."

I was instructed in a more subtle Magic if the time ever came when I was confronted with *The Blight*. I had to prepare myself for an out of body experience. Following my dad's instructions, I shut off every lamp from her room. Lighting the wick of a single candle with a quick flick of my finger where a small flame of *Green Fire* curled around my finger tip, I sat cross–legged on the floor opposite. In the shadows dancing around the room I had to locate one dark visitor.

Feeling totally absorbed by the inky atmosphere of the room I reached my hands to the wooden floor and felt the *Mother's* strength flow up my arms and through my body. I began to create a ward against the Dark Shadow that I knew was lurking in the room with me. Using the rising pillar of smoke from my candle I formed a glowing shield to surround myself. It felt warm and smelt of candle wax and I knew it couldn't be penetrated. The *Green Mother's* energies still coursed through me while I peered intently into the darkness with my inner eye. *There you are you little bugger.* I smiled and felt somewhat relieved. This was no ugly bear. She had sent a *Dream Snatcher* to do her foul bidding.

Outside of the exclusive circle of Celtic Mages, my father was considered an ordinary man of non-specific talents. But inside that elite group of Magic Users, my father was the sorcerer who destroyed *Dream Snatchers*, no easy feat even among the best wizards.

Dream Snatchers were a wily bunch. They are conjured for the sole purpose of stealing the dreams of the unsuspecting sleeper and twisting them into horrific night terrors. Not so terrible at first glance, but when you put that into the context of enduring terrifying dreams night after night, even the most stalwart of beings will shatter under the strain. Being visited every night while you sleep, by monsters, demons, and creatures, you'll have some issues.

That's of course the main job of the insidious *Dream Snatcher*. His creator is usually a disgruntled wizard or sulking sorcerer, both wanting to injure their perceived enemies by driving them to a mental breakdown and making them suffer along the way. These are definitely not nice guys and now I was looking through my grey shield at one of these creatures. I began to study the *Dream Snatcher*. Tufts of coarse black hair were jutting out in a haphazard pattern all over its short, thickset body; even the tops of his square shaped feet and all six toes. His head came to a severe point that I realized was a sharp horn that could kill quite effectively.

Nice, I thought, as I tried to asses this creature's ability more realistically than my *initiate's kinda cute* theory.

During my observations, it had been using razor sharp claws, likely poison tipped by the discoloration that streaked down the face of my dome, to try to extract me from the safety of my smoky cocoon. I was staring into its gaping mouth filled with serrated-edged teeth and dripping some kind of yellow scum onto the wiry black fur. Kinda cute? No way.

After a good minute of scratching and dropping gobs of thick drool all over itself, the monster decided on a different tact, so not as dumb as it looked after all. It rose up from a crouch to a rather surprising height. Looking down on me like a bug it was about to squash, or perhaps an appetizer about to be devoured, it wrapped its hairy muscular arms around my cone shaped shield and tried to squeeze it.

I think the *Green Mother* had had enough and when I whispered a supplication for her energy to surround me, my cone was immediately turned into a giant transformer, charged with an enormous amount of green energy. The creature had been taunting me with a toothy grin when it was lit up like my dad's cheap cigars and smelled just as bad. I murmured a quick thanks to the *Mother* who in her wisdom had turned off the juice so I could exit my cone.

I knew my last task of a very busy day would be to check in on everyone before I could let myself sleep. I found them all secure behind the wards I had placed around them earlier and sleeping peacefully.

I knew I could lure Ursa into some kind of action if I looked like easy pickings to her, so I purposely told the others within Jemma's hearing ,that I wouldn't need my own ward as I was no threat to her since I was outside the coven. No one challenged that thin logic, but then, they weren't familiar with the corruption of a spirit that's fallen under the influence of the Dark Arts.

Jemma was now in her spell-induced slumber, but I knew Ursa had heard and seen everything through her up until then. She may have even activated some kind of *Watcher Churl* to just hang around and report on our doings. I'd be alert to that possibility, but for now, my charges were snug in bed and that's where I headed for some much needed rest. *Magic is so tiring* I was thinking as I drifted into a peaceful sleep and my own sweet dreams.

Chapter 10

Morning came tearing in with gusts of wind and swirling pale red dust. The wind had increased over night from balmy breezes, to a steady wail, racing close to the ground, shoving ahead of itself any particles of desert debris it encountered that wasn't solidly rooted.

I didn't much care for the attitude of the weather. It blew hard and gritty. My first cup of coffee in hand, I peeked out the kitchen door to study conditions and was greeted by a low ceiling of fast moving cumulous. Their brownish color made them seem stuffed full of *desert* rather than rain, but in any case, it would keep us cooped up inside pretty much the whole day unless we wanted a mouth full of old dirt.

I had poked my head into Jemma's room earlier after I had dressed. The sun was meekly stroking the rock formations and struggling to pierce the dust-burdened overhang of clouds. She slept soundly so I returned to the small travel mirror I carried on trips, to put on a bit of make-up; protecting my face from the dry climate, at least that was my reasoning. Truthfully, I am too vain to be seen without it even in these badlands. My mother was never one to, "dawdle over a make-up table," as she often reminded me, but I somehow felt incomplete unless I had put my face on to meet the day, even one as grim as this one was proving itself to be. Besides, my mom hardly needed anything other than what the *Mother* had already endowed her with, but she didn't seem to know that or even much care.

When the others were finally up and about, Jemma joined us saying she had a good night and slept well. She did look like herself again, young, pretty and non-threatening. I still didn't trust her around anything sharper than my wit so I kept a close, but discrete eye on her as the day passed from wind storm to the rare rain storm.

"These rains can be dangerous," Wynn was saying as we lounged around with various books, magazines and the occasional solo card game. "They can cause deadly flash flooding especially in old gullies and ravines." It was hard to imagine such an occurrence in this arid place, but I had no experience with this terrain and was content that we were located on flat land without any signs of past flooding. Drowning in the desert just sounded wrong.

Joanie sat at the kitchen table and fiddled with a large detailed map of the Valley of the Gods. "I think we should put on our hiking boots, tie scarves over our mouths and noses and wear those protective eye goggles that are stored in the shed if we need to and *then* we should visit the *Goddess* in her Valley!"

She seemed almost jubilant and her mood quickly infected the rest of us. It was surely more enticing then sitting around a gloomy, creaky house. The rain had slacked off to a light drizzle that the bright yellow slickers they pulled from the hall closet could easily protect them against.

We all donned the rough-weather gear and although we looked like a bunch of school crossing guards, we were happy to escape the boredom of being trapped indoors. Joanie had made up a first aid kit from items stored in the bathroom and Wynn and Jemma packed a portable feast to keep us from starving during the three to four hours we'd be gone exploring.

And exploring is what we did. It took us nearly an hour to actually enter the Valley of the Goddess, since the compound sat a good brisk walk from the boarder it shared. Yesterday we hadn't gone into it as far as we intended on this trek. I knew this was an exquisitely beautiful area at various seasons and we were in one of the loveliest, the beginning of early spring.

According to my research, this was considered some of the most scenic backcountry in southeastern Utah. It's been called a natural gem for vacation goers who don't need informational signs, pre-cut trails, or civilized campgrounds; in other words they don't mind roughing it along with snakes, lizards, scorpions and other slithery creatures.

Our self-reliance was rewarded as we discovered towering pinnacles and flat-topped buttes the color of sepia photographs dotting wide-open spaces; it felt like eternity had swallowed this place in one cosmic gulp.

There were many words of praise for the gorgeous spectacle of the Valley even though the three Wiccans had been there on other retreats, but then there are always surprises to be found even in the everyday of living.

I slowly became aware of how isolated we were. I watched Wynn's back as she led the way with her own version of a long walking stick. We walked without much conversation, looking around, moving single file, deeper into the valley. Any rain had passed hours before from the look of our self-made trail, as we now trekked over dry, cracked ground. We had seen no other hikers since starting out. Even the wildlife seemed to be holed-up out of sight. Nothing scurried ahead of our foot falls; nothing cooed or chirped in the snarl-toothed branches of the pigmy scrub, or poked a scaly head from under the scattered balls of sage brush or rock piles. We appeared to be the only life forms besides what plants managed to survive in the unyielding soil.

I suggested we stop to rest as the sun was getting pretty intense, since the rain blew out with the last somber cloud. We rolled our yellow slickers up and packed them tightly inside the canvas tote we took along for that purpose, looking ahead optimistically to clear weather.

Wynn and Jemma broke open their carefully packed cold storage bag and Joanie and I scoured the area to plant our blanket for our upcoming picnic. We needed to be sure it was flat and didn't have any rocks nearby that might harbor anything that could bite, sting, or take up too much room. I was hungry as a bear, but that was a bad thought so I thought Gator instead. No sense in calling down trouble on our peaceful amble.

As we sat in the informal circle favored by Wiccans, there were welcome sighs of contentment as we ate and rested, but little conversation. I explained to the girls earlier that going on this long hike would help me get a feel for the land where their friends had disappeared. I'd be watching and using my Magic to pick up any traces of the missing girls. Looking around at the downcast faces of the three Wiccans remaining, I sensed that they understood this wasn't a nature hike for me, but a reconnaissance.

After eating I was ready to jump up and continue. I looked over at Jemma and noticed she'd eaten very little. I hoped she wasn't having any residual effects from being slapped with so many spells and charms over the past few days. As we all began to get up and start repacking Jemma looked up and asked "Do you think I could just rest my eyes for a few minutes guys? I feel so tired." With that she pitched face forward into the now empty plate of sandwiches.

"That can't be good!" Joanie said.

We all jumped up, looking down at our sleeping companion. We knew that when she woke, we would not be facing our gentle friend, but likely we would be meeting her evil controller in some diabolic form. For a witch who could take people over while they slept and then sculpt their dreams like some wicked Michael Angelo, Ursa wasn't too bright.

Though I'd never been to the Valley of the Goddess it was renowned as a power site among Magic users who studied such things. This sandstone valley dates back to the Permian period, a whopping 250 million years ago. The *Mother* has lavished this place with rich colors and fantastic formations to captivate the imagination and bring the soul closer to experiencing *Her* great bounty. There is a subtlety in the variety and brilliance of the colors and fragrances that stun the senses and gives testament to the *Mother's* presence in the totality of creation.

I knelt down on the rust-colored earth and called upon the power of millennia and shaping my hands into a sphere, placed Jemma inside a red-tinted bubble of energy. I drew the spirit that had invaded her out into the open by forcing Jemma's heart to slow and then seemingly stop. She wasn't dead or dying, but the malevolent being didn't know that and was forced to abandon its host.

It came out of Jemma's slightly opened mouth (something none of us would ever tell her) like a snake leaving its hole in the earth. Slithering, mud-brown with raised warts along its back ridge, it began to wind itself around Jemma's arm and pushed its thick body against the round transparent cage I had created.

The fiend moved away from Jemma, using its claws to hold onto the dome while staying tethered to her arm. I collapsed the bubble and threw *Green Fire* at it. Not wanting to burn Jemma, I used my outstretched hand, twisted the air around its body, pulling it clear of her completely while it twitched and burned to a foul-smelling pile of ash.

Within a heartbeat, I had Jemma's own heart beating strongly again. She looked around herself at our concerned faces and said, "Not again! This is really beginning to tick me off guys!"

We helped her to her feet and I said, "Jemma, you need to keep hold of that anger. It's a perfect way to stop Ursa from using you so easily. If you resist, she may be forced to stop."

Joanie and Wynn had moved off to a discrete talking distance so I tuned in with refined Magic to over-hear. "We can't keep Jemma locked away Joanie, but I'm afraid she's our weak link when we eventually have to fight Ursa."

I noted the concern my friend had for Wynn's dilemma, but as usual her response was direct and logical. "We need to let Cathleen call the shots on how to handle this, Wynn. That's why she's here after all. Her Magic can beat Ursa and keep us all safe."

I was glad to hear the loyalty Joanie felt toward me and my Celtic powers; now I just needed to live up to her expectations.

We hurriedly repacked the leftovers of our desert picnic and decided after much discussion to continue on until we made it to a particularly awesome formation. Made of sandstone and the elements of the desert over enumerable millennia *Sort of like Celtic Magic* I was thinking as I appraised its power of durability.

We had grossly underestimated the distance to this alluring monolith as we had trudged another hour and a half before it towered over us in all its majesty. As the sun moved in its arc pushing time ahead of it, the wide shadow cast by the butte stretched out like a cool, inviting lawn. I started to walk toward its beckoning respite from the sun, when Jemma grabbed my arm. "Don't go over there yet, Cathleen, until we throw some rocks to scare off any resting snakes." I'd forgotten how snakes like to cool down in the shade of rocks and I thanked Jemma for her timely warning.

It was definitely a good sign. Jemma wasn't totally under the control of Ursa's corrupting influence. Maybe that meant she wouldn't pose any physical threat now. I thought about placing another ward over her, but I wanted to deal with her demons as quickly as possible and needed to keep her vulnerable so we wouldn't be. Hard decisions are part of my trade.

We still had plenty of water left and some power bars which sounded pretty good right about then as our lunches had been walked off a few miles ago. Joanie and I started throwing rocks into the inviting shaded area as I scoured it with my inner eye to discern any creepy crawly thing that might have resisted our rock-slinging assault. When we were certain our butts were safe from ground attack we threw the blanket back down and then we all flopped in various poses of a reclining circle, munching our bars and gulping the rather tepid, but welcome water.

I turned to Wynn with a question that had been nettling me since I got there. I asked softly so she wouldn't feel interrogated.

"When did the rest of your coven leave the compound Wynn?"

She paused a moment before answering. "Almost as soon as Joanie and Jemma left to pick you up in Durango." I had a twinge of guilt when I heard that, but the clear blue eyes she leveled on me held no accusation.

"Everyone was still in bed except me when the first two girls left about two-thirty that morning. I was alone in the Meditation room when I heard the front door opening. I saw them as they followed one another out the door into the dark. When I called out to them they never said a word, like they were sleep-walking. It was as if they'd been infected with contagious hysteria, only there was no screaming just dead silence, and then they were gone."

As peculiar as that sounded, her analogy to mass hysteria wasn't too farfetched. Each of the coven members had heard the same mesmerizing siren call and each had responded in a mindless, unthinking fashion. Ursa called while they slept and they obeyed.

I suspected that like Jemma, Ursa had invaded their dreams and through her devious sculpting spell, had changed their allegiance from Wynn to herself. By channeling her commands when they were most vulnerable in sleep, she was able to destroy the coven and Wynn's leadership without exposing herself to any physical dangers or Magical challenges. The perfect crime. Magic style.

Of course, she didn't count on my Celtic Magic trumping her Dark Magic. But I warned myself not to get too giddy with pride as I hadn't crossed Magical swords with Ursa in the flesh and that could be a whole different ending if I wasn't careful.

We were all lounging in various stages of rest when our attention was drawn upward with the shrill cry of what looked like a very large eagle. The bird was soaring on the warm air currents and though it had an enormous wing span, it didn't seem to need to flap them much as it coasted in a serene, circling pattern above us.

"That's got to be one big bird," Joanie commented.

"I've seen lots of eagles in my mountain country," I added, "but that's got to be the "mother of all eagles.""

Wynn stood up and putting her hand to her forehead to block the sun more efficiently than her floppy hat, she studied the bird as it seemed to be on cruise control over our butte. "Why is it so intent on our spot do you think?" she quizzed no one in particular.

Jemma stood up then and in a trembling voice said, "I think it's Rain."

"There isn't a cloud in the sky, sweetie," Joanie shot back over her shoulder and then continued watching our winged interloper.

"I don't mean like the water kind of rain," Jemma said, with a tremor in her voice "Rain, our coven sister. She told me her spirit animal was the eagle."

"Oh," I said, nonchalantly, "*That* Rain."

Wynn began to wave her big straw hat about like she was beating out brush fires as she said, "Let's test that theory."

It was like waving a bright red flag in front of a bull. The soaring raptor tucked its wings in close to its body and came hurtling down at us at lip-curling speed. We all abandoned our blanket and jumped back against the base of the jagged sandstone pillar. I had a quick flashback as I recalled the demon-built, man-eating ant hills on the African Savannah, but that's another story.

We were pressed so tightly against the rock face that I was sure we'd all have permanent divot marks. The bird pulled up from its very impressive comet streaking dive at the last death-defying moment, leading me to surmise that it was sent to demonstrate how fearless it was in the face of certain destruction. I pulled a quick spell out of my, "things you might need someday," file and using my hands like twin magnets, pulled up a wall of stone particles gathered from the sandy floor around our feet, just tall enough to shield us, bending it to enclose our bodies like a coral.

I know birds aren't renowned for their big brains, but this guy (or gal) barely saved its feathers from decorating some Wiccan jewelry, when it charged head first at the barrier. Shimmering like a pale veil under the shadow of the butte, it didn't look like much of a deterrent, but it was reinforced with some strong Magic.

The bird seemed determined to peck and claw its way through to the cowering group and was repaid for such determination with chipped talons and cracked beak. I urged everyone to stand very still. While my ward protected us inside, a foot breeching the barrier would be bird food. This eagle stood close to six feet, covered in pearly white and black feathers with beady eyes the color of the obsidian in a Pharos's tomb.

I began to study this monster more closely and noticed a tacky looking band drawn around one of its scaly legs. It looked identical to the one drawn around Wynn back at the house. *Hmm* I thought as I filed that bit of information away.

I have always had a great admiration for raptors. As birds of prey they are peerless among their feathered brethren. But this particular beastie was all beak and no brain as it kept hammering away at an indestructible object. I decided I had looked it over long enough and I needed to get back to the compound to test a theory that had been germinating for a time.

I raised my arms causing a sand devil to form a few yards away and like a whirling Dervish it spun across the open ground directly toward the attacking bird.

The gritty sand seemed to devour the beast whole, as it swirled in ever tighter circles around it. Inside a crushing volume of wind, the hapless bird didn't stop its mindless attack until it was rendered into a pile of feathers.

Just as suddenly as the giant eagle had appeared above our little group, what was left of it disappeared into a fading blue sky. The Wiccans seemed rooted to the spot, hypnotized by the scene and I only got them to move when I dropped our shelter back to the ground.

"We are definitely going back to the house," Wynn was saying. The others were nodding their heads, but no words came from their open mouths.

I had the red rock barrier reabsorbed back into the earth and with only a few comments about this most recent attack, we headed back to the relative safety of the Wicca compound.

I had noticed that Jemma kept close to Wynn as we journeyed back, but Wynn seemed more distant to her than before Rain's attack. Jemma seemed unaware of the chill coming off Wynn's aura, but I certainly noted it and wondered about Wynn's lack of compassion for the girl so desperate for comfort.

These Wiccans are an odd sort I thought as I plucked a beautiful rock off the dessert floor and slipped it into my jacket. *A gift for my Sheriff.* That conjured his face and I couldn't help but smile. Joanie caught my eye and raised her brows in an unspoken question. I kept smiling and she whispered close to my ear, "Jason, right?" My grin broadened and she had her answer.

Chapter 11

The trip back to the house was not only very quiet as we all seemed to be holding inner dialogues, but it felt like there had been a death in the Wiccan family. As the destruction of the eagle was finally sinking into their consciousness each of the women became more and more withdrawn. Wynn had fallen behind slightly as we saw the low stucco walls of the house come into view. I slowed my own pace to let her catch up with me and when she fell into step, asked her what was on her mind.

"Cathleen, I don't know how much more we can take of these attacks. Even Joanie seems scared and at wits end. I'm thinking of disbanding our coven and just abandoning the compound. There's just the three of us now. I know the local Indian clans would like to have it returned to a natural state."

"Wynn, if you leave now that will become the open invitation Ursa has been looking for. She'll increase her powers and the sisters you guided and mentored for all these years will be lost to the Dark Arts. Only the *Mother* knows where that will all lead to, but I can assure you, it won't be safe for other Wicca followers anywhere. The Black Witch will hunt them down and subvert them as she's trying to do here."

Wynn seemed to be taking this all in and with each step I saw less defeat and more determination return to her stride. "I can't allow that to happen!" She had said this so loudly that the other two turned to look back at her.

They looked over at me and I smiled and said, "Your leader has spoken girls." They look bewildered and tired, mostly tired. When we reached the front door I put my hands out and asked them to stop for one minute. "*Mother,*" I said softly, because She has great hearing. "Make clean this building so that all know your purifying touch." A slow downpour began and blew itself against the poop-smeared front wall until it glistened in the last rays of the sun.

I was allowed to shower first since I was a guest at the compound and didn't argue as I felt pretty gritty. My long, naturally curly hair was like a heavy curtain and would surely capture anything that blew or crawled into it. I couldn't wait to rid myself of the buggy feeling that kept me scratching at my head.

I had just finished unpacking my suitcase when I heard a hesitant foot fall outside the door. Reaching out with my inner eye I saw Jemma turning away from my door. I yanked it open and she jumped. "What's up Jemma?" I asked.

"I…I…would you…can I…?" This was going to be as annoying as people who pop bubble wrap sheets for fun.

"Jemma, it's ok, really. Just say what you need to and I'll be happy to try to help you."

"Can I sleep in your room, Cathleen? I'll sleep on the floor, I really don't mind. I just can't sleep alone, please."

There goes my minute of privacy I thought, but quickly quashed that selfish response and instead told her absolutely she could sleep there. I insisted that we move her own twin-size bed for her so she needn't sleep on a cold, hard floor. After we completed that relatively easy task she went off to shower and get ready for a quiet evening of Wicca stuff I guessed.

I took advantage of her absence to call Jason back in Iron Mountain to see how he was and how Oliver was faring. Jason reported they got hit by a small blizzard; it was only late February, so probably a mere eight inch snow fall currently smothered the deep mountain forest around my home. I lived in a charming historic town, nestled in the Appalachian Mountain range near the famous Appalachian Trail. Jason, as the town's Sheriff was not what you'd call charming, being direct and curious, but I liked him that way.

After some obvious probing, I got Jason to admit that he was missing his "Magic Girl" and I reciprocated with my own lonely heart confession, suggestive and spoken softly into the phone, wishing my lips were pressed to his ear instead.

"Ah, you're working your magic on me now, Cathleen. Seems like you've been gone a long time already. Are you taking care of yourself, so far away from me, out there in the desert?"

After I assured him I was in great health and drinking lots of water, I also filled him in a little on my investigation at the compound. "I haven't got any leads on the missing girls yet, but I do have some theories. I miss your insights Jason, along with your company."

He laughed softly and said, "The only thing I can see from here is a white-out covering the mountain. Great time to snuggle down under a downy comforter with a sweet Irish lass. But alas you prefer dust and dirt to snow. Just keep your eyes open and listen to those fine instincts you have, Cathleen. You'll be safe. The sooner you solve the mystery, the sooner you'll be back here, where you belong."

"Believe me, I can't wait to get home to you and Oliver. How's he doing, anyway?

He assured me that my dog Oliver was definitely not pining away for me as he should have been, but rather he was being treated like a furry potentate by the Vet staff. I smiled at that news and was relieved that his advancing years hadn't curbed his own special charms.

I was getting ready to make a smart comment when my mind switched gears and I blurted out, "I miss you, Jason. Please take care of yourself until I get back to take over the job." We both laughed and I had to say goodbye as I heard my new roomy approach. Jason gave me a crisp "Take care of yourself, my Cathleen, and call again soon to tell me you're on your way home."

I promised Jason I'd hurry, and then helped Jemma get a few other things moved into the shrinking room. I tried to think of my over-occupied room as cozy despite my rising claustrophobia. After her travel everywhere with it pillow came a special rock she'd found that morning and then her brush and mirror. I was waiting for the chair and desk, but then I think even she noticed it was getting a bit cramped.

Joanie had been watching the parade of items and just smiled her knowing smile and went to help Wynn with dinner. That little miracle called a Bread Machine had been busy as we trudged around the valley. The wonderful fragrance wafted through the house causing our mouths to water when we got back from our wandering. With only the four of us to feed rather than the coven of thirteen, food preparation went fairly quickly and a lovely fresh vegetable casserole with a side of Angel Hair pasta and home baked bread awaited our ravenous appetites.

Joanie was putting the last fork and knife in place when Jemma and I came into the very fragrant smelling kitchen and took our seats. We knew we'd have wash-up duty, but the feast laid out before us dried up any snarky comments about dish pan hands.

As we ate with appropriate zeal, I was carefully monitoring the rest of the house for any signs of intrusion, or tampering with our personal auras. We each have these mystical halos or in lay terms, gauges, of the present and future. They are visible to people like me with access to their inner eye, allowing access to the spiritual well being of any individual along with mortal concerns like death and danger. All seemed in order as I made my scan with the tiny exception of a small tear in Joanie's aura. *Hmm* I thought as I surreptitiously observed her sucking in the tender shoots of spaghetti strands from the spicy tomato sauce they were buried under.

What's going on with that I wondered. I couldn't fit anybody else in my bedroom so I'd have to place a special ward around her as soon as we all went to our rooms. Until then, I thought everything was in the acceptable range of safe for now.

Around eleven, after they had shared a small, but revitalizing circle along with prayers to their *Goddess* for safe passage through the dark of night, we all went to our rooms. I told Jemma I would be in shortly and went to Joanie's room. I knocked a few times in case she had her ear buds in, but when she didn't respond I called her name and opened the door.

Joanie was kneeling in front of her personal altar with candles and incense burning, turning the room into a potpourri holder with a bed. I could scarcely breathe and wondered briefly if she'd been overcome by the thick, pungent smoke.

"Joanie," I was saying as I approached my kneeling friend. "What's going on with you? Are you alright?" Joanie looked up at me with a stricken look etched on her face; hard to do with all those freckles.

"Cathleen there's something I haven't shared with you since we got here and I think I should have told you, but I didn't think it was important and I wasn't sure if you'd think it was…"

"Whoa," I said, taking her by the elbow and seating her on her narrow bed. (*Nuns must have lived here once* I thought randomly).

"Tell me now what this is all about. " She took a shuddering breath that along with her braided red hair made her look about eleven. *Geez I feel old around these girls* I was thinking.

She retold how Ursa had been thrown out after the first night and Wynn ejected her from the coven and the compound. This would have been the night before Joanie had arrived with Jemma. When she had gone to bed with all the stories of Ursa and Black Magic buzzing in her head she had a dream about me.

"About me?" I asked alarmed. "But I wasn't even on your radar back then kiddo." She was bobbing her head in agreement, but insisted the dream occurred the night after the big blow-up.

"I think Ursa knew I was afraid of her, Cathleen, and when I'm afraid I usually think of you. Sorry." She said this last with downcast eyes, like she hated to admit that she needed her best friend to help her out of tight places.

"Hey, what are best friends for if not to have each other's backs? So don't you ever feel guilty about that for one minute" I gave her a quick hug and asked her to tell me what the dream was about, dreading what I was about to hear.

She told me she had to close her eyes to remember more clearly and with the soft lighting from the two candles on her altar painting her face in fluid shadows she began.

"I dreamt I was sleeping when something woke me. I heard a noise coming from inside the house. When I opened my bedroom door a crack I saw the reflection of fire in the kitchen windows, so in my dream I thought there had to be a fire in the front room, our gathering place.

Instead of running out of my room to warn the rest of the girls about the fire, I left my room and went toward the flames. I stood there a few seconds and felt the cold floor under my feet, even with the huge fire that seemed to tower over me like a living thing. As I watched it I felt a presence inside the unnatural colors of the flames. That's when I focused as hard as I could to see what was trapped inside.

And there you were Cathleen O'Brien surrounded by this massive pillar of fire. I also knew that there was Black Magic at work and that the witch using it was very powerful. I could feel her hate and the chaos of her spirit as surely as if she'd touched me."

At this point Joanie's eyes flew open and she looked dazed and afraid. I was trying to digest the fact that she saw me being roasted like a Cornish hen.

After a few calming breaths, Joanie was ready to resume. Closing her eyes again she continued, "I saw you standing very still, frozen inside those awful flames. You weren't burning, or moving to try to escape either.

I wanted to rescue you so I started to move toward the fire, but when I stepped closer I saw there was a circle of blood drawn on the floor and you and the fire were inside of it. I tried to cross it, but felt like a huge hand pushed me back and then I heard it. It was Ursa's smug voice. She told me I was powerless to help you and she laughed. That's when I woke up and I swear there was the smell of that freakish dream fire in my room." Joanie's eyes had popped open and were riveted on me.

My turn to be afraid? I've never liked the sound of feet running away, especially when they were mine.

Chapter 12

It cost me some energy to get Joanie to calm down after reliving such a vivid and heart thumping dream. I put new wards in place and nothing would get through to her dream state without setting off the alarms I planted around her room, keeping a thread attached to me so I would know of any attempts by an intruder.

I needed to replenish my Magical energies, so after leaving Joanie curled up like a cat under her quilt, I quietly opened the front door and stepped into the night. It was an awesome sight that awaited me. The dome of the universe was extravagantly studded with uncountable stars, reminding me of the multi-hued stones I'd seen glinting under the concentrated intensity of the sun earlier that day. Their collective light and the luminous glow of the moon, gave me a clear view of the grounds around the adobe house so I walked until I reached the nearest open area.

Kneeling down and sitting back on my heels I bent forward and stretched my arms out touching the earth with my palms. I immediately began to commune with the *Green Mother* and draw energy from Her gifts. I was so absorbed in my ritual that I barely felt the presence behind me.

I spun around on my knees and was facing three young women, all wearing the long skirts and silver and turquoise jewelry favored by the Wiccans; all were holding the Scottish Highlander's Dirk. *What's with these ancient weapons?* I immediately wondered. I needed to ask one of these ladies after I disarmed them. I let them approach and as they closed on me, I saw the vacancy sign flashing in their empty eyes. *They were robots doing the dirty jobs around the house* I thought with not a little pity.

"OK, girls. That's quite close enough," I said sharply. They paused to consider their next move I supposed. That's when I saw that annoying jumbo-sized eagle appear from around the back of the house. "Geez," I said glumly, "I thought we plucked your feathers back in the desert!" The bird opened its newly sharpened beak and surprisingly a dark, rough voice came out.

"I can bring life from death and as you see, Rain lives."

"Yeah, very impressive for a Black Witch; of course you couldn't do that unless you had the Dark Masters to aid your Magic," I said gamely. I was hoping she'd try to test my own powers about now because the grit and rocks were starting to bother my knees. Not one to suffer well or in silence I said, "Look Rain, or Ursa, or whatever is fluffing your feathers, we both know that your Magic is corrupted by the chaos that rules it. Let the sisters return to their coven and I'll help free you from your Dark Masters."

Having said that mouthful I figured she'd take at least a minute to consider my generous offer. Instead, one of her minions rushed at me with the deadly Dirk held high for a downward slice. Rather than lose my nose or some other part I was fond of, I raised one hand and threw a ton of sand at the wicked Wiccan. When I say a ton, I mean literally, a ton. It would be awhile before they dug that one out. That left two plus the cuckoo bird that seemed transfixed and hadn't moved a scaly foot.

Ursa's voice came through the eagle's open beak once more. "Very amusing my Celtic friend, but she's not needed to dispatch you."

"First off," I said with some heat in my voice, "I am *anything* but your *friend*. In fact as Clint Eastwood said once, "I am your worst nightmare!"

Without further ado I reached deep inside myself and down through the earth until I found what I was searching for, molten rock. I drew this boiling sludge up and letting the *Mother* guide my hands, caused it to congeal into a mighty fountain of death. The two girls stepped back as one. Ursa wanted them alive. I desperately wanted to rescue these women because I knew they were innocent and merely being used in Ursa's dirty war on the coven.

The eagle, however, was not so smart, or perhaps wasn't favored by her, because Ursa let it attempt to attack me through the fountain. Maybe she was testing my power. The effect was immediate and complete. The bird wasn't even fricasseed, it was just gone. *Good grief, Rain is not the brightest bulb in Ursa's pack* I thought, with some regret for her searing end.

While I kept the fountain raining down lethal showers of steaming death, I decided to grab one of the ex-coven sisters so that we might interrogate her and perhaps release her from the she-bear she worked for. While the fountain poured forth I focused on the shed directly behind the sister on my right. It was glowing in the reflective light of the lava and I was able to surround it with a protective ward before I reached out my hand again. Bending the air tightly around her waist, my target minion was flying like a balsa wood plane and thrown none- too -gently through the open door of the shed. There was a resounding snap of a Magic infused lock and that was that.

With her parrot gone, Ursa had no one to speak her words. The buried follower had freed herself from the sandy mound, emerging like a blind mole. She tried to flee with the last sister when suddenly they were tripping into a heap of long skirts and flailing arms on the chilled ground. I hadn't done that particular, though favorite Magic, so I quickly looked toward the front door of the house sensing the source. I shut down my fountain and said, "Hey, Wynn."

She approached the struggling women with a scowl creasing her face. Her white hair had been brushed out and fell like a bridal veil down her back, while her pale night gown billowed out behind her as she walked toward the two Wiccans like some avenging angel in the nocturnal light.

She stopped next to the writhing mass of clothes and limbs as the ex-sisters tried to free themselves. Looking down at them Wynn's voice dripped sarcasm. "Welcome back Maud and Alana." They didn't respond. But it was clear they felt anything but welcome.

I went over to the shed and after breaking my bonds on it, retrieved my captive. It turned out it was Luna, the coven sister who had first made Joanie aware of the disappearances and strife within the coven. She was snatched while they were driving to pick me up at La Plata.

We marched the girls back inside and Wynn left to wake the others while I held them all in Magic foot wear. They looked fine, but were rooted to the spot. My father used this charm on me as a very curious 4 year old. It was his specialty while babysitting me for my unsuspecting mom. It never hurt, but was quite frustrating when I had unicorns to hunt.

With all of us assembled in the front room in various stages of dress and night wear, I decided to let Wynn begin the questioning since these were her coven members at one time. She had them all sitting on the lumpy burgundy coach and began with a prayer of thanksgiving to their *Goddess* for releasing these three sisters back into her care. Looking from face to face, I wasn't sure they thought it was such a dandy turn of events. Nevertheless, they all sat quietly and didn't interrupt their former leader's prayers. It could have been good manners, but most likely it was the collection of dirks I had floating in an elliptical orbit over their heads, ready to deploy at a thought of danger to the others.

I still had to inquire into the use of this peculiar weapon, but I suspected it had something to do with Ursa's real name, other than her sacred Wiccan name. *Hmm a mystery within a conundrum* I was thinking as I turned my attention on the circle that still decorated the floor a few feet away.

The red coloring was still evident though a bit faded and definitely didn't look tacky to the touch. I got down of the floor and like a nine month old, started to crawl slowly around the drawing. My face was inches away when I smelled something familiar, something metallic and salty, something human.

OK, I know what that is now I thought sitting back on my heels. The question that needed answered was *whose blood was mixed with the ochre colored sand to form the circle.* I didn't have an answer as yet, but I had a hunch and when I had those, I got a bit of a twitch under my left eye which was acting very quirky at the moment. Jason always teased me saying it was "eyeball sympathy," for his own empty eye socket. That man had a weird sense of humor sometimes.

I didn't want to disclose my findings until I was sure Wynn was through questioning the wayward coven members. As I returned to stand alongside of Jemma and Joanie just a bit apart from Wynn, I noticed Maud had been crying. Tears were still wet on her face and she was looking at Wynn the way you do when you know you've hurt a good friend. Wynn asked Maud to repeat her story for me. She told her to take her time, not to leave out any of the details.

I looked over at the other girls, Luna and Alana, sitting so rigidly it looked like someone had placed them into cement casings. "Would you feel more comfortable talking to me Maud if the other two girls weren't listening?"

"No" she responded firmly "they know what happened to us and we all need to tell you what's going on. I don't want to forget anything. I just want to get this out of me!" She made the last comment like she had swallowed something disgusting like a big hairy spider. I shivered and nodded for her to begin.

Chapter 13

"We all wanted to be part of this coven, Cathleen and acknowledged Wynn as the coven leader. When we came to this holy Valley, we were looking forward to exploring the sacred places she had told us about in our meetings and sharing a true spiritual journey while we were together. This was the first trip out here for most of us.

Maud stopped long enough to take a long breath, as if she needed to collect her thoughts. "It all started to change when Ursa began her rants during our Group Gatherings. She kept shouting Wynn down and saying her own Magic was very powerful and we were a weak, misguided coven. At the last Gathering, she claimed that she was the rightful leader of the coven.

This went on for the first two days we were all together, but had actually started back home at the last several coven meetings when Ursa had approached each of us individually about forming our own coven. We never told anyone, not even one another that Ursa was trying to recruit us.

After the last big blow-up with Wynn, Ursa left slamming the front door so hard it rattled the windows. We could still hear her cursing us all and calling down Darkness upon our coven. We were stunned by her behavior and figured she'd be back long enough to get her things. She didn't return that night."

During this long description the room had gone so silent that I could hear the drip from the faucet in the kitchen. The others were transfixed by the tale, but I noticed that Wynn looked more unsettled and agitated in reliving the details, her hands knotting and unknotting in her lap. Maud continued, all of us riveted to every word.

"We'd all gone to bed after that horrible episode, pretty much exhausted by all the fighting and screaming. When we met outside the next morning for our sunrise ritual, we realized that Alana hadn't joined us. Wynn sent Rain inside to make sure she wasn't feeling ill.

When Rain rejoined us she reported that Alana was gone. All of her things were still in her room, but she was gone." I noticed Alana was now looking down at her lap as if searching it for some clue to her own disappearance.

Maud continued. "We all thought she'd likely gotten up very early to explore our compound in peace, so we weren't too concerned when she didn't show up even by dusk. She always was an adventuring sort." With that she gave Alana a small smile. Alana was listening intently, but she returned the gesture when she heard the compliment from her friend.

Maud continued. "That night after our Sharing Circle we all went to our rooms for private meditation and then sleep. The next day we were told by Wynn that Rain had also gone missing. Wynn told us all to scour the countryside around the compound as she was now very alarmed." She shot Wynn a quick look as if to confirm this observation and then continued. "Rain doesn't like to wander around unknown places alone. And she never would have left without her sacred talisman. We found it hanging on the mirror in her room.

I was the last to be taken. Then the others followed after Joanie and Jemma went to get you, Cathleen and well you know what happened to Wynn. Guess that's it." She leaned back like she was drained and she probably was, but I had some serious questions to be asked and answered.

"Maude, how were you all *taken*, not just the three of you, but all the others too?"

She said in a small voice, "In our dreams. She came for us when we were sleeping and then entered our dreams and somehow made us get out of bed and go to her."

"Where exactly did you go, Maude? Was it close by?"

Suddenly, one of the others spoke up. It was Alana. "All of us were told the same thing; to go to our special gathering place just outside of this compound and then to *follow the fire*. There was this red glow in the distance and I guess I went in that direction." Maud and Luna were shaking their heads up and down to show they had the same experience.

"The fire seemed to become clearer as I got closer and that's when I saw her. Ursa. She stood with her arms stretched out inside the flames. She was standing in front of a huge Butte. It has a name."

"The Scotsman Butte," supplied Luna.

Joanie offered in a stage whisper, how she had found that on her map of this area when they first arrived.

Alana's eyes were fixed on some distant space as she described what she had seen. "Ursa stood *inside* the red flames with a horrible smile on her face. And I could hear her voice inside my head."

Wynn was standing silently to the side. "You girls haven't mentioned this fire to me before now," she said, with her brow furrowed deeply in concern.

Maud answered for the three. "Talking with Cathleen seems to be easier because we haven't betrayed her." Wynn looked down and shook her head as if to deny such a hurt existed.

"Get back to the fire, please," I said as I was anxious to examine as much of my adversary's arsenal as possible, before I had to face her.

Maud continued her version of their shared experience. "The fire seemed to move like something alive over Ursa's body. She screamed out some words I didn't understand. The next thing I knew the fire seemed to leap over to where we were standing and then I was somewhere in the dark inside the Butte with Luna and Alana."

"Anything else to add about the fire?" I asked patiently though I was anxious to hear every last remark.

"Only that it never felt hot or burned us" said Luna. The other girls nodded their heads in unison to this fact. Since Rain was not with them, I had to assume she'd had a similar experience as these three.

"Sorcerer's Fire," I was thinking to myself, but must have unconsciously mumbled it aloud.

"What did you call it, Cathleen?" Wynn asked with a curious look.

"It's not something for you to worry about, Wynn. Let's sort out what we're going to do with our long lost sheep here," I said, looking from one girl to the other down the row as they sat like castaways in a life raft. They looked numb and exhausted by their shared experience, and fear no doubt.

Joanie cleared her throat to get our attention and said, "We could have Cathleen put them into some kind of frozen state until we deal with Ursa." The three would-be statues all spoke at once, begging not to be reduced to that condition and I had to agree with them. It wasn't their fault they were used by dark forces and they certainly couldn't be responsible for trying to kill me off with those darn dirks.

"Hey, you three," I said a bit sternly. "I want to know why you were wielding those ancient weapons, the dirks. Satisfy my curiosity and I'll come up with something more comfortable for you than becoming inanimate objects."

They couldn't talk fast enough and I had to appoint Maud as spokesperson. "Ursa's non- Magical name is Tira Duff, if that helps."

I smiled and said, "Well, that helps explain the use of a Highlander's famous weapon. Tira Duff is very Scottish; her family name comes from the Gaelic meaning *dark*. Her Scottish ancestors were very resourceful at creating their treasured dirk from used or broken weapons such as swords, very inventive and very deadly."

"What's on the round hilt? It looks like runes," asked Joanie as she looked up to study the suspended weapons.

"They used the runes to decorate them, but I'd say these knives had special marking that held the Dark Magic Ursa put on them." I answered. With that said I waved my hand over the three seated women; they flinched as did the others, but I merely gathered up the would-be assassin tools onto the floor beside me.

"I'll tuck these away until I can give them back to their owner. " Lots of side-long glances were made at that remark. I like to keep people on their toes.

We were all thinking about how the Dirks could be used on our ursine adversary when Jemma's small voice said, "I never saw that fire, but I went someplace dark and full of howling sounds, someplace that made me believe that I'd never find my way back. I can't imagine how awful it was for you three." Joanie took Jemma's hand and squeezed it to show her she was safe, but I felt her fear still moving like a slow all-consuming iceberg through her life.

In the end, we all ate around the much-used kitchen table, some of us standing at the counter with our plates. I had used my inner eye to scan the three returned sisters for any nasty tag-along riders that Ursa might have attached to them. They came up clean and seemed relieved to be back among their old coven friends as they shyly joined into some of the laughter over stories of patients they had cared for at their various hospitals.

While they chatted in soft voices, I started to focus again on a very salient fact; these girls were all nurses. Now this interesting point had not evaded my notice, but was tucked back there in my *interesting clues* file. I started to rummage about in that part of my brain and found something else of note. Ursa was a member of another coven, according to what she had told Wynn when they had first met. She had said she respected Wynn's reputation and wanted to join her circle of sisters. Where was the first coven she belonged to? Did she leave willingly, or was she forced to leave? Lots of questions. I suspected I would have the opportunity to ask them of her very soon.

My plan had been fermenting for some time now, but I couldn't take the chance of having any of the others aware of my strategy just yet. Especially the three returned members. Even with my wards over the group and Wynn's own protective spells, I still was insecure about sharing too much information with them, or even with sweet Jemma for that matter. It seemed the only people I had full confidence in were Joanie and I hoped Wynn. I needed as many allies as I could get to face Ursa. I knew the Black Witch was gaining more power by the day from the feats of Magic she'd already performed.

The girls all seemed more relaxed with one another as the tension leaked out of the atmosphere like stale air from a released balloon. I stayed on my guard. Ursa was more than a pure Wiccan now. She had blended their benign Magic with something dark and evil, bringing chaos to the order of Nature and I was certain *Mother* wasn't happy.

Chapter 14

We cleaned up the dishes and then all six sisters and I went to the front room to hold a Sharing Circle. They prepared the room by lighting enough candles to perform surgery, and began to approach the red circle. It reflected the shifting flames from the fireplace and seemed to beckon all to enter its welcoming warmth.

"Stop," I shouted. "The circle has been contaminated by Dark Magic and I'm certain that's what held Wynn in the Zombie spell when we found her."

They all stared at me with alarm and fear, eyes darting back and forth to the ominous space. Their earlier camaraderie was shattered by sidelong looks of renewed distrust; it was three against three again. I had to change that equation and make them a healthy group before I could expect any help from them.

"You are all Wiccan sisters. You have all been through a lot together and separately these last several days. It's obvious that three of you are mistrustful of the three sisters who were dream-knapped by Ursa, but there is no trace of her influence on them right now. I think by holding your ceremonies including a *cleansing spirit chant,* you will all feel purified and stronger."

"What about the circle?" Wynn asked looking down at the object of concern as if it was a coiled snake.

"I will first test my theory and then I'll destroy any trace of Dark Magic on it," I answered. "Meanwhile, I suggest you go outside and perform your rituals in a pure environment."

They all paraded outside pulling on sweaters and jackets as they went, with Luna, Maude and Alana following behind like obedient children.   When I saw them take one another's hand and begin their ceremony, I went back inside to work on the contaminated circle.

The first thing I had to do was determine if the dried red stuff was indeed blood and if so, whose blood. I got down on my knees yet again and pressing my palms to the wood called to the *Green Mother* to help decipher the circle's content. To do that, I needed to borrow her Faeries once more. These tiny creatures had a highly refined sense of taste and smell and I knew they could use both without harm to themselves if they tested the circle for the presence of human matter, even if it belonged to a Black Witch.

My eyes were screwed shut tightly so I wouldn't be distracted by the candles cheery dance. At first I thought I just had an itch on my nose, then it moved to my bowed neck and then my hair was tugged none too gently and I knew Her Faerie Troop had arrived.

I opened my eyes and smiled broadly, totally forgetting they were terrified of a human flashing a mouth full of teeth at them. They immediately bunched together under an old fashioned lamp shade with long tassels that must have been popular in the late 1800s. It was rather endearing seeing them as they surreptitiously peered out between the gaudy fringe. I bowed low and in old Celtic begged their forgiveness. You can't be too careful around these little guys. They may be tiny, but they know how to carry a grudge into the next millennium.

When they were suitably placated by my bowing and scraping (such an annoying remnant from the time of Faerie rule over Magic in Celtic lands), I asked them in the old tongue if they could spare me some of their time and test the makeup of the circle. By now, I was getting flat-kneed from the hard wooden floor and was relieved when they quickly agreed.

They were again, thirty-three in number, likely the same gang that showed up last time. They moved so fast they were a blur of rainbow colors to my human eye. I switched to my inner eye to clarify their movements.

They had each scooped up a particle as big as a drop of water and were busy sniffing with their upturned noses while their long butterfly–like tongues, unfurled and pricked the sample in their tiny webbed hands.   They reminded me of Crime Scene Investigators handling evidence. When the buzz of activity came to an abrupt stop, I knew they had finished and I could now quiz them about their findings. I put on my most officious face, since Fairies love pomp and ceremony.

"Will you be so kind as to share your information with this humble human Mage?" I asked, trying my best to look humble. Hard to do when you're looking at thirty-three beings the size of a rather long finger.

A voice penetrated my wandering attention and I turned in time to have their leader alight on my open palm. "This human blood, indeed it is and still it smells corrupted."

"Are you saying it has been touched by the Dark Ones?" I asked, already knowing the answer.

He resumed. "Four flavors of human blood and each with evil mixed."

My mind was racing. Four blood types, four dream-knapped girls and one Witch practicing the Dark Arts. So, I reasoned, she took blood from each victim and herself and mixed it all together with some kind of evil incantation. She painted the circle and tossed Wynn inside to rot. She sent the girls back here to kill, maim, or capture other Wiccan sisters. That solved the questions about the circle. Now to destroy it.

I was still kneeling. In fact I felt like my legs would be in this bent knee formation permanently. I touched the wood of the floor and the *Mother* was quick to respond to my plea. The floor directly under the drawn circle opened like the mouth of a giant clam and when it closed again, the floor was as scuffed and worn as the rest of the room. *WOW! That was pretty cool. If only I could get rid of the clutter in my house that easily.* Sometimes I have flights of fancy.

Their work done, I was surprised to see the gang still hanging about until I remembered my manners and in the old Celtic tongue invited them all into the kitchen to finish off what remained of a very sweet coffee cake from breakfast. I blinked and they were all over the gooey mess flitting around like a flock of humming birds enjoying their favorite nectar.

I left them after many more bows and scrapings and went outside to find the Wiccans chanting and swaying in time. They looked and felt peaceful to me and I knew things were starting to fall back into place as some of the unrest in the group was beginning to subside. At the sound of my approach, Wynn, standing in the middle of the circle looked up at me and nodded. That's when a howling wind suddenly swept in from the stillness of the desert, pushing large heaving waves of sand, filled with rock and scrub in front, like a great storm surge, propelling it unerringly toward the vulnerable women.

They were screaming out in alarm and went hurtling toward the front door. I could see Joanie struggling desperately to help Maud who had tripped over a hidden rock to get away from the oncoming sand tsunami. They were directly in its path when I shouted out a powerful spell used only against a nature that had been turned unnatural, no longer responding to the orderly ebb and flow of the natural design. *"Cas farc neart."*

Using the Language of the Celtic Mages from antiquity is both daring and dangerous; one word placed in the wrong construction could rain disaster upon the Magic user. One wrong inflection could corrupt the word and hence, the meaning. When I was training under my father's watchful eye he would constantly try to rattle me into using the wrong verb or construction, with some hair-raising experiences ensuing. I never forgot those lessons and they have served me well on innumerable occasions. This was one of them.

The would-be deadly inundation of desert elements dropped like a heavy curtain when I shouted the last syllable of the incantation. The ear shattering wind became a gently moving breeze filled with all the sweetness of the yucca plant, wind sculpted bluffs and sun drenched earth. The *Mother* was content and so was I. As I approached the house behind me I saw all six Wiccans lined up at the large front window their mouths open and their eyes wide with amazement. I felt like bowing, but even I' m not that vain. Besides, the *Green Mother* doesn't appreciate arrogance in mortals, but especially not in Magic Users.

I came into the front room where I was immediately surrounded by a gaggle of women all trying to ask me something at the same time. I held my hand up and they quieted down long enough for me to say, "Guys, we really have to keep calm or we just invite chaos into our midst. I think that's one way Ursa has used you, by attaching her black Magic to any upheaval or stressful situation. She draws power from this negative energy just like plugging into a physic outlet. Let's take a breath and have some soothing herbal tea."

I was beginning to feel like Little Bo Peep as the girls lined up or went in twos to follow me into the kitchen. I've always believed that the *Great Spirit*, or whatever *Mother* is called by some, created kitchens so that mortals could rest themselves and find a few moments of peace. People don't usually argue and fuss when they are sipping a wonderful cup of Green Tea, or slurping up my personal favorite, the rich flavor of heavily creamed coffee. It just wouldn't be natural.

As we all pulled out cups, spoons, teas and what the Fairies had left of the coffee cake, we took our earlier places around the table and counter. It felt good to stand after all my kneeling so I found myself next to Joanie by the sink. She gave me one of her, *I have something to tell you,* looks so I reached over and ran the water while pretending to rinse my cup.

"Cathleen, meet me outside by the shed after dark."

We both knew the schedule for the coven included some private meditation time in their respective rooms. Now that Jemma had more or less moved into my room I had the perfect excuse to be outside for a bit. I nodded at her and turned off the faucet. As I turned full around I caught Wynn's eye. She had slightly raised her brows and her curiosity was evident in her look so she must not have bought my cup rinsing diversion. *Oh well. She is a Wiccan after all* I thought, so it figured she might have a certain amount of insight into the unspoken.

The group was discussing in a fairly animated fashion, the near disaster of the last hour. "I don't feel safe outside anymore," Jemma was saying. Her arms were crossed tightly across her chest and I saw goose bumps rising on them like a chill had settled inside her.

Luna was a quiet girl, but she radiated concern for her younger Wiccan sister and put her arm around Jemma's shoulder for a brief hug. "Jemma, three of us here have already seen the Black Witch and she is not invincible."

I need to talk to her, I was thinking when Maud and Alana both affirmed her statement. "She's right, Jemma," Alana was saying.

"And with Cathleen's help," interjected Maud, "We can defeat and destroy her and her Dark Magic." I almost said something modest, but felt it was best not to shake their confidence.

"None of us will be safe unless we work together," she went on and all their heads were nodding in agreement.

Wynn sat straighter in her chair and said, "As leader of this coven it's my responsibility to guide and protect all of you. I have deiced to meet fire with fire. I won't let her challenge to me go unanswered." Everyone including me was shocked that this woman with such a timid spirit would consider a confrontation. There was a barrage of concern for her safety, but Wynn was adamant.

"This is not a decision for the coven, but for the leader alone and I have made it. I know I may look weak to you at times, especially since Ursa bested me with that circle of blood, but I am prepared to do what I must to fight for our safety and Wiccan beliefs."

That fiery speech was followed by the scraping of her chair as she left the group with concern and questions written across every face. Except mine of course, because I had already determined that Wynn would attempt some sort of foolishly heroic act. I had every intention of being on hand to save her snowy white head when she went up against a power I was certain was too great for her to defeat.

In the few moments of stunned silence after Wynn left us all wondering about her safety, and me, about her sanity, I felt Joanie begin to stir next to me. There was something she needed to show me and before things got more complicated, I thought I'd best see what new surprise awaited.

I took Joanie's arm and steered her out of the buzz that had begun in the kitchen. "OK," I began, "Here's what's going to happen."

But before I could lay out my strategy, Joanie said, "There's something you have to see in the shed first." So we quietly left the others to talk and fret over the fate of their leader; their personal meditation time, forgotten.

Stepping outside and going around to the back of the house, I saw the shed was giving off a greenish glow like the dial on an alarm clock through every crack and warped wood. Looking more closely at the shack it was clear to me it was in the last stages of a useful life before it collapsed and was recycled into the red earth. It was windowless and had only the one door for access and exit. I had successfully used it earlier when I had to restrain Luna without harming her, or frightening her witless with some scary toad-like guard.

As we approached the glowing wooden heap, I noticed that Joanie had stopped keeping pace with me. My attention was focused on the time-worn shed, studying it in the hazy light of a shrouded moon. I still had my inner eye open to see all that might be waiting for us in the darkened corners of the decrepit wooden structure.

I paused mid-step when I realized Joanie must have fallen behind. I didn't want any of the girls to be by themselves out here and that went double for Joanie.

Turning slightly to look over my shoulder, I saw her frozen like a garden gnome under the feeble lunar light. As if that wasn't shocking enough, standing beside her was the last person I expected to see.

"Mom!" I screamed like a kid on her first roller coaster ride.

*That likely gave me at least two white hai*rs I thought bleakly, trying to regain some composure. It doesn't look good for a Wizard to whimper. *Darn you, mom.*

Chapter 15

She was shimmering in her own version of a Communications Hologram, perfected so that she could interact and not just be heard like a recorded message. It had been created using her Magical essence so was as real-life as one could get without actually being present. It was a very cool innovation, as she often reminded me.

My mother hovered next to the stiff body of my best friend while I recovered from the shock of seeing her. While my father was a first class Celtic Wizard, my Mother was a practitioner of *This and That Magic* as she so quaintly named it. She could take a pinch of Wicca, a plop of Druid, a pound of Celtic, a squirt of east and an ounce of west and stir it all together for her own brand of smelly, foul tasting, very, *very* potent Magic.

My father envied her skill and I often heard him asking for her secret recipes as she referred to some of the most blood curdling things I've ever seen crawl out of a caldron. Mom had unsuccessfully tried to persuade my father to allow me to do her form of training, using her *This and That* approach, but as envious as he was of her skills, he refused to have my Celtic roots polluted. My parents never approached Magic the same way, but they both used it in the services of the *Green Mother* and any other deity they happened to acknowledge.

When I was able to move, after the initial smack-down moment of surprise, I quickly went to help my friend.

"Oh, not to worry about her, pet," my mother said while hanging over us both with her beautiful smile firmly in place.

"She's fine, just sleeping a wee bit and from the looks of her, she needed the rest."

With that charming Irish brogue of hers, mom could convince anyone of her innocence even when caught red handed at some mischievous form of enchantment by the Guild of the Green Wizards. But right now my concern wasn't with her slapping some lout silly with the animated switch from an apple tree (I was 7 when I witnessed that particular act).

"Mom, what were you thinking? Joanie could have been seriously injured if something had gone wrong with your spell."

"Oh, tosh! She'll be fine and if you want I'll wake her now."

"No," I said quickly, not wanting Joanie to endure another jolt of my mom's brewed Magic until I had a chance to question her presence at the Wiccan compound. "I think we need to talk in private first, Mom. I have some questions for you like, why are you here?"

"You always were a most determined little munchkin, pet. Alright, this is obviously a wee surprise to see your Ma here in hologram projection, but I needed to let you know that I've already arrived in mortal form too!"

"What?" I shouted again, making her projection quiver in the process.

"Now dear, I knew you were in need of a bit more spice for your own wonderful Magic and I am here to add that." She was wrapping a pale fringed shawl around her bare shoulders as she spoke, leading me to speculate briefly if she was already in Utah's temperate climate.

"Mom, this is something that needs to happen as quickly as yesterday and can't wait for you to get here. This coven is already under attack."

"I know," she answered. "In fact it would appear you have an unwanted visitor waiting for you in that shed over there. Oh, toad stools! I'm beginning to fade, pet. I'll have to tinker with this hologram spell just a smidgen. I'll see you by noon tomorrow. Hugs and kisses, my sweet lass."

With that last comment, she blinked out. I saw only open space where she had been hovering like Joanie's side-kick. Then my friend stirred. She saw me and said almost laughingly "For goodness sake, Cathleen, what are we doing back here? We were almost to the shed. It's like time stopped for us."

"It's ok, Joanie," I said quickly. "My Mom used your energy for just a minute so she could tell me she'll be here tomorrow by noon. I'm really sorry she took advantage of you like that."

"That's great news, sweetie! And I'm fine. Nothing seems to be working strangely, see?" With that she raised her foot and wobbled as I grabbed her arm to steady her. "You know she'll help us out and more importantly, keep *you* safe."

That reminded me of my mom's warning about the shed having an unwanted visitor. Trying not to scare her, I told Joanie to stand still for a moment while I did one of my "just in case" wards on the shed.

It wasn't a particularly strong ward, but I didn't expect much by way of nasty Magic waiting for us. Was I ever wrong!

I motioned to Joanie that it was safe to proceed and opened the warped wooden door. Peering inside with her human vision alone Joanie announced "All clear, Cathleen. I was viewing the same area with my inner eye and there in a corner, dressed in the darkest shadows, stood a *Bleak Phantom*.

Renowned throughout the Magic world as a formidable Dark Magic creature, the *Bleak Phantom* was used by evil wizards to erase the human memory of anything that brought happiness and joy on the mortal plane, to be replaced with night terrors, unfounded guilt and a life without hope, or meaning.

I saw the mass of shadow shift and knew Joanie was directly in its path and soon would be within its reach. Without begging her pardon I shoved her out of the shed and ignoring the yelp as her body met the ground, I spun around and threw one of my nastiest spells into the now gyrating darkness. Screaming *"Gathgorum!"* with my arms held up like an umpire calling a safe touchdown, caused a gaping hole to appear in the shed's old roofing as rotted shingles flew off in every direction. Having done that, I proceeded to the real work of sucking the shed clean like a giant sized Hoover.

I was surrounded by a roaring sound, my ears popped and my mouth went dry, as a vacuum formed directly above the *Bleak Phantom*, distorting any shape it had inside the shadows and pulling it like strings of black gunk through the newly made opening. It struggled to throw one of those slimy strings my way, but I quickly increased the suction and it was pulled upward with a long piercing howl.

"Holy crapski!" Joanie shouted in a strangled voice. Getting back up and dusting the red dirt off her jeans she was looking at me in horror and admiration. I liked the admiration part.

"Not to worry Joanie, that was just a little *Bleak Phantom* that was likely attached to Luna when I locked her in here earlier. Our friendly Black Witch sent it as a special surprise. It likely dropped off Luna when I put the binding wards around the place to hold her. They hate any Green Magic and are really cowards that have to hide in dark places."

"Do you think we can go back now, Cathleen? I've had just about all the Magic I want to see for one day."

We turned to walk back to the kitchen when I stopped and asked "By the way Joanie, what was it you had to tell me about the shed that got us out here in the first place?"

She looked embarrassed and answered, "Darned if I know."

Mom and her subliminal messages. She's as addicted to those as I am to email.

As we walked toward the back of the house, Joanie picked up the thread of our previous conversation. "So is your mom going to like *oversee* your Magic, Cathleen? Not that you need that, sweetie," she added quickly. She knew how hard I have tried to gain my independence from my mother.

"She told me she's going to blend her special Magic with mine to make it stronger. I'm still trying to figure out how she knew about my being here." I paused mid-step. "Oh, yeah, the Faeries. She's very close to our visiting clan over in Ireland, so they must have warned her about the new Black Witch on the block."

"Your Mom is quite a character, Cathleen, but I know she loves you very much and would never let you come to any harm." Joanie was definitely part of my family. She practically lived at our old farm house while both my parents were alive and was well aware that Magic was at the heart of O'Brien family life.

She never expressed any fear when we'd conjure the occasional *House Buddy* to do the needed repairs my father had to neglect due to his busy schedule. "Making up excuses was time consuming after all, pet," mom would tell me in his defense and with a loving chuckle. She was no Home Beautiful diva herself so they were well suited in temperament.

Even the assorted creatures that popped up at my mom's beckoning to pickle the vegetables from the garden mom never weeded put Joanie off. All in all, Joanie was the perfect, nonjudgmental friend, accepting me and mine where she found us, even if that was making disappearing lotion on our kitchen stove, or conferring with Faeries while dining on tea biscuits and warm milk.

We tried to be quiet coming into the house, but it was a needless exercise as all the coven sisters were back in the kitchen with mugs of hot chocolate and a much more relaxed air. I wasn't planning to share the latest run-in with the *Bleak Phantom* with them, so that should continue. It was good for us all to go to our happy place for a while.

"Hey you two," Jemma called, "We saved some hot chocolate for you." She went on to pour two fresh mugs of the frothy liquid and we gratefully sat in the recently vacated chairs of Luna and Wynn.

"You were out there counting stars, right?" asked Wynn, giving us both a look that seemed a little more wary then teasing to me.

"Yep, and there are even more than last time I counted," I said with what I hoped was a cheerful grin.

She was wise enough to pursue another topic. "The girls and I have decided to do a thorough cleansing of the house and wanted you to join our ceremony, Cathleen." I told her I'd be honored, believing that any Magic that serves the *Green Mother* was a source of good to all.

We finished slurping up the tasty "drink of the gods" as the Mayan believed it to be, elevating their intelligence in my book. Contented, we then sauntered in slow procession out to the front room and a newly drawn circle. I noticed it was the same shade of azure blue as the skies earlier today.

"How did you capture such a true sky color, Wynn?" I asked, with admiration in my voice.

She smiled sweetly, and said, "We all have our little secrets, right, Cathleen?"

Guess I deserved that since I knew she suspected there had been bad Magic afoot during our prolonged absence and I had chosen not to share my information. I was somewhat surprised at Wynn's attitude, however, and maybe even a bit hurt at her dismissive comment.

Oh well, I like purple skies better anyway I thought with a mental *Humph!*

Chapter 16

They had small bundles of fragrant White Sage in the center of the sky-blue circle and small clay pots with burning coals giving out a soft glow. *So that's why they had the grill going earlier. And I was looking forward to hot dogs* I was thinking while I watched them prepare for their ceremony.

Dozens of white candles were placed all around the room and I could hear the softly chanting voice of Wynn as all was being made ready.

Each sister entered the circle, picking up the small pots by the rounded handles that jutted out from their sides. They all held a bundle of sage and holding them over their single brick of white-hot charcoal, set them to smoking. This process took only a few minutes and soon the front room was awash in the pungent aroma of the sage as it drifted out enclosing us in its own circle of smoke and sweet bouquet.

I took a place inside as soon as they had accomplished the sage burning part of the cleansing and stood quietly waiting for them to place the small pots back on the hearth's stone work. That done they returned to the circle and bowed to Wynn who reminded the coven sisters of their responsibility to a basic Wiccan belief similar to the old fashioned Golden Rule. "An it harm none, do what ye will."

Like any preacher or prelate, Wynn gave a short sermon on the creative power in the universe that the Wiccans conceived as masculine and feminine, without bias toward either. She spoke of both outer and inner worlds and the interaction between them which helps Wiccans tap into the Magical in both.

All in all, it seemed to me that the Wiccans were very close to my own beliefs about keeping in harmony with the natural world we live in as mortals. One of my insights at the conclusion of the circle rites was that Wiccans really believed in Karma so I guessed they all were thinking of their nemesis, Ursa about then. *For a peace-loving religion, there was definitely room for pay back* I thought with a smile I hid by bowing my head.

By the time the house cleansing was complete and all the rituals observed, it was nearly mid-night and we were all ready to call it a day and seek out our beds. Jemma retreated back to my room, now our room, and crawled into bed saying a mumbled "good night" to me before totally conking out.

I had already gone through the house placing wards around each bedroom and the front and back doors. I also set a motion spell around the windows in case there was any attempt to enter the sleeping house that way. I was feeling pretty secure in the work I had done when I heard a quiet tapping on the bedroom door.

It was Wynn.

"Wynn, what's wrong? Did you hear something?" I asked looking over her shoulder toward the front room. She stood in the defused light coming through the front room windows. Her hair had been drawn back into a tight braid and her night gown had a home-spun look in its simplicity giving her the look of a frontier woman.

Without any preamble she said, "I found this, Cathleen and thought I'd best show it to you. I didn't want to alarm the others, but I felt it could be a warning." She handed me a crinkled parchment paper that reminded me of some I'd handled at an Egyptian Mystics conclave I'd attended some years ago. But that's another story.

I fumbled open the ancient looking paper as I was only half awake. It was written in black ink in a beautiful script. *"Close your eyes if you need. Sleep if you dare."* I reread it and took in the complete impact of the message. I looked up from the sheet into Wynn's concerned eyes. "When and where did you find this, Wynn?" I asked, not bothering to keep my brow from furrowing with worry.

"I found it when we all retired to our rooms for the night. It was on my pillow."

"Was there anything out of order in your room, or anything missing?" I asked.

"My hairbrush was moved from the night stand to my dresser, but I didn't even consider that, Cathleen. Do you think someone from our group is involved?"

I did not think any of the present coven members could have left the note since they were in constant contact all day. It had to have happened while we were all outside since I placed my wards only *after* we came back together this evening. I mentioned all of this to Wynn and added, "Someone had to have left this while we were in your circle to cleanse the house and before I set my wards." And to my mind only Ursa could conjure an intruder to slip in and place the note. This was a threat to Wynn, and she looked appropriately scared.

"Wynn, I'd like you to sleep in my room with Jemma for tonight. Don't worry though, as it has already been protected by me."

"Where will you be?"

"Your room of course." I saw a question flash across her face and disappear as she slipped past me into my room where she saw a sleeping Jemma. I nodded my approval of her move and closed the door behind her quietly.

Wynn's room was at the end of the long hallway where mine was closest to the front door. Hers was also closest to the much coveted bathroom. With only one full bath and seven females there was lots of jockeying for bath time.

I decided to arm myself further by stepping out the front door for a moment. Touching the ground, a surge of energy filled me as I crouched in the creamy yellow light of the moon. I felt rather than heard a stirring behind me, and spun in time to see another kind of shadow, a *Leach Phantom*! I'd only seen drawings of these creatures in my dad's *Conjuring Demons from the Pit: Encyclopedia of Dark Wizardry*. I'd heard that dad successfully dispatched a few, but I never had an opportunity to replicate his spell until my current situation. *Guess Ursa is throwing it all at us,* I thought grimly as I wearily gathered myself for yet another confrontation.

It was translucent and I shuddered as I watched an oily black sludge course sluggishly throughout its fog-gray body. It was headless, with long tentacles springing in every direction from where that part of its anatomy should have been. Its torso was studded with the most rudimentary of eyes over a mouth that seemed to be in a continuous scream of agony. Of course, if I looked like that I'd be screaming too!

It had a pair of claw-tipped appendages jutting out from its sides, and they looked strong, the claws likely poisonous. I was surprised at how short it was, but then realized it was moving toward me on some kind of rollers where legs should have been. *Ursa must be getting better at sending these spooky creatures,* I thought just before I flung *a Many Colored String* spell at it.

Immediately it was bathed in a rainbow of cheerful colors, like an upended crayon box, which phantoms like this one hated with a passion. They avoided all color and any hint of happy. I had gathered the strings from the huge over-stuffed chair that matched the coach in its drab burgundy color. *That's no loss to the décor* I thought, smiling tightly as I kept pulling the long tendrils through the open front door and kept adding new and vibrant colors as I worked my Magic.

The strings wrapped themselves around the *Leach Phantom* with a cyclone force never allowing it to even attempt to escape, or fight back. This was one of my favorite spells as it was both pretty and effective. It's good to enjoy your work.

When the chair had been reduced to four wooden claw feet and a pile of springs, the cyclone stopped abruptly and the phantom had been turned into a very colorful mummy. It wasn't terribly grateful to me for the face lift as it tried desperately to attack me when I got closer, managing to poke one bony claw out between some blue and orange strings. But I was more than enough match for a dummy mummy.

I merely raised my palm in a shoving motion and the creature hit the ground where it lay like a huge moth chrysalis, pretty humiliating to a phantom of this caliber. I wasn't gloating too much though as I still had to figure out how this particular monster invaded the coven compound undetected by me, or even some of the others with higher forms of sensitivity to spiritual doings.

I decided to drag the intruder further into open grounds away from the house, so that I could question it about its mission. As I bent down to grab hold of some dangling strings, the entire mummy casing caved in on itself and the phantom was no longer my guest. *Hmm* I thought. *Someone has pulled a few strings herself!*

I went to my room to check on Wynn and Jemma and found them both in a deep sleep. *Glad someone is getting some rest*, I thought, with a huge yawn to mark my own sleepless state.

I went back toward the living room and stopping at the linen closet along the way, picked out a particularly cozy looking quilt to curl up in on the only soft furniture left, the lumpy burgundy couch. My back twanged at the thought, but my choice was that or the floor as I ruled out Wynn's room because my wards obviously hadn't held there for some reason. Another mystery I was too tired to think about. *Was I having fun yet?*

Chapter 17

Morning came buzzing in on Faerie wings and I nearly swallowed one of the small creatures when it flew too close to my bleary-eyed yawn. "Wake up my darlin' lass. I've arrived and just in the nick of time, so I'm told."

My mother stood in the flesh at the foot of the coach with a big grin on her beautiful face and a Troop of Faeries covering her arms and shoulders like swallow tail butterflies, hovering around her head, in a hallo of iridescent color.

Her wavy dark red hair was held back with a yellow head band and hanging coyly over one shoulder, showing off large, gold hoop earrings. She looked quite at home in the outfit she'd chosen for her introduction to the Wiccans, a long skirt, the sunny yellow of my kitchen back home, topped with a gauzy white blouse embroidered with small moon and stars. She had layered so many strands of multi colored beads around her neck that I feared she'd do herself bodily harm. She wore rings on most of her fingers that flashed in the sparkle of the Faerie light, diamonds and her favorite emeralds. All in all she looked like part of a wandering minstrel show.

Before she could raise a ruckus I jumped up, almost tripping over the quilt in my haste to get her outside before she woke the whole house as she started to burble with that special laugh of hers. I love her dearly, but mom's laugh is like a cross between a braying donkey and a nanny goat. As beautiful as she is that seems her only real physical flaw. Or maybe I'm just ultra-sensitive to unearthly sounds. Guess dad was able to use Magic to stopper his ears when needed because they laughed a lot when he was still with us.

"Mom," I said, steering her outside into the predawn of the desert, "I didn't expect you until later, much later. How did you get here so fast?" She gave me one of her quirky smiles and pointed a perfectly manicured finger to a shiny red Corvette nestled close to the recently vacated shed.

"I rented that beauty, dear, and it is almost as much fun as zooming about as a hologram. It certainly attracted the attention of the local constabulary though and I fear they may be hunting it and me still, as I wouldn't acknowledge their annoying sirens and flashing lights. I really can't abide such harassment, and me, a visitor to this country."

That explained the charm she placed over the car as it cooled its engine. I swore I heard it panting as heat shimmered around the hood. She must have gone at warp speed to get here. The candy-apple-red sports car sat snugly under an invisibility cloak and I only knew it was there because I still had my inner eye open to any new mischief by Ursa and her minions.

"Mom, you really have to be more careful. What if you'd had an accident driving here?"

"Well," she replied with that annoying little grin she uses on me when she knows I've caught her out, "Oh, aye, I suppose I could use me broom, but that's a wee bit old fashioned don' ye tink?" Now, she said this using her most quaint Irish brogue, so of course it sounded even more innocent somehow.

I sighed deeply, and without another word we were giving each other big hugs and kisses as she patted my back and crooned softly, "Oh, sweet lass, it's so wonderful to see you." She stroked my hair like I always loved as a little girl and I felt calm and safe for the first time in days.

"It's really wonderful to see you, Mom." And I hugged her tighter. I hadn't realized how much I missed my mother after she returned to Ireland.

When we lost dad to the waters of the mighty Alleghany River, she turned to me one day shortly after and said, "Time for your ma to return to the Emerald Isle, dear girl. You are a woman grown and I need to be among the heather and Faeries once more."

The next morning she kissed my forehead, gave me her blessing and was gone. I sold our farm house and our never farmed 20 acres for her and sent her the money, even though she cheats and conjures some up from time to time when she doesn't approve of a certain sales technique. Once a merchant had placed it in his money bag it would disappear just like she had. I must admit my mother did have a bit of a felonious streak in her.

We held hands as we began to amble into the beautiful stillness of the desert at dawn. Many of the stars were still visible though fading by the second with the slow rising of another hot sun. As we approached a large outcropping of rock surrounded by the ubiquitous tumble weed of the area, she stopped and holding both of my hands in hers she said, "Now listen lass, the little folk have been telling me tales about a Black Witch here about, who has begun to conjure some pretty scary beasties. They say she was a Wiccan at one time, but gave her spirit to the Dark Lords so she'd become more powerful. They also tell me she has an alter ego who is far more dangerous than even this Black Witch."

I saw the concern in her eyes and tried to allay her fears somewhat. "Mom, it's all true about Ursa, that's her name…"

"Oh," my mom was mouthing, "A potent name for a Magic user, pet."

"Well, yes," I said, "but she's got her weaknesses too. She's vain and thinks she's too powerful to be beaten by any other

Magic. I know that I can best her, but I am concerned about trying to protect this coven while I work that out."

"Speaking of this coven dear, I feel the presence of only six. Where are the others?"

"Five are still under Ursa's control, one more was destroyed and then, of course, Ursa made thirteen," I said.

"Well, sweet girl, nothing to concern yer darlin' head about, protecting this clutch of Wiccan women. I will stir up a little something to help in the guarding o' the place."

"Oh, mom," I said, perhaps too anxiously, "You are naturally welcome to stay as long as you want I'm sure, but I think I have this well in hand."

"Huh!" she said. "That's not what the wee folk are tellin' me, pet. And besides, I haven't done any decent Magic since my last run in with the Guild Masters, the old stuffed shirts!" *Guess that explains a lot,* I thought with a sigh of resignation.

We were still standing by the rock cluster when I heard my name being yelled out with panic brought on by some form of distress.

"Better get back there, mom. That didn't sound like good news about to break!" We spun on our heels, at least she did. I still had only my socks on and had no intention of spinning on the hard dirt and sharp pebbles.

We both rushed toward the front door where Joanie was standing. "Oh thank the *Goddess,*" she was saying, her voice rising to near-hysteria.

"Joanie, what's happened, girl?" Mom grabbed Joanie by her outstretched hand. Joanie was so upset it didn't seem to register with her that my mom was there at all.

"I think that Maud has been taken again!"

I raced past them both and dashed to Maud's room. The door was open and she was nowhere in sight. It looked like her bed hadn't been slept in at all. I couldn't believe my wards and spells could have been so easily compromised, but her absence indicated something unknown was at play.

Mom and Joanie had come up behind me, trying to peer past my shoulders through the narrow doorway. "So love, what doings do you suspect?" Mom asked softly.

Turning to them both, I said, "Maud could not have been abducted like before. My spells and wards are still in place. I can feel them." I said this last adamantly as indeed I could sense they were un-tampered with and still working. "But I do sense another of Ursa's little buddies."

My mother stopped me, taking my arm for a second as I turned to go back to the front room. "Listen lass, there is a presence in the kitchen my wee friends have told me." The Faeries had vanished after mom and I went outdoors as they get notoriously out of sorts in hot desert air. "They've been enjoying the pots and pans hanging around the stove, playing a bit of "Look for the pretty Faerie" don't you know." I rolled my eyes to encourage less diversion. "Well," she went on, "that's when they saw a *Pitted Choker* hanging about under the table."

That was definitely bad news. Those little buggers were made to poison food, pollute water and drinks and make a person feel just generally miserable if not dead! The fact that they were here and Maud was gone made one wonder. *Hmm maybe she didn't want to eat the cooking this morning* I thought with genuine disappointment as I liked Maud and thought she was trying to get beyond her recent experience.

That's when Maud came strolling through the back kitchen door, humming quietly to herself and holding a basket of fresh

White Sage for the house. She stopped in her tracks and stared across the room at us, trying to figure out what was going on.

"Hey guys. I got up early to get some more of our sage inside from the shed. With that new hole, I figured it might get damaged out there and--" She stopped and stared openly at the new face.

"Maude, this is my mother, Brighid O'Brien."

She crossed the room and putting her basket down on the table top, came over to where we all stood. Unfortunately, when she deposited the basket it vibrated the table enough to bring the *Pitted Choker* to its feet if that's what those slimy green chunks were. I grabbed for Maud's hand like I was going for the gold ring on a Merry-Go-Round and jerked her unceremoniously into the front room.

She yelped and nearly sprawled onto the floor. Luckily mom caught her and setting her aright, turned her attention back to her only offspring, who really needed some attention by then!

The *Pitted Choker* had moved into the kitchen proper and was looking none too happy with me. I suspect it planned to add some unwanted ingredients to the morning's oatmeal and place some unwelcome poisons as seasoning to anything in the refrigerator that struck its fancy. These particular creatures were made to wreak havoc on the mortal constitution and thoroughly enjoyed watching folks writhing around on the floor in utter agony. A bit of frothing at the mouth of their victims was like icing on their poisonous cake.

Mom was beside me in a heartbeat and with out-stretched hands, she called down a lovely little spell that literally pickled the *Pitted Choker* on the spot. I could taste the strong smell of brine on my tongue and got a bit of a whiff of dill along with it.

"Why a pickle, Mom?"

"Well, it *is* green, dear."

Joanie and Maud came hesitantly back into the kitchen, staring open mouthed at the very ugly pickle firmly affixed to the linoleum. "Now you girls aren't to worry your heads a bit." Mom said cheerily like she had just baked a chocolate cake for them. "I'll have this annoying creature out o' your breakfast room straight away!" Mom believed every meal should be eaten in its own designated room; hence, we had three separate eating areas in our house and a small room for snacks. And I wonder why I seem too maladjusted at times for normal relationships.

With that said, mom snapped her bejeweled fingers and the green beastie was gone while the smell of pickle brine lingered on.

Maud was standing close to Joanie for comfort I suspected when I asked, "Maud, did you come through here when you left the house this morning?"

"No, after I got ready I just went out the front door and right to the shed." She hesitated for a moment. "By the way, it's probably nothing, but I bumped into something near the shed door and I can't see anything there. Do you think it was another creature?" I felt badly about any bruised shins, but didn't want to explain about the cloaked Corvette either, so I just shrugged my shoulders and looked perplexed.

After calming down her fear of other intruders, I asked Maud to return to her room for a bit while I scoured the grounds with my mother just to be sure all was in order. We were ready to leave when Joanie seemed to wake up to my mom's presence.

"Oh, dear *Goddess*!" she cried as she came over to mom and threw her freckled arms about her shoulders.

"Hello, dear." My mom gave her a big kiss on each cheek and holding her at arm's length said, "We have some catching up to do, lass, but let's go with Cathleen first and lay down some wee surprises for any unwanted visitors around the grounds before the other girls get up to breakfast."

Joanie seemed delighted with mom's enthusiastic plans to deal with the Black Witch and be part of our team even in a minor role. I, on the other hand, was wishing we could be planning a cook out rather than a war.

Chapter 18

By the time we set out for our stroll along the compound perimeter, the stars had blurred in the muted light of a welcome dawn. The air was soft in these early morning hours and I inhaled deeply. It helped clear the stench of pickle brine from my nose and I began to feel hopeful it would prove to be a productive day. In spite of mom's presence, I knew I was still responsible to get to the bottom of the mystery of the missing coven members.

I had told Maud I was taking Joanie and mom on a short reconnaissance so mom could get acquainted with the area, but we needed her to remain behind as our home guard. She seemed pleased with that task. I suspected our trust in her provided a needed boost to her self-confidence.

Knowing my mother would not be satisfied with playing a minor role in the battle between Ursa and the coven, I planted her between Joanie and myself as we walked so she'd be included in our conversation and any strategizing.

"I'm convinced we need to lure Ursa to the compound so we can clobber her with Magic," I said firmly. "As of now she's sent her minions to do her dirty work and protected herself from any direct confrontations."

"Do you think she knows your mom is here now?" Joanie asked looking at mom and then me.

"Aye, of course she knows, lass. I sent her a messenger to announce my arrival." *So that's where the Pickled Pitted Choker went* I thought with a tiny smile, glad I didn't have to say that out loud.

"I wanted her to understand that she had more than wee lass on her own, to deal with. No offense, darlin' girl." she added quickly. I smiled at her and she knew I was happy and comforted to have her strong Magic at my side. Moms are made to protect, she always told me and my mom was more than up to the task.

We decided to split our forces, though I'd keep Joanie with me for two reasons; she didn't have the Magic needed to deal with the bad guys that kept showing up around the place and she was really scared. I felt I could at least give her a bit of comfort in my being close by and I knew she'd have my back if there was any trouble.

Mom and I both used our inner eye, though I doubted she ever went abroad without her guiding eye engaged. She would go to the right, covering a half circle until we met in the middle as we came in from the left. The boundaries of the compound were fairly blurred, but there was a remnant of an old barbed wire fence either lying on the ground or dangling from rotted posts that would indicate the extent of the compound property.

I looked over at my mother to see how she was doing in this unfamiliar environment before we went our separate ways. There was a mild breeze stirring the loose hair around her neck and she looked so vulnerable wearing that I'm-a-delicate-woman outfit. *Boy will she surprise any fool who threatens her,* I thought with grim satisfaction.

We began our Demon reconnaissance just as the light wind stiffened slightly. I only noticed because Joanie was clutching her hat to keep it on her head; with her long red hair shoved up under it, the hat was precariously set at best. As we walked I put my far reaching senses into motion and pushing them farther ahead, following like a hound dog on scent.

The dry gray sage brush was blowing around our feet and scratching against our legs as the wind buffeted them like a bunch of deflated punching balloons. These bristly incursions on our progress turned from annoying to downright threatening. We were suddenly surrounded by a sea of the brittle scrub that was mounting one upon another until they formed a thorny wall that curved into itself, effectively cutting us off from the outside world.

Joanie began to look around herself with wild concern blooming in her eyes. "Cathleen…what's happening?" she whimpered. I could barely hear her even with my enhanced hearing, as the wind had now become an aggressive roar and the prickly brush was pushed higher and tighter around us.

The air inside the now towering hedge became heavy with the scent of putrefying meat. I turned in a quick circle to see dozens of human arms poking through the scrub like sickly Halloween decorations, hands grasping blindly. The flesh was a gangrenous green and black and sloughing off the straining, disembodied arms. I knew the grasping hands and fingers on these other-worldly limbs belonged to those who had forfeited their souls to the Dark Pit and were brought up by the Black Witch.

By now Joanie was nearly hysterical as one of the garish hands brushed across her face. I quickly held my own arms out to my sides, narrowly avoiding the grasp of a probing hand. I pushed back against the tremendous volume and pressing weight. This barrier with its rotting limbs was a perversion of Nature in the *Mother's* eye and *Mother* didn't take kindly to mortals perverting her plan with bad Magic.

The sage brush seemed to blow apart and in a blink we were free and staring at acres of natural desert. I could hear Joanie's heart begin to slow down from its panic-induced tempo. We looked around us for anything else out the ordinary and finding nothing, walked on. This time it was my friend who used her intercessions to her *Goddess* to keep us safe and protect us from the Darkness.

She had taken my hand in a strong grip and squeezing it said, "I think we can say we had a close "brush" with death, Cathleen." I laughed as much with relief at her humorous response to this attack, as to our escape.

It was pleasing to listen to her melodic chanting as we walked on and it helped to soothe our somewhat fraying nerves.

Twenty more minutes of walking and we met up with my mother, completing the circle we'd made. We told her about the sage brush trying to turn us into mulch. She scowled at the mention of the rotting limbs saying, "Death seems to be Ursa's calling card, my dears."

As we began to walk back to the house my thoughts strayed from demons to Sheriffs. *I need to check in with Jason and see how Ollie* is doing I thought, sorry for my dereliction of duty in spite of best intentions.

I missed both my guys and wanted nothing more than to get back to my reasonably normal life. With the exception of a few werewolves, an occasional banshee and the rare rogue Wizard, it really was a fairly mellow life in Iron Mountain. I liked it that way, until I got invited to investigate a mystery with Dark Magic undertones. I still had no clue as to underground grape vine that carried my particular talents along to the uninitiated, but was grateful for the chances to use my training to sort out situations most humans aren't equipped to cope with.

Mom must have caught the dreamy look in my eye when she said, "Cathleen, thinking of that man of yours, dear?" She smiled smugly because she knew Jason had captured my heart. She was just thrilled he had captured my *attention,* considering how fussy I always was. Why compromise in life is my motto, and Jason was second best to no man.

My Magic had become a natural part of our relationship almost from the beginning. He is strong and loyal and he always has my back if we get into any trouble. But I would not give my mother the opportunity to try some funny stuff like *love lusters,* or *bedazzlers* on the poor guy and she was definitely not above that kind of meddling.

I smiled brightly back at her and said, "I think we should do a wider sweep, mom," trying to divert her attention. "There are just too many things Ursa can throw at us if we're not alert to them."

She answered while gazing distractedly into the far horizon. "I've been planting wee surprises around the area Cathleen, so I think the Black Witch will be stepping into some nasty poo, if she comes inside my mine field." She took in a deep breath and said, "This is so invigorating dear!" She smiled and putting her arm through mine we started back to the house.

We joined the others for breakfast after all the introductions were made. No one seemed very surprised at my mom's presence. In fact, they seemed happy to have an extra pair of Magic hands available against Ursa's scheming.

I had asked mom earlier to keep her Magic feelers out for anything that might have attached itself to any of the coven members, without alarming any of them. We determined that was how the *Pitted Choker* had gotten through my wards into the house. Ursa must have found a way to allow her minions to get in under my radar.

Mom was an instant favorite with the girls of the coven and she and Wynn seemed to hit it off like sister witches around a friendly caldron. They were nothing alike outwardly as my mother was flamboyant and glamorous, while Wynn, though attractive, favored the more conservative styles and was very soft spoken. That old saw "Opposites attract" came to mind.

With the cleanup done after breakfast, more tea and coffee were brewed and we all returned to the front room with our steaming mugs. Unfortunately, since I had unraveled the lumpy side chair, which they all thought was cool Magic, some of us were forced to sit on the floor while others grabbed the four kitchen chairs or shared the even lumpier couch.

"I think we need to discuss our strategy to defend against Ursa," Wynn said opening the floor to whoever wanted to jump in with suggestions. Maud and the other two returned sisters looked uncomfortable and gave each other sidelong glances.

I don't know if Wynn caught them, but mom certainly did and said, "Three of you girls have intimate knowledge of this Black Witch and need to share that with us all." She said this last while looking directly from one to the other.

Maud was first to answer this restrained challenge. "I know that Ursa is terrified of any light brighter than candles. She has become deathly pale because she never goes outside except at night…or maybe she's dead…"

Mom looked at her and said "Oh, she isn't dead in a "natural" sense dear, but certainly her spirit is taken and her humanity is now deceased."

The group sat in silence for a minute before anyone else spoke. The old clock sitting on the fireplace mantle ticked its seconds and minutes into a bleak stillness.

"And even if she goes out at night she wears a cape with a cowl," added Luna. "She looks like some kind of creepy monk," she finished with a shiver.

We all looked over at Alana knowing she would be the next to speak. "I noticed that Ursa's eyes have changed color. They have a strange inner glow coming from them too."

"Yeah," said Luna "we think that's how she can see in the dark."

"What color are her eyes now?" mom asked, she had clearly taken over this subtle interrogation.

"They're a dark red, like…like congealed blood." answered Maud with a desolate almost haggard look on her young face.

Mom looked down at my upturned face as she had naturally taken the heavy captain's chair from the kitchen for herself and I sat at her feet *like the Queen's daughter should* I thought.

"Cathleen and I will need to confer, ladies, as this is no ordinary Black Arts user at work here. My little friends warned me that your coven was under attack by a powerful witch and although my Cathleen is quite capable, she may need a wee bit of help from her old ma." I was hoping for more than a tad of help at this point, having realized that Ursa and her Dark allies had a great deal more evil power than I first believed.

We decided to go on a long walk together into the Valley of the Gods and leave the house under *Alarm Wards*. If someone, or something, tried to enter the house, or even come closer than the shed, the alarms would sound. These would be set at a pitch even a blue tick hound dog couldn't hear, but mom and I certainly would. These were put into place along with some "*Merry Chimes*" as mom so quaintly calls these lethal little bells. If they are triggered and not disarmed, they will cause ear drums to burst and eye balls to spin in their sockets leaving the victim pretty much dead, or at least incapacitated. My mother loves noise makers.

The other sound alarm was guaranteed to set teeth on edge. It was formulated by my dad years ago to scare off some annoying coyotes that kept eating our chickens. He called it the *Celebration* charm. These alarms were placed close to the ground and when stepped on would sound like the predator was transformed into part of a July 4th celebration as one of the exploding firecrackers! If the sound of the booms didn't rattle your teeth, you didn't have any in your head.

The Magic done by myself and my mother completed, the eight of us set out with a movable feast prepared by Jemma and Wynn, our acknowledged chefs, jackets and sweaters for the expected evening chill, enough water to supply a Roman cohort, walking sticks when available and hats for everyone. Mom was not keen on the offer of a baseball cap, but it provided shade for her eyes and I told her would protect her from wrinkles. That naturally persuaded her.

We all casually looked back at the empty house as we moved out in loose formation; Wynn and mom leading and as I noted, beginning a quiet conversation. I decided not to listen in as I didn't want to be distracted from my careful surveillance of the area as we trekked along. Mom could fill me in later. Joanie and I took up the rear position with the rest of the girls sandwiched safely inside.

A churning sun was bearing down on us with the weight of its intense heat by the time we stopped to eat our lunch. After I took precautions that no poisons were secreted into our food by the *Pitted Choker,* Jemma and Wynn finished their buffet preparations. It was close to one before we sat down to our buttery croissants, fruits and cheeses. "Very continental," my mother purred approvingly about the delightful spread.

Looking down at the tempting food laid out in the center of a pale pink blanket, I thought a long hike would do me good. I was in serious need of exercise before I started to look like a cactus.

The heat was building as the sun reflected back from the mirror like surface created by the hard packed sandy earth. We had seen a fair number of scuttling and slithering things along the way and I was glad for my heavy mountain hiking boots while I looked over the assorted tennis shoes sported by most of the others. Mom was too practical not to have her own rugged wear on her size 5 feet.

We sat under the shade provided by one of the fantastic flat top buttes scattered around the area and seen like a city skyline off in the distance. Mom turned slowly in place making a full circle while her eyes took in the exquisite beauty of the natural rock formations.

"These could rival the Clannish in Scotland, ladies," she said with clear admiration on her face and in her voice.

"What are they?" Luna asked.

"Well dear, they are a set of ancient standing stones, sort of like these, where lovers go to declare their vows. At least they did many centuries ago. Of course we have only the word of the Scots so…"

Mom blithely let that politically incorrect remark hang between us, but I did notice a few heads bobbing in agreement. By now some of the women were referring to Ursa as "The Black Scot," but they likely wouldn't care for haggis either.

As we cooled down from our exertions, Wynn decided this was a good place to do a circle so we could pool our energies and commune with their *Goddess*. The Valley of the Gods was certainly considered a sacred spot to them and a Power center for many who follow the spiritual aspects of nature. By making their circle of energy they could pick up the earth's pulse, its life force.

Wynn looked around at her coven sisters and said "I've seen this place in my dreams of late. We have been linked like this. I was aware of a strange Magic though, very powerful and very protective of the Mother Earth. I didn't know why that Magic was always present with us in those dreams, but now I understand." She looked at me and my mother who had joined hands earlier. For a breath, I thought I detected a flicker of jealousy in Wynn's eyes, but dismissed that as shy admiration as she quickly lowered her head.

The sisters had all closed their eyes in order to block out the corporal world around them and commune more closely with the spiritual. Mom and I kept our eyes open and vigilant for any surprises that might materialize. I had shared with her earlier that ever since the *Pitted Choker* incident I felt a presence and believed we'd been followed and watched. She confirmed my senses were definitely picking up something Magic, but advised we keep it to ourselves until we knew what we were dealing with.

It is believed by many witches and shamans that they can move between the physical and spiritual words via holy power sites like the Valley of the Gods where we currently stood. They believe these earthly spots act like borders between the Real and the Magical and they can cross over to either world, either to do Magic, or to escape from it.

I was thrilled to be in the physical presence of such power emanating from the *Green Mother,* but realized how that opportunity worked both ways. As we stood quietly wrapped within the hum of chanting voices, my mother and I snapped a quick look at each other and looking down saw the earth shift ever so slightly.

By now the sun had moved off toward the west making it around three-thirty. We knew we had a bit more time before our expected visitor showed itself. These creatures favor "shadow time" as Magic users refer to sundown. The deep silky spread of darkness would conceal any Demon creature waiting to perform its master's bidding. One thing my parents drummed into me as a fledgling wizard was that what came from the Dark, loved being part of the dark and they were very patient while they waited there to do harm in this realm.

Just as I was starting to get a little fidgety, Wynn clapped her hands and the chanting stopped abruptly. The girls around the circle dropped hands and smiled at one another as if they'd been renewed by the power around them and cleansed in spirit.

That was a good thing because now the real challenge was ahead of us and we needed all their energies and our Magic, to stay alive in a valley of the sacred, where a Demon of the Dark hid from the sacred light.

Chapter 19

We were picking up our various backpacks and canvas totes, discussed dinner and decided to eat around eight o'clock and then head back before it got too dark. A good plan and I must give my mother the credit as she engineered the conversation in her subtle way.

Once more, Wynn and Mom led us, with Joanie and me following the others like faithful sheep dogs. In some ways I felt like we were on an army patrol instead of a nature hike because I had to keep a constant vigilance as we walked along. The day was still very warm, but we kept a good quantity of water flowing down dry throats so no one got dehydrated.   I heard snippets of conversation between the girls in the middle of our convoy and all seemed natural and back to easy relationships between coven sisters. I knew it would be hard for the returned coven members to reconnect with Jemma, Joanie and Wynn, but time is a perfect distiller of memory.

Jemma was saying that she needed a quick potty break since her consumption of water was catching up to her. We were near a cluster of small dirt mounds and after she checked it out for unwanted voyeurs she ducked down behind it. We all took the opportunity to look around us and identify the more famous buttes in the area. From our vantage point in the Valley we easily recognized Setting Hen Butte, and Seven Salons Butte, and Devils Window at which point someone said, "That one right down from Devils Butte is Scotsman Butte."

In the silence that followed all heads and eyes turned to a point in the distance that was all too familiar to a few of us and very scary to the rest. That's when we realized that Jemma wasn't back from her personal tour of duty.

I looked over at mom and she gave an imperceptible nod. I walked over as casually as I could to the small towers of red dirt. "Jemma, is everything ok?" No answer. Not good. "Jemma did you hear me?" No answer. Really bad.

Now I know private potty time is part of our DNA as females, but putting that aside I rushed to look behind the dirt screen. Jemma was gone and there was a huge hole in the ground that was slowly filling up with the gritty makings of the Valley floor.

"What should we do?" It was Wynn's pleading voice to my mother who looked as perplexed as I felt. We were all standing around the quickly filling hole where our friend should have been, with everyone huddled together for comfort. Joanie and I exchanged looks and I said, "Jemma has been taken by Ursa as you all must know. Right now is not a good time to panic though. You are all Wiccans and your connection to the earth is a strong one, especially in this sacred place."

My mother took up the pep talk. "We need you to link your energies and draw power from the *Mother* while Cathleen and I have a bit of a chat."

We moved off and I heard Wynn shout after us, "May the Goddess be with you."

"She is ever thoughtful, that one," mother said, but I thought I detected a bit of sarcasm in her tone. *Hm.*

We waited to do any Magic until the Wiccans had moved far off from the site of the disappearance. Whatever we planned would be significantly more like a "rotor rooter" than pick and shovel work.

Facing each other across the now mostly filled hole we joined hands. There were only a few shifting grains of sand and dirt still moving, so it was obvious the job of snatching our Wicca friend was complete.

We held out our free hands, arms extended over the now settled area and began our spell to displace all that had filled in the space. We had to be general, not just calling it dirt, or sand as it was likely scrub, pebbles and even creepy crawlers too. In spell casting you can't be too careful, or too specific.

This was my mother's favorite thing, casting spells and counter-spells. She excelled at it and as my father often remarked, "Brighid, you are splendid my love at forcing your spells down any throat or hole known to the Magic world!" He was very proud of her Magical talents and I prayed to the *Mother* she had kept her skills sharp.

From what I understood since moving back to Ireland, my mother had turned her Magic to the more mundane like baking the best pastries in the history of the county fair. She hinted that she might have cheated just a smidge by using some special ingredients to win, but she always shared the prizes with the Faeries. No wonder she was their favorite Wizard!

The ground that had swallowed Jemma began to tremble. At first just a few grains of sand sloughed off to the side, followed by a significant shudder, and then a hole began to form. It shot straight down with the sides holding fast as they were being shorn-up by our combined Magic. The shaft became immensely deep and we could see with our inner eye that it suddenly veered off to the left in a direct path to the Scotsman Butte. Not breaking our concentration, my mother and I fixed our spell in place like mortar and returned to a chorus of chanting Wiccans.

"Wynn," Mom said in a calm voice impressing me with her sense of control. "We need your lasses to keep up their prayers and chants and whatever Magic you do, dear. My girl and I have to leave you for a bit and go investigate a clue."

A clue? I thought. *That hole must go down seventy feet and who knows how far till we get to Scotsman Butte…another mile?* Myself, I thought of a clue as something not quite as significant in size, but that was mom speak for not to worry, pet.

Wynn and the rest of the coven seemed content enough with that plan of action and I saw some of them taking their talismans out from under shirts and tops and holding them as they began to chant once more.

These girls had to be our rear action guard. I hoped they could protect themselves in our absence while keeping our way back above ground, clear of unwanted visitors. I knew my mom's plan was to descend into the new tunnel, making our way by using it as our back door so that we could benefit from the element of surprise. Ursa was surely aware of our Magic and she'd be waiting for us with Jemma as her bait.

As we stood over the gaping hole we'd just prepared, my mother turned to me and with a motherly hand, brushed my curls away from my eyes. "Now Cathleen," she said brusquely, "we need to keep connected at all times, dear, so that our power remains unbroken. And use only your inner eye lass, as I don't want the dirt getting into those pretty hazel eyes of yours. You certainly inherited those from your Da." Mom's eyes were a sea green that always held the promised mystery of sea monsters in them when I was a child.

We clasped hands once again and I squeezed my eyes shut, sensing our being levitated over the hole and then with a fantastic swoosh of air being displaced by our bodies, we were beneath the earth and standing at the bottom of a tunnel.

Mom spoke softly in my ear, "Time to open your eyes, pet" As I did so I saw we stood directly in front of the left-hand tunnel opening that would lead us to Scotsman Butte.

"Mom," I said, in equally soft tones, "I sense some stirrings up ahead."

"Why yes, love, that would be Ursa's nasty minion creature. I believe we'll find a *Blood Blodget* waiting patiently on us."

I inhaled a shaky breath of stale air.

Blood Blodgets were a particularly nasty type of Demon. I had had only one experience confronting such a creature, and was luckily in my father's company. I was around fourteen then and fairly advanced in my Magical powers, or at least I thought so. My dad and I had set up my training in a cave site probably abandoned by the original peoples inhabiting that area, deep in the Alleghany woods. We were practicing some pretty potent spells and must have caught the attention of a Black Magic user who sent the *Blood Blodget* to investigate and curtail our intrusion with brute force. My dad made short shrift of the wizard's assassin, but not before it did some nearly lethal damage.

These things stand seven feet tall, on three legs. Their scaly bodies are covered in spike-like growths tipped with wicked barbs that they enjoy leaving inside their victims. Unusual enough with their three legged stance, these guys also have three arms, one which projects from their chest, accordion like, striking out and back in rapid motion. Dad was hit in his vulnerable torso by a barb and almost couldn't finish his spell to destroy the Demon. I moved quickly to apply the antidote charm as he had started to blacken around his mouth, and his ears and nose began to detach from his head. Not an attractive way to go, just rotting away, piece by piece. He recovered, but I've never forgotten the *Blood Blodget*. I would never underestimate its deadly abilities.

We stood in utter darkness, but with our Inner vision we were able to negotiate the tunnel without incident; that is until we encountered the lurking Demon. It was acting as Ursa's sentinel I supposed and would be our executioner if we didn't dispatch it quickly. Mom squeezed my hand in a signal to stop. We each held out our free hand, palm out and our combined power shot bright *green fire* directly at the bulk of the scaly creature.

The *Blood Blodget* was wreathed in green flame, but continued to stand there, unmoving and unfortunately, not dying.

Again my mother squeezed my hand, but this time not with fire. A sulfurous smelling slime shot out across the space separating us from it. The Blood Blodget made a snorting sound deep in his chest. "I do believe the little bugger is laughing at us, Cathleen," my mother said indignantly.

Since these guys have no mouth, I couldn't confirm this observation visually, but it seemed reasonable since the monster had no reaction to our slime either.

"Hm, perhaps we'll need your Da's famous recipe for *Blood Blodget* destruction." I shot her a quick glance and she said, "Oh, yes. I knew about that encounter in the cave, dear, and was none too pleased I might add. But you did a fine job at saving your Da from further harm."   They really had no secrets from each other, I realized.

The big guy became restless waiting for us as we tried to dispatch him with a few other disappointing spells, so it moved forward in our direction. On its three legs it had covered a good bit of ground, but then we were in the process of backing up rather quickly so that it only looked like it was moving fast. It had extended its arms, pointing those dangerous barbs toward our faces. I noticed the slime we had shot out earlier had dried to a kind of crust around the *Blodget's* head, giving the impression that he'd suddenly sprouted a head full of white, smelly hair.

The Demon was closing the gap between us, so my mother decided on a new tact without consulting me. She jerked her arm upward in a sudden gesture and since the hand I was holding was attached to that arm, I was suddenly propelled a few feet forward, closer that is to the Demon. I must have yelped out my surprise, but to my own amazement, the *Blodget* stepped back in reaction to my sudden close proximity.

This time it was me who shouted out the spell I had learned from my dad that day in the cave so many years ago. "Begay Flatulitum!" Instantly, there was an explosion as the *Blood Blodget* was blown apart like a punctured gas-filled balloon. The narrow tunnel was instantly filled with an obnoxious odor that practically knocked me to the ground. I didn't realize I was dripping *Blodget* scales until my mother was suddenly at my side picking icky things out of my hair.

"Well, now I remember that part of your da's story, pet. The exploding *Flatulitum* part. Most effective I must say." She was actually chortling like a magpie at this point, and I continued to pick unsavory items from my person.

"Mom," I said, "a little help here?" She didn't hesitate at the note of concern in my voice and immediately produced a *Clean-up* spell to rid me of the goo and gristle. Being a Magic user was messy business at times. *Those little charms of hers come in handy* I thought and made a mental note to ask for that particular recipe.

"I don't think we'll encounter more of these creatures, Cathleen, but Ursa's been up to no good while we were engaged. I sense some dark creature at the end of this tunnel."

"I think that might be Ursa's alter ego, mom. I felt it lurking around the outside of the house earlier and I think it's what followed us into the Valley."

"She must be using it to block our entrance, pet, so let's be very careful shall we, dear?" I guess she expected an argument, but stealth was obviously our best tactic.

"Mom, how about using that cloaking spell you threw over the Corvette? We could pass right by the dark being and then have undetected access to the Butte."

"That's very good thinking, Cathleen, but that particular spell is only good for one object at a time. So, I will conceal myself and you will wait until I dispatch the creature from behind." While I didn't much like that solution it seemed the only reasonable way to proceed. My own cloaking device wasn't as full proof as hers and had on occasion left parts of me showing. A real disadvantage when facing a creature wanting to do you bodily harm. *I really have to work on that* I thought with the benefit of hindsight, my usual vantage point in life.

I knew we'd have to go with her suggested plan and said, "OK, but I will have my ears on you and if there's anything you can't handle, just sing out so I can help you!"

With that said my mother breathed out the ancient Druid words, "*Fulla fiada*" and disappeared from view at least the view of those without inner vision. She looked rather funny hunched down low as if trying to make herself smaller. She moved off toward the target and after a moment I sensed the Dark One stir at the slight shift in the air currents.

That's also when I heard La-La-La over and over, and I realized Mom was singing! Good grief...she had taken me literally!

I drew power into my arms as I ran my hands over the dirt walls of the narrow tunnel and begged the *Green Mother* to give my Magic a boost. When I got to her, my mom was standing, her back flat against the tunnel wall and looming in front of her, Ursa's Alter Ego. The Dark One was being held inches from her face by several thick roots winding over and over, around its black form. Its body was thick and long, reminding me of a Moray eel in its sinuous motion. It was as black as the eye of a newt and though naked was totally covered in weeping sores.

It struggled against the constricting fibrous roping. Its long arms pinioned to its oozing sides.   As I watched, a pale knotted root shot straight out of the dirt next to the Dark One's knobby head. With the twisting motion of a boa constrictor, it wrapped around the Alter Ego's neck until its energy faded and it fell like soot from a chimney.

My mother seemed none the worse for the fright she gave me, so I questioned her loss of concealment. "Oh goodness, dear, I think Ursa has the inner eye herself and likely, the cheeky little devil gave it to her Alter Ego as a safe guard against our slippery Magic. Can't be helped, I suppose."

"By the way, mom, if I tell you to sing out again, don't. I'll explain later." She looked perplexed, but nodded her head in agreement and we moved on.

Although the Alter Ego Ursa had used to extend her personal greeting was reduced to ash under our feet, Ursa was very much as potent as ever. I wondered what her next move was going to be and since there was no way to predict what a Dark Witch will do, I just figured it would be very nasty.

Chapter 20

We stood outside once more, close to the base of the Scotsman Butte. After failing to locate Jemma in any of the chambers we discovered, we decided on a different tactic and returned to the chill but welcome night air. Stretching our senses, we tried to pick up any other evil creatures that might be lurking about outside the Butte, since no new ones had turned up during our search. There were none and that meant Ursa had flown the coop. But there was a faint life force, a pulse beating slowly, like a clock beginning to wind down. It had to be Jemma.

We linked hands once again and used the wind currents captured in the desert breeze to rise to the top of the flat Butte. We didn't actually move through the air by our own power, but used the power of the wind like an elastic band to sling ourselves to the top. We never disturb *Mother* unnecessarily.

Jemma was lying in a circle that seemed made of the same red sand and blood as the one that had captured Wynn. My mother put out her hand to stop me from entering as she wanted to first cleanse it of the dark forces that held Jemma inside. With a quick gesture of her hand she was able to pierce the circle's continuity. I stepped through the broken band and dragged an unconscious Jemma away from the circle and onto the weathered roof of the red monolith.

"We need to return to the others quickly, Cathleen, so I suggest you and I hold her between us and I'll do a *Gliding* spell."

"Mom," I said with some concern in my voice, "You had a few mishaps with that spell, don't you remember?"

"Oh, Dragon Twicky!" she said, using her strongest vulgarity, "I've had lots of practice since your Da's tiny incident."

That "tiny incident" nearly cost him two legs and one arm as she glided him into a fast spinning wind mill. Luckily he was able to stop the thing before any real damage could be incurred, but he told mom she wasn't to drive him anywhere ever again. It's a man thing.

I couldn't really suggest any alternative mode of transport that would accommodate all three of us, so we hooked our arms under Jemma's and locked them in place by holding hands. Before I could sneeze from the dust we kicked up with all our activity, my mother had called out in her best witchy voice, "Cas cuai feach!" and we were launched.

"Oh I do love to travel," she was saying. I tightened my grip on her hand which she returned in kind as we began to descend near the circle of chanting Wiccans.

While it felt like we'd only been gone a short while, Joanie dissuaded us of that notion, telling us we'd been away more than two hours and they were worried sick. The others had taken Jemma into the shade of the rocks and laid her on our picnic blanket. She'd gotten par boiled up there on that exposed surface and they began to hydrate her and put cold compresses on her wrists, using the frozen cooler cubes to bring down her body temperature. She started to come around and when she spotted Wynn said in a weak, but clear voice, "I quit!" With that she said she was starving and we'd better have saved her some food.

It was way past the time we said we'd be heading back, but everyone was so relieved to have their sister back among them, the joy and excitement turned into sharp hunger pangs. With little fanfare, they broke out the food and we all dug into the goodies like fire ants at a Texas picnic.

The sunset that evening painted the endless sky in a blaze of glorious color, turning the rocks a heart-blood red and dappling the purplish scorpion weed and Yucca plants in a rosy golden blush. The dessert was being transformed before our eyes and I felt content with my good fortune to share in this bounty of beauty.

With the sun moving into its evening hibernation, the stars began to pop into view; countless silver fish swimming in a great ocean of deepest blue. We didn't want to leave this natural miracle of the cycle of time and space, but we needed to get off the desert and home to our beds.

The packing up was more disorganized than the original process, with things stuffed into anyone's open back pack or bag. The long journey home took on a feel of warriors returning from battle to the safety of their fort.

Maud walked with Mom directly behind Wynn and Jemma. Except for a whispered conversation between Wynn and returned girl when we started back, all of the others were silent. I held my position at the rear of the group with Joanie as my walking partner.

"Can you tell me how you got Jemma back to us, Cathleen?" Joanie knew me well enough, that I didn't share too many details of my Magical exploits or those of my parents when we were younger, but her curiosity always triggered the question anyway.

"I'll tell you this, Joanie, Ursa is one mean Witch and I'm glad my mom's here to do some of the heavy lifting." With that said Joanie showed her intelligence and asked no more. We saved our energy for the long hike home.

"Only another hour to go, ladies," Wynn called out from the front of our rather tattered caravan. There was a collective sigh as we all trudged on into the gathering night.

Happily, we had left the lights on in the kitchen and front room so we were not returning to a dark house. I flashed a quick look in the direction of the Corvette and saw it was still under its Magical wrap and unmolested by any Chevy hating Demons. We filed through the front door and the air of relief was palpable.

"Can I have the first shower?" Jemma asked in a small I-can't-take-any-more-of-this voice. It was quickly agreed that she would be the first to run the hot water down and she went back to our room to collect her pajamas and robe.

Ever since she moved in with me, I felt I had no ownership over that tiny space and tried to spend as little time there as possible which wasn't too difficult. Jason has referred to me as a nocturnal being, saying I didn't seem to require as much sleep as most folks. This from a guy who began a serious study of the night sky with his first telescope as a very young boy; guess he hasn't slept a full night since he was seven.

While the others were putting things back into cupboards and into laundry baskets, or just stretching out on beds waiting their turns in the coveted shower, I went to my mother's room. They had kindly installed her in the Meditation Room as they called the closet-like space where they had wedged a narrow cot for her unexpected visit. She seemed quite content with the accommodations as I found her with her pillow tucked behind her leaning against the wall. In her hand was her treasured box of recipes. Indeed, my dad referring to her spells as recipes was quite correct. She was going through them one by one with a frown creasing her otherwise flawless forehead. *Magic or Botox*? I wondered.

"Hi mom, do you mind if I sit with you for a minute?"

"Of course, my sweet girl. I am always happy to see you. Here, sit down. I'll make space." She tucked her feet under her long skirt and drew them up to her chin. I hoped I would be that limber at her age, whatever age that was. She'd never tell me her age and my dad kept her secret out of his love for her quirky ways. After today's excursions I just hoped I'd be limber at *my* age!

I was thinking earlier that I'd better get my mother up to date on some of the facts surrounding Ursa and her split with the coven. After a twenty minute recap of the story of the power dispute and Ursa's mission to convert the Wiccan sisters to the Black Arts, my mother said, "Ursa sounds a bit of a fraud, dear."

"What do you mean, mom?" I asked. She had my full attention when I heard feet hammering down the hallway in our direction.

Before Mom could explain, Alana poked her head into the room and finding us both staring up at her said, "There's something in the fireplace!"

My mom popped out of the bed so quickly we nearly collided at the doorway. We raced into the front room and found some of the girls up against the far wall looking fearfully toward the fireplace.

Joanie spoke first. "Cathleen, we decided to start a fire and when Alana was putting more wood in the fireplace she screamed because... "

"I saw a face!" Alana finished breathlessly. "It was inside the smoke that started to rise when I added the new log to the fire."

"Can you describe what it looked like?" I asked.

I wondered if this was what mom and I both sensed was attached to Jemma as we hauled her off the Butte earlier. We were unable to determine if it was still there when we arrived back here. Now I guessed it had been hiding somewhere on her like in a pocket. For that matter, it might have attached itself to a less-obvious host after Jemma was gathered up with the rest of the girls.

After listening to a halting description of the newest intruder, mom and I decided it was likely a *Budgie Phantom*. Kept as favorite pets by some Dark Magic sorcerers, they were used to subdue unsuspecting victims. They are remarkably adapt at appearing harmless, even charming. They are small and friendly when first encountered, but you didn't want to extend a hand to them. They would probably bite it off! Mom agreed that we'd likely be finding one of these creatures coyly peeking back at us through the shimmering heat of the fire.

The other girls had been alerted to trouble by Alan's scream and had joined the huddled group at the far wall. They all seemed to be looking at me and that's when I realized my mom was nowhere in sight. *Uh Oh,* I thought as I tried to find the right spell in my tired noggin. Finally feeling prepared for the tiny, but lethal intruder, I approached the fireplace. The flames were gyrating in the air currents flowing through the hearth. As I got closer I could clearly see the *Budgie* clinging to the brick work at the back.

It looked enchantingly sweet, with fuzzy pink hair covering a plump body. A touch of pink fuzz covered a small round head, emphasizing its oversized ears and making it even more endearing.

It saw me through the flames and gave me a winning grin. It shouldn't have done that because I spied a double row of tiny, sharp looking teeth gleaming back at me. Just as I was about to cast a spell I knew would turn the miniature rogue into soot, my mother pushed in front of me and threw a *Net spell* over the darn thing.

"Mom!" I yelled, "What the heck are you doing? I could have turned you into a smoke smudge!"

"Sorry pet, no time to explain. Had to make sure my recipe was correct. Help me drag this furry fellow outside and into that shed for a wee bit of interrogation."

Getting the pink *Budgie* out of the fireplace was easy enough after mom waived her hand to reduce the flames to embers, but getting him into the shed proved a challenge. The girls kept saying how adorable it looked and it kept whimpering with fat tears dropping from its big yellow eyes. We convinced the Wiccans of its lethal nature by allowing it to think mom had relaxed her grip on the *Net charm*. It charged me like a hungry lion with all four rows of teeth flashing and greenish drool speckling its furry cheeks. After that, there were no more objections, only stunned looks from the group.

When we got it installed in the only corner of the shed that still had a roof, I said, "So mom…what's up with the *Netting Spell*?"

"We need some information dear and this is our only link back to Ursa. And you know lass, how witches love their pet *Budgies*. I wouldn't be surprised if Ursa tried some sort of rescue."

The *Budgie* must have thought so too as he was fairly complacent with the turn of events. It was squatted down on its round belly with its four legs spread out. It looked pretty relaxed for being a hairs breath away from becoming an ash pile.

Mom wrestled over an old rain barrel and upending it, perched lady-like on the round seat it made. "Now," she said lightly, "shall we begin? You are the pet Demon of Ursa the Black Witch, who is attacking this coven." When the Budgie tried to open its toothy mouth mom simply said, "Not yet dear," and slapped a *Gag spell* on it. It made a guttural sound, as its eyes bulged bigger, and then was still.

"Ursa has captured five other coven members and we want them returned safely to their Wiccan sisters."

I added, "Their names are Skye, Morning Bird, Niamh, Aileen and Aeron." My mom shot me a quick smile of approval.

"Now that you know their names, you will give us their location."

She rose suddenly and raising her hands slapped the *Budgie* with yet another of her favorite recipes, *The Truth Inquisitor*. "Gabala Escal!" At the same time she disengaged the gag spell and the Budgie began to speak.

I am not as conversant in the various languages found in the realm of Magic as mom, so she translated its gabble into human speak.

"It says that Ursa has the Wiccan sisters in a dark place beneath the big red rock. The name of the giant rock is…Scotsman Butte." She shot me a quick look with raised eye brows and said, "We'll need to dig deeper this time, love."

Turning back to the *Budgie* she commanded it to continue. "My mistress has a black flower that she grows for strength."

"I know that flower," Mom said, turning her worried face to me after translating. "It's the Black Scaborious Rose. It's named after the Druid women warriors who followed the Black path. It is forbidden to be cultivated by the Green Guild Masters because of its evil powers." Looking at her prisoner she indicated for it to finish. "The Mistress will keep the Wiccans as her own followers after they eat from the dark flower in another two sunsets."

"We are done here, Cathleen. Would you clean this up, dear?" With that she exited the shed and I was left staring at the pleading look of the *Budgie*. Almost regretfully, I spoke the spell and reduced its fuzzy pink form to black dust thinking *that was probably how Ursa made it too.* Life can get rough in the world of Magic.

That chore taken care of, I went back inside to find my mother relating her information to the gathered girls. Wynn asked a few questions regarding plans and mom just casually looked over at me and replied, "My daughter, Cathleen, will first give us her ideas of how to proceed won't you love?' I wondered why she kept downplaying her own part in all this, but felt sure she had her reasons.

I cleared my throat and sounding much more confident than I felt began, "I think it best if the group stays here and binds this house and grounds with any kind of spiritual purification you can, so that nothing and no one can be attached, or used to infiltrate the compound. I believe that the five sisters being held are in no real danger until they are forced to eat the Black Scaborious Rose petals and then they are lost to us. We have only two sun downs to act, but there's still a little time to sleep. I suggest we get up before dawn to start our work."

Joanie asked, "What will you and your mom be doing, Cathleen?"

"We'll be doing our Magic," I said, looking over at my mother who smiled sweetly, bobbing her head in agreement. It sounded ominous enough that the group seemed relieved and satisfied as they padded off to bed.

Chapter 21

"By the way, I checked Jemma, dear," mom was saying when the others had gone. "She's quite healthy and there seems to be no more free-loading riders on her person, thank the *Mother*. I do dislike those *Budgies*!" she said this with a sour look on her face. "It's off to bed for you, pet. I'll take the first watch and see you in two hours. That will give us each two hours of sleep before we need to rouse the house to work."

I knew we'd be doing guard shifts since mom had shared that with me earlier when we discussed protecting the house more effectively. The idea of sleep sounded great to me, but when I opened the door to my room I saw a shadow crouching in the corner near my bed. Wynn had returned to her own room feeling safe now to do so and it was just Jemma and I sharing the tiny room. She was accounted for in her bed. My bed was empty. When I slipped back into my inner eye, I saw a pyramid of Faeries hovering like tiny helicopters in the space of the corner. They knew I could see them and started to wave their little webbed hands frantically for my attention.

"I see you, friends," I whispered as loudly as I dared without waking Jemma. They all made a bee line over to me, which a fair description since they were buzzing with excitement. I needed to calm them and find one Faerie to talk for the Troop.

"I will speak with your leader only, my friends. So please choose so I can hear your words." They were suddenly still while one emerald green clad Faerie detached itself from the Troop and alighted on my outstretched palm. Using this as his platform he bowed and began. After several misunderstood words in its archaic language, I was able to make sense of the message and it wasn't good.

Ursa had nearly completed the flowering process for her Black Scaborious Rose. Our time-table had suddenly been moved up. I told the Troop to follow me and ran for the front room and mom.

I knew mom would quickly move into action. She wanted the Faeries to, "stand by, wee friends." They adored her, Brighid, beloved of the Celtic Goddess, Dagda. They bowed down to their tiny toes and stood on the fireplace mantle like a row of multi-colored Christmas ornaments, some resting on the mantle clock as Faeries have a true fondness for any kind of time-keeping devise. The Green Guild had to ask them not to cover Big Ben in London, as it was noticed that it was slightly off its chiming of the hours.

"This changes our plans, dear," mom was calmly telling me as I refocused my attention. "We'll need to rouse the others and set them to the task of warding the house and grounds. We don't want to have to concern ourselves with these girls when we are trying to rescue the other five."

I agreed that our challenge was immediate and we went off to each of the girls and roused them, giving a brisk order to meet up in the front room in twenty minutes. They were dressed and back together in under fifteen minutes. They understood we faced a calamity and time was of the essence.

"My mother and I want you to begin your wards and spells to protect this house and the compound against intruders. We will place our own spells on the way out, but there is no longer any time left on the clock. Ursa's going to have her dark blooms ready very soon so we have to act!"

Mom added, "I suggest that each of you keep a partner in sight at all times and when the spells are in place, return to the safety of your circle."

"What should we do there?" Jemma asked mom timidly.

"Pray, dear."

Since neither of us had undressed we were pretty much ready to leave for the Valley when Maud approached us, carrying two ponchos. They were of a heavy, dark brown weave, with a swirling sun pattern on their backs and would give us some warmth out in the desert night. "I made them myself," she told us with a hint of pride in her fine work. "They were both blessed by the waters from our very own Niagara Falls. The Iroquois warriors worshiped at the site in order to strengthen their courage and keep them strong. I hope they will do the same for you."

She told us all of this while we shoved our heads into them and shouldering mine into place around my body. I definitely felt a surge from what the Native Americans called Thundering Falls.

Mom placed her best Protection ward at the front door while I went around to the kitchen door and did the same. I looked over at mom's cloaked Corvette and threw a quick second cloak over it just in case hers might be weakening over time, and I needed the practice.

We each had fifteen Faeries riding on our shoulders and holding on to the hair on our heads like corn tassels. We decided to leave three of their Troop behind and stationed them inconspicuously around the house so they wouldn't give the others a fright by flitting about the place.

The *Green Mother* was showing how much she valued my mom and me by sending Her tiny champions to our aid. She is aware of the perversion of even the smallest flower and the Black Scaborious Roses would be on Her radar for sure.

When we could no longer see the lights from the Wiccan compound my mother stopped for a brief conference between us and the Faerie Troop. "This would be a good place to send some scouts up ahead I believe, Cathleen and also to use our own camouflage." With that said the Troop's leader sprang into action and tugging the selected five candidates they were gone in a wink.

As for us, my ever creative mother was working out a spell to conceal our very human forms. "Why can't we just use a cloaking spell?" I asked, wondering what she had planned.

"Oh tosh!" she said, "We need to blend in, dear. I think if Ursa sees any humans she'll become a black bird in the wind."

I noticed her hands were quite busy as they jutted out of her poncho. Suddenly there was a small tornado of red dirt heading our way and mixed in with it some scraggy looking brush. This desert mulch was hovering over me when mom said sharply, "Close your eyes, my pet." After dumping the yucky mix all over me, my mother smiled and watered it with more Magic so it would stay in place. While I stood speechless she performed the same trick on herself. She had placed a thin red layer over our faces so we could still recognize one another and read expressions.

Now that we were both encased in our dessert camouflage, looking like mobile ant mounds, we moved closer to the Scotsman Butte. It jutted upward like the craggy arm of a red giant, resting on the desert floor. My senses started to tingle and when she became still and squatted down, I followed my mom's example. I gazed at the sea of stars as they floated serenely in an endless night. Something passed in front of the moon, casting a recognizable black silhouette. It looked like a very large vulture and I knew then that Ursa was leaving her lair and her captives. She probably felt her tunnels and secrets were secure under the rock-solid Butte. This was a stroke of luck for us, but I knew this meant she was on her way to the Wicca compound to do as much mischief as she could and we had no way to warn the coven. All we could do was hope all their wards and spells were strong and they were praying hard to their *Goddess.*

Mom stood up and we continued to move toward the Butte until we heard the return of our scouts from the Faerie Troop. They seemed very agitated as they didn't know how to land on us, but soon settled on some brush planted on our shoulders. "Let me hear your news, little friends," my mother said. There was much gesticulating with arms and hands flying about as they related what they found up ahead and nearer to the Scotsman Butte.

From the look of alarm on my mother's face, though somewhat muted by the dirt, I knew there was a challenge we hadn't counted on. I thought we'd just pull our tunneling trick and pluck the girls out from under Ursa's pointy nose. But from the far away gaze and set of her jaw, I knew mom had other plans.

"What's going on, mom? I only caught bits and pieces of their report, but it almost sounded like wall, or was it fall?"

She squared her shoulders mentally because she certainly couldn't move them any other way and said, "It's a wall, dear, and it's just ahead of us a tad. It would appear that the Black Witch has placed a high barrier all round the Scotsman Butte, but we, my darling lass, can get close enough to plant a few spells and break through. We only need to find its weakness."

"But mom those other girls may be forced to eat the petals from the Scaborious Rose before we can break through to them."

"Ah! No dear, I'll have another task for our wee friends here before that can happen." With that she squatted down and looked like an ordinary mound in the desert landscape. The Faeries all perched at various sites and she instructed them on the art of pruning, flowers that is.

The moon was still high and splashed the desert with thick syrupy shadows that spread across a few thousand millennia of compressed earth, blasted sand and fantastic stone sculptures. My mother completed her instructions and then turned and said, "Close your eyes again, Cathleen. We won't be in need of this uncomfortable desert wardrobe after all."

"Well thank the *Mother* for that," I sighed as the earth sloughed off me and back to where it belonged. "What's changed?" I asked, scratching at some sand that found its way under my sweater.

"For starters dear, Ursa has taken to altering her appearance by turning into a very large bird of prey and is headed back to the compound to pull off some cleverness there if she can. Also dear, she has stationed a small army of *Trogladytes* around the perimeter we need to penetrate. Only a wee bit of alteration is needed in our approach, lass."

That almost sounded comforting to me except for the *Trogladytes'* part. These were particularly nasty critters and even though they disdained the use of modern Magic, they were extremely adapted at twisting perfectly good charms and spells by infusing their evil machinations into them as they were spoken. The trick to beating these guys was to get the spells in place before they could tamper with them. *Geez...do I hate these guys* I was thinking. Mom must have read the apprehension on my face as she patted my shoulder and said confidently, "Not to worry, dear. I have this one in hand."

My mother was a Wizard's Wizard my dad repeated over the years to me. He knew she could be relied upon in extreme circumstances that would sorely test the Magic of other Mages, not to mention their courage. Now, we were definitely faced with a challenge that called for both bravery and Magical know-how.

Using our strong bond, we spoke in hushed tones, "*Scaaathnearrrt*" into the night. We reached out our hands and started dragging the shadows and pools of inky darkness from beneath outcroppings of rock formations and from under tangled brush leaving a faint glow of Magic behind. We then draped ourselves in this natural darkness until we were one with the night. There was no sense in announcing our visit to the Demon militia. They were a brutish lot and our hope was they would be easily fooled by our new camouflage.

We were on the move once more. The Faeries that had come to warn us of the guards quickly reattached themselves to our shoulders and heads just before the cloaking was complete so they too benefited from our *Shadow Charm.*

The *Trogladytes* are notorious in their hatred of the Faerie folk, probably because they were as ugly as the little folk were beautiful. In any case, the Faeries understood that they would be in grave peril if they were captured by one of these monsters. Pulling off wings was just one of the terrors they would suffer at their hands.

The *Trogladytes* were a particularly gruesome breed of Magic creature. They were built to perform as superior soldiers. With coarse, blackish brown hair covering long heavily muscled arms and short thick legs, they had the look of plodding, stout oxen, but were both physically powerful and quick on their hairy feet. Their heads were not exactly flat, but slopped back from the bridge of a bulbous nose, as if they'd had an anvil dropped from great heights repeatedly on them as they slept, which of course was impossible as they never slept since they too were conjured from the Pit of the Sleepless Dead.

A brief history of the *Trogladytes* flashed through my subconscious as I recalled they supposedly were cursed by the great Wizard, Merlin with a lifetime of sleeplessness for really ticking him off; something to do with dragon's blood and slain sorcerers. Their constant state of alertness probably had a lot to do with the very testy temperament of these guys. It could make anyone a bit grumpy.

The Faeries gave my hair a tug and brought me out of my reminiscing and must have given my mother a signal because she stopped in her tracks. Looming straight ahead was the base of the Scotsman Butte and in the subtlest of life force glow, my senses picked up a force of 30 *Trogladytes* arrayed around the broad foundation of the Butte.

Our little friends scouted the area again just in case any formation changes had taken place, finding all in the same order, we huddled together to plan our way past them. Mom seemed very calm as she spoke into my ear and said, "You go first, dear."

Huh! I thought she'd clear a path through the hairy louts, but instead she left it to me to organize some kind of stealth-like entry.

I knew better than to begin a discussion on tactics as time was ticking away like the annoying twinge that had begun under my left eye. This was my internal radar reacting to the close proximity of danger and though Jason always found it an endearing compliment to the loss of his own left eye, I just found it aggravating.

I did a quick survey of my options of magical weapons and began to move forward toward the waiting army of the night.

Chapter 22

I focused my senses like radar on the east side of this desert fortress, where the milky light spilling down from the moon was less of a factor. Using my interior feelers to probe the spaces between guards, I realized they stayed in one place at all times, only shifting from hairy foot to hairy foot to relieve the burden of their weight. It's little known, but a Magical creature can still feel mighty uncomfortable just like a mortal if the circumstances are bad enough. Standing guard duty at the base of a desert butte must qualify, as the ones I was scoping out all seemed to be bored and shuffling around.

After some hesitation, I decided to distract the three guards closest to me by conjuring a harmless *House Buddy*. Mom loved these little creatures as they were fast and efficient at house work, which she thoroughly detested, except for baking at which she truly excelled. Dad once confided in me if she wasn't so beautiful he would have married her anyway for her Triple Chocolate Threat.

I placed the *House Buddy* out of reach of any of the three guards I had targeted and had it sweeping up the desert floor. Soon, in a frenzy of motion there was a growing pile of scrub brush, sand, lizards, scorpions, rocks and the occasional irate Faerie. They are very curious and a few of them had zoomed over to check out the commotion. The speed of my *Buddy's* broom was as fast as the beating wings on the inquisitive Troopers and when they came within range it merely scooped them up in the swirling vortex it created. I hurriedly fashioned an *air scooper* yanking them free before the *Trogladytes* could hear their reedy voices, as they loudly protested the indignity.

It was rather convenient that our little friends came over just then, as I needed them to scurry inside the hole I was making, planning on catching up with them there.

The three guards had left their posts to investigate the manic cleaner. They approached cautiously at first, not as dumb as they looked, I conceded. The biggest one came within striking distance …of the broom that is. It was soon spinning like a top along with the debris whirling inside the fury of motion created by my *House Buddy*. I almost laughed out loud, but luckily my mom pinched my arm and I winced instead.

She'd been standing quietly, slightly behind me while I did my Magic, most unusual for my take charge mother. But I appreciated the courtesy as it wasn't considered polite to crowd a Wizard while he or she was at work.

The two other guards I had targeted watched their big cohort while he was in the spin cycle and moved forward from their own posts, probably glad for the distraction. Their flat beady eyes seemed mesmerized by the swirling of this cyclone which included a blur that could barely be identified as the big guard.

When they came closer to investigate they were sucked into the spinning mass and became part of a widening tornado base. I sent a Faerie to enter the hole I'd made and continued to drill it down until it hit open space. I had asked it to scout the area until it came to the room holding the five Wiccan sisters. I knew it would return with the information quickly and turned to my mother. "Would you mind freezing them all, mom? I'm pretty tired and need to rest and recharge a minute?"

Smiling her agreement she stepped forward and when she was within touching range of the *Trogladytes,* she threw a small dome over the scene and froze the whole thing in place. Nothing moved, nothing twirled or swept, every particle of dirt was suspended in a golden sap, like a mosquito in prehistoric amber. Most ingenious I thought proudly.

I knelt down on the chilly ground and was communing with our *Mother* to restore myself before we entered the Butte. Mom looked down with some concern showing in her eyes. "Are you alright, Cathleen? It isn't like you to tire so easily, dear." I hadn't thought of that fact, but put it down to no sleep for almost twenty-four hours. "I'll be fine, mom, just need a minute to regroup."

Inexplicably, while we were talking, mom's spell suffered some kind of malfunction and not only did it release the guards, it also put an abrupt stop to the *House Buddy's* frantic sweeping as the dome fell to the ground like crystallized confetti. The rotating tornado stopped so abruptly that its entire load was deposited on top of the little guy. This left the *Trogladytes* quite free and greatly put out.

They were milling about for a minute, trying to understand what had just happened. Luckily this type of Magic creature is as imaginative as a wad of used Kleenex, giving mom and I time to scoot toward the hole I had made earlier. I had tweaked it just a bit to accommodate our squeezing through.

As we moved toward the opening, I looked over and saw the guards were moving too...right for us. It was as if our cloaking spells had stopped working. "Uh, Mom," I said, "I think they can see us."

"Don't be silly, dear. They can't pierce our spell." Just then the one big guard said something in their guttural tongue and they all turned toward mom. She had moved slightly ahead of me in her desire to enter the hole quickly. Just as she was stepping through the entry one of the *Trogladytes* threw a heavy mesh net over her.

She stood there looking stunned and not a little concerned. She didn't struggle as the netting was being pulled tighter and I think I stopped breathing as the long, heavy arm of the first guard shot out to secure his captured Wizard.

None of the creatures seemed aware of my presence so I had to believe my own cloaking device was working.

What's going on with my mom's Magic, I was thinking frantically as I watched the net being pulled toward the *Trogladytes'* waiting arms.

Chapter 23

With mom wrapped up like a Thanksgiving turkey, I was relieved my own cloaking spell was still holding. It was like something was interfering with mom's Magic. The guards were moving toward her in their slow, deliberate shuffle. Mom seemed calm under the weight of netting. In fact if I wasn't seeing things, she had a tight little smile in place. *Hm,* I was thinking, *what's she up to?* I knew the stumpy *Trogladytes* were no match for mom's Magic, even if they threw a thousand steel nets over her. They approached her with some caution and I saw the big one shove a smaller guard closer to her as if testing the water.

She shouted so suddenly that the guards jumped back a foot. "Get to the compound, Cathleen! I can handle this." It sure didn't look as if she was handling much of anything as the *Trogladyte* pulled the net tighter and making it into a bundle, toppled her onto the ground. The big guard then swung it and my mother over his hairy hump of a shoulder.

"Mom!" I shouted, truly alarmed that she had let herself be scooped up like a trout by a hungry bear. I immediately thought of Ursa and groaned as I stood rooted in place. Luckily the three guards couldn't hear my high pitched voice, so never noted my presence in the tunnel.

Since they're an unimaginative bunch, they weren't looking for mom's point of entry. These creatures are also known to be very near sighted, so could not have seen that far off. Mom yelled again, "Run girl! Get to the compound before Ursa destroys the Wiccans."

I was torn between helping my mother who was now bumping along on the hunched back of the big guard as they slowly made their way to some unseen access leading further underground. I knew that she would never allow herself to be captured unless it was a planned scheme to get into Ursa's fortified burrow. I spun around and ran, the whole time concealed from their view and chanting a spell to help speed my progress. Luckily they never saw the dust I was kicking up as I hustled back into the dry air of the sleeping Valley.

I had fashioned my own spell out of the wind to race back to the compound. I spoke the words of my spell over and over. *"Casnearth casfarcnert,"* Using the power emanating from the earth's aura and tapping into any tremors, I am able to ride the surge of the combined forces to the place I visualize in my mind. It's actually pretty low-level Magic, but I wasn't being fussy as I needed that speed boost to get back to the vulnerable Wiccans. My mother must have picked up some information from the Faeries that she didn't share with me. She's a trifle annoying that way.

I was within spitting distance of the old shed when I saw a pulsating glow coming through the sheer curtains of the front window. *Must be the fireplace* I thought. It made me nervous that mom thought the girls were in imminent danger considering all the wards and spells they would have in place; not to mention ours. I stood still, just another shadow falling across the dirt yard and put my senses into high gear. I heard voices I identified as Wynn and Joanie with Maud's in the background, saying that they would not leave the circle. This was spoken in the adamant, but frightened tone of people under pressure to conform to an order they knew would mean certain disaster would befall them.

The next voice was laced with scorn, spoken in a deep, throaty growl that sounded more animal than human. It was a threat to

Wynn. "You will likely die in a most painful manner, but I can lessen your physical pain if you cooperate with me. Break your circle and come to me and I may even allow you to live in my service."

I heard Wynn respond with a slight quiver in her voice, "You can't frighten me Ursa and we are NOT leaving the circle!" There was a scream of anger as Ursa tried to hurl yet another of her spells which included balls of red fire. This tirade and exchange must have been going on for a while from the scorched look of the walls and flooring around the circle. The fact that the Wiccans had remained safe from her threats and fire only added to Ursa's inflamed frustration.

I still couldn't figure out how she had disarmed the house to get in, but she was a Black Witch and they were known for the dark power behind their sinister art. I also wondered if she had some insider help, but when I approached the window and carefully peered in, I could see all the sisters' present and gripping hands in their circle. They were sitting on the floor and in their long skirts and peasant tops they might have been a band of gypsies around a camp fire; except for the terror etched upon their tired faces.

Some of the girls showed signs of dehydration as they seemed to sway slightly and there was a damp sheen on their arms and faces as if ready to faint. I looked at Joanie and saw my friend's eyes squeezed shut as if that would make Ursa disappear.

The fireplace was giving off that pulsating glow I had seen through the window and smelled of burning sulfur along with logs. It turned Ursa's shadow into a huge menacing presence as she stood with her arms outstretched as close as she could to the circle of Wiccans. Because of the power of the circle created by the natural forces called upon by the sisters, Ursa was powerless to enter their safe haven.

I heard her grind out another spell from between clenched teeth. As it was hurled against the invisible barrier of their faith and nature's great powers, it bounced back and hit the evil one squarely in the chest. She reeled back and pushed the fireplace screen into the fire, her own long skirt catching fire. At a quick gesture from her hand, the flames were smothered and only a thin scrap of smoke hung near the floor.

It was time for an intervention before the girls all succumbed to their fears and weakened physical state. I quickly thought back to one particular spell taught to me during my apprenticeship that dealt a mortal blow to a Wizard practicing the Dark Arts.

I was enjoying my sixth winter and my third as an apprentice. My dad and I were in our cave in the upper reaches of the mountains; concealed from the view of the curious by heavy brush and the furry branches of the thick pine trees that fronted it. We had just begun practicing some basic charms for levitation of objects, when we heard a spell being carried on the wind and scudding along the ground with tremendous velocity, fashioning a killing ball from snow and ice and hurtling toward us.

My dad shouted, "It's Black Magic, lass, and we are right in its path!" With that he grabbed my arm and before I knew what was happening he had me shielded behind a frosted pane of thick blue ice. I knew it was ice because I saw my breath puff out in panting bursts, hanging in front of me as if I'd swallowed some wispy clouds. My father quickly retreated to the front of the cave to intercept the attacking weapon. Before he could open his mouth to shout a protective charm, a great ball studded with sharp limbs and grey boulders jutting from a ton of compressed snow and ice burst through the natural barriers to the cave's opening flattening tress that had stood for a hundred years to pulp.

My dad was on his back and using his hands and feet to motor backward away from the crushing weight of the deadly sphere. He was never one to quake in the presence of strong Magic and I remembered his words and actions as I watched Ursa try to break through the Wiccan circle. *"Terminatous Bellicous!"*

I wasn't even aware that I had moved from the front window to the front door, slamming it open against the wall. I screamed out my father's spell and repeated it even louder a second time as my lungs filled with the scent of evil. Ursa had spun around in my direction when I burst into the room and had obviously not been expecting my intrusion. She seemed to wink out like a light turned on and off and she was gone.

I know the Wiccans were all jumping with joy at her disappearing act, thinking she was destroyed, so I had the unhappy task of explaining that what had been harassing them all this time was a spell Ursa had created and personified with her own form and face. It was never-the-less destroyed, but she, unfortunately, was not.

This information left all anxiously looking at me as I told them they were free to leave the   safety of their circle. We gathered around the kitchen table after everyone had a few minutes for much needed breaks and stretching of taut muscles. Joanie helped ease us into a more relaxed group when she blurted out, "Ursa's body double was even uglier than she is in real life. She missed a good opportunity to improve on her looks."

After the subdued snickers ended, I brought them up to date on what had happened with my mother and me when we got to the Scotsman Butte and tried to quell their alarm at hearing my mother was likely a prisoner. "I'm not sure," I assured them, "but I believe my mother planned to be taken by the *Trogladytes* so she could penetrate Ursa's domain. She didn't seem concerned for her own safety and was adamant that I return here."

Joanie said, "And it's a darn good thing you arrived when you did, Cathleen. I'm not sure how much longer we could have held the circle."

Luna piped up from her perch on the counter, "Cathleen, I remembered something from the time we were being held by Ursa and both Maud and Alana think you should hear it." She said this looking over at the other two girls to see tem shaking their heads in agreement.

I snapped a quick look at Wynn to gauge her reaction to this new information. Her face seemed closed off, so I couldn't tell if she was annoyed at their forgetfulness, or just tired of the whole Wiccan mess she was in.

"Go ahead, Luna," I said, somewhat apprehensive at what I might hear.

She resumed, "Ursa is not alone in the Scotsman Butte, Cathleen. We're certain she is working with a second Black Witch." I was stunned, but nodded for her to continue. "We all heard Ursa talking to someone…someone that seemed to be in charge."

"Did you hear another voice?" I asked.

"No, just a low murmur and occasionally a kind of dragging sound like something heavy moving along the ground. It was very creepy. Whenever we heard Ursa speaking it was clear she was definitely not the one in control, but the one taking the orders."

Now this was an interesting turn of the coin. Ursa on the one side and a mysterious presence on the other. I knew that practitioners of the Black Arts often called on Demons and creatures from the Dark Pit of the Sleepless Dead. They would raise them up to be used in some evil machinations.

If Ursa had indeed brought up a Demon from the Pit, she may have stirred a pot that threatened to boil over on her. Perhaps we had been over estimating Ursa's power as a Black Witch. Was something else was at the helm of her Dark Ship? If this was so, I could only hope my mother figured it out before she encountered this new enemy. I looked up from my ruminating and noticed Wynn watching me, an inscrutable intensity in her eyes.

"Cathleen," she asked, "what are your thoughts on the possibility of yet another sorcerer working with Ursa?"

I knew I couldn't dodge the answer as it was likely pretty obvious to the group. "It would seem that Ursa is no longer calling the shots ladies, but that does not make her any less of a threat. Whatever she has conjured to join her is definitely from the Dark Pit of the Sleepless Dead and won't want to go back there to hibernate another thousand years. It will want to control the outcome of Ursa's assault on this coven, so it can assume a place among the living once more. We can't *ever* let that happen!" I said this last as an admonition so the girls got the message along with some insight into a future of chaos for all life forms in this world if they succeeded.

"What do you want us to do?" Alana asked in a rare moment of speaking up.

"I need all of you to perform a purification, but this time place your various blessed talismans and sacred objects on the outside of your circle; then return to your circle for prayer and mutual support. While you perform your ceremony I will place wards around the outside of the house." *I also have to try to figure out why my mother's earlier spells were not working*, but I kept that thought to myself.

I had changed out of the still sandy shirt I'd been wearing and donned a T shirt and heavy Harvard sweatshirt; a gift from a Rhodes Scholar I'd met while studying "Folk Lore of the British Isles" for a semester in Scotland. He was very forward thinking and though he never learned I was a trained Mage, he accepted the concept of Magic like any other phenomena that didn't have obvious explanations.

I slipped back outside as the girls were burning their white sage in every corner of the house as well as in the fire place. It smelled wonderful. I wished I could stay inside to enjoy the calming influence the incense was producing. They would rejoin within a half hour inside their circle so were focused and didn't notice my exit.

The night sky, like the dark throat of an ancient Nubian Queen, was richly bejeweled with celestial gems. I took in a deep breath of the cool desert air to open my senses and renew myself. I had decided that if Ursa had indeed called up a Demon not within her power to control, then she had some shortfalls in her Black Magic capabilities. I would use these to undermine her scheme and to destroy her if I had to. I still hoped she could be saved, but as dad always said of the evil doers, "Those who would do evil upon the earth's creatures and the *Green Mother* will find no mercy in Her heart when they surrender."

As I made my way in the shadow of the house, the moon journeying on its mysterious course, cast a brighter light on the shed and the Corvette parked close by. I had never closed off my inner eye and could see the wooden structure clearly, leaning somewhat like a cartoon version of Pisa, with a full Troop of faeries perched atop it like forgotten holiday decorations.

They knew I spotted them and started to wave and jester for me to join them. As I got closer some of them flew over to sit upon my shoulders and head while they played with my messy curls.

"Hey," I said indignantly which seemed to divert their miniscule attention back to why I was skulking in the dark in the first place. "My mother has been captured by the Dark Witch," I said with obvious concern making their sudden squeals of laughter rather surprising. "This is serious friends…my mom is in real danger!" Again, peals of laughter like the tinkle of water over a pebbled stream. I guess my look of total disbelief in their amusement encouraged the Troop Leader to speak up. After a few agonizing minutes working out a translation, I finally came away understanding that the Faeries knew my mother had engineered her capture, as I had suspected. She was in no danger. In fact, they found that idea utterly absurd. They were literally tittering at the thought of mom not being the real threat in the situation.

I was somewhat mollified by their information and asked them to please send a small party from the Troop over to the Scotsman Butte to do some reconnoitering and reporting back to me. As five of them flew off in the direction of the open desert, I turned my attention again to placing wards around the building. The Faeries that occupied front row seats on my head decided to come along for the ride.

As I turned the corner to reach the back door my little gang of riders began to pull my hair until it was downright painful. "Ouch," I said. That's when my own alarm system went into hyper drive and I jerked to a stop so fast I nearly lost one or two of my passengers. "Mom!"

"Well, not exactly dear," she said. That's when I noticed the shimmer effect around her and realized this was yet another personal hologram.

"Mom, are you still at the Scotsman Butte?" I asked as I stood a few feet away from her projection.

"I am Cathleen, but you aren't to worry about me, dear. I have been busy rounding up the girls taken from the coven and they are on their way back to you."

"Is it going to be safe for them to return here without some protection?" I asked in wonderment at her achievement.

"I've already taken precautions and sent along the Faerie Troop you were so good to send to me dear. Oh, and there is that especially good ward your da' taught me… the *Mother* love his bones…It will see them back, no worry."

My parents were always exchanging Magic, but I wasn't sure which one mom was referring to. Dad always turned to mom's This and That Magic when he got stumped by a particularly nasty Demon. She always laughed and said he was, "just learn' the trade" and this to a man who stood as a Grand Protector in the Guild of the Green Wizards.

I told her about the visit from Ursa through a kind of physical copy of herself which I dispatched with dad's famous *"Terminatous Bellicous"* spell. I saw her smile and wished again for the comfort of her presence.

"Tell me what's going on there, mom. Do you need my help, or more Faeries, as you see we have another contingent?"

"Ah, no pet, no more of our little friends are needed, but there is one wee favor you might do me, Cathleen."

"Of course," I said immediately.

"When the five girls get back to their Wiccan sisters, be sure to *check them* for any…irregularities."

That wasn't exactly what I'd call clear instructions, but then my mother loved ambiguity. "Care to be more specific mom? Anyone in particular and what should I look for?"

"Too many questions love. Got to go now, but do be careful."

I was suddenly staring into far space. I really hated those projections, but they beat e-mail. I told the Faeries that had been listening that we'd have the rescued girls here in a bit and I needed help checking them for attached Magical creatures.

The return of the others would bring the coven back to eleven unless Rain was back in one piece, but I think her last eagle trick may have been her undoing. She was definitely a disciple of Ursa's as she proved by coming back after her first run in with us. I felt little sympathy for her and the fate she brought down on herself.

The Faeries were more than happy to join in my search and destroy mission if we found any uninvited guests tagging along with the lost sisters. I was thinking that I had forgotten to tell my mother something…something very important.

Oh dear Mother, I thought frantically. Ursa was not alone, but my mother was!

Chapter 24

I had only one way to let my mom know about Ursa's accomplice, or master, whatever the case was. I had to send another two of the little folk back to the Scotsman Butte. I knew they wouldn't hesitate to aid my mother, so I merely told them I needed two of their fastest Troop members to alert my mom to a danger she might not be aware of as yet. I felt awful for neglecting to tell her of the presence of a mystery sorcerer, but then she might already have dealt with that problem since the five Wiccans were free. *Hm. something just doesn't add up. Why didn't mom tell* **me** *about finding a second Black Witch? Unless...*

It was too late to stop the speeding scouts and now, I might have sent them to an awful death at the hands of an unknown Demon. Why hadn't I wondered at how easily my mother had achieved freedom for the five Wiccans? The fact that she told me to be watchful of any tag-along creatures was a pretty good diversion to keep me out of the way too. Or had she unwittingly sent five allies of the Dark Ones?

I had to get back to the Scotsman Butte and fast. Not only for the Faeries sake, but for mom who was likely going to need my help whether she knew it or not.

I returned through the kitchen door after I warded it using a stronger form of the spell that would not only stop an intruder, but warn the others with a piercing siren sound so that they could return to the safety of their circle if they were out for some reason.

The girls were finishing up their purification and the house was filled with the fragrances of white sage and jasmine, and there was another fragrance this time. I stood still for a second and then identified it as the comforting smell of chamomile. They had brewed a huge pot which was steeping on the stove top. When I asked why so much they told me they intended to keep it warm and sip it while they prayed and waited inside their circle. It would impart its calming remedy for their ordeal of waiting. *Wiccans must have remarkable bladder control* I speculated to myself.

They were thrilled with my news about the returning five Wiccans from their imprisonment by Ursa and her accomplice. It was beginning to look like the Black Witch could be beaten.

I then told them in as few words as I'm capable of, which was way too many, that I was returning to Scotsman Butte to find my mother and bring her out of there. "But that means we'll be alone," Maud said with alarm ringing in the air like a death knell.

"I will be leaving a number of my little friends here to watch over you and to check out the five girls that are on their way back here."

Wynn had a quizzical look on her face and asked "What do you mean by *check out,* Cathleen?"

"There may be some unwanted guests attached to them and the Faeries will detect and destroy them," I said. Wynn looked skeptical, but held her peace. The others just looked scared.

As I was readying myself for the trip back to the Scotsman Butte, Joanie approached me and said, "Hey, kiddo. I want to go with you this time. I know you wouldn't be going back unless you believed your mom was in trouble she might not be able to handle.

I gave her a quick grin saying, "Thanks, Joanie. While I appreciate your offer, I want you to stay here with the others. They'll need your courage and faith to get through this."

She looked a bit crestfallen, but quietly said, "Yeah, I guess you're right." She left me to join the others in preparing for the coming demon storm.

In the jumble of my thoughts about mom, I gave a quick thought to Jason and Ollie. I knew from our last conversation the weather had turned truly nasty there, with heavier snow and arctic cold, but Jason was a true mountain man and Ollie would be in his special bunk made up of quilts and pillows at his favorite Vet's. Right about then I was thinking *dogs might be on to something.*

I still wore the warm Harvard sweatshirt and put my woolen socks back on. No sense being uncomfortable when facing evil doers. I'd taken off the poncho Maud had given me as it felt too gritty. She understood and said she'd give it a good shake. I was glad mom still had hers as I knew the bottom of a butte would be unpleasantly cold.

I asked Wynn to gather her group for me so I could just say a few things. She quickly had them assembled in the front room, some near to the quivering flames of the fireplace. It was definitely a good time for a little extra heat.

"I want you to keep the fire going strong, ladies," I said firmly. "It will prohibit any Demon not of that element from entering the house through that channel. Should any get through they will be met by the Faeries and dispatched with very reliable Magic. I know you are all a trifle bit uncomfortable with the idea of Faeries because you have no experience with them, but I can assure you they are dedicated to the task of protecting you as our *Mother* would want. "Please reenter your circle at the first sign of any trouble."

I scooted to the front door with a wave of goodbye before they could register my leaving. As I went the Faeries were placing themselves around the women in what they believed to be a charming and friendly looking group. Except for the sharp pointy teeth they might have succeeded.

I didn't stay long enough to hear anything but the closing of the front door as I began the protective ward. The sisters that were returning would likely be here by sunrise if they traveled at a moderate pace. I hoped they weren't all covered in Demon creatures that needed to be eradicated as it would certainly put a damper on their homecoming to say the least.

I took the well-used path back to the dreaded Butte, made unnatural when it was appropriated for evil purposes. I stirred things up some as I employed my *Wind and Aura* spell. Other than my trail of dust swirling in my wake, nothing seemed to be moving on the dessert floor. An unnatural quiet seemed to have fallen, encasing the land and all of life in a leaden blanket of darkness.

The dessert was waiting.

When I got to Ursa's hide-away, I decided not to go charging ahead with a rescue plan. I had noticed that all the *Trogladytes* were gone …at least gone from sight…and the hole in the side of the Butte still gaped open like a baby's mouth expecting sweet peach cobbler. It seemed to me like an invitation to get inside and to get into trouble.

I had reconsidered my mom's instructions for the umpteenth time during my trip back. She asked me to check for any irregularities. Like a jolt along a fault line, I suddenly understood what mom was trying to say to me. She had been taken! She never mentioned the other presence at Ursa's stronghold. I had it backwards! She would have told *me*, not the other way round. She would have told me, if she was free to speak.

Now I knew the truth. Mom had been captured and while she said not to come, she was counting on my doing just that. *At least I got that part right* I thought.

It also meant the five captive Wiccans were not on their return trip. They were still secreted away inside the Butte. Mom wanted her captors to believe she had freed the girls and had herself stowed them away for safe keeping.

I was more than alarmed when I began thinking about the kind of creature Ursa had unwittingly conjured up from the Dark Pit of Sleepless Dead. The thought that it was walking freely in this realm, brought on shivers that had nothing to do with the nippy night air.

My mom had coded her hologram message so that it would appear she was being cooperative to the Dark being that had taken her captive after she hid the girls away.

If I'd had a bugle I would have blown it. The cavalry is on its way, mom! But then, I've never liked blowing my own horn.

Chapter 25

Time for a reconnaissance mission I told my less careful self.
I'd be no help to mom if I was turned over to Ursa and her
unidentified accomplice. I had employed my improved cloaking
spell so I wasn't concerned about being spotted. I was worried,
however, about having my use of Magic detected by a super-
sensitive wizard. I had to take that chance as my mother's life
could well depend on Magic to rescue her.

I had taken only two of the Faeries with me as they were a
chatty bunch when there was no way to separate them. I had asked
each one to take hold on either side of my head and they dutifully
still clung to my ears like head phones.

These were Greens; Faeries that were totally green except for
their vivid blue eyes. I thought them very beautiful in normal
circumstances, but right now I only valued their Magic and their
sharp little teeth.

As I neared the opening I'd made at the base of the red
monolith, I strained my hearing to better pick up any voices in the
depths beneath the Butte. As I stepped through the hole I was
immediately confronted with two lounging *Trogladytes*. They
seemed to be fascinated by the long rods they gripped in their
hands; probably had some energy current running through them.
They were unaware of my presence which was a good thing since I
had nowhere to hide. I would have to pass between them as they
stood directly across from each other in the narrow passage way.

I had to create some kind of diversion. I assured the Faeries I'd
keep them cloaked and asked them to harass the two brutish guards
long enough for me to pass further into the tunnel and then to

rejoin me when they'd seen me accomplish that. They were nearly giggling with delight at the prospect of annoying just about anything.

With that they let go of my ears and shot to the top of the tunnel just above the heads of the unsuspecting duo. They each took a guard and first pulled tuffs of hair from each head, then bit into pulpy noses and floppy ears. They had the guards jumping and swatting at the air like they had stepped into a bee swarm. The result was quite effective for my needs, as I raced down the tunnel toward a faintly flickering light. I slowed my pace so I wouldn't run into any wandering guards, or the mysterious wizard who likely held my mother prisoner.

I turned the first corner I came to finding the light was from a series of sconces affixed to the walls on either side. Each held a squat black candle that sputtered, its flame twitching in the dank air in response to my body movements. A collection of melted black wax oozed around each flame, threatening to smother them altogether.

These candles had been burning for some time. I wondered if I followed them down the corridor if they'd lead me to my mother. I decided that was way too easy a road to take and instead used my inner eye to scout further ahead. There, in the flickering light, I picked up the unmistakable aura of a human.

Normally, I would have welcomed the presence of another human amongst the creatures I'd encountered in this clammy place, but this time, not so much!

Coming toward me like a submerged swimmer rising out of the murky tunnel, Ursa walked with the quiet step of the phantom she'd become. Her skin was dead white with an undertone of yellow. Her eyes held a reddish cast and had the look of two burnt holes in her drawn, nearly skeletal face.

She was leading a *Dungeon Dog* on a very short leash attached to a collar studded with sharp spikes aimed inward toward the dog's exposed neck. This was a cruel way to slow it down, or make it respond to a command. Pain seemed the favorite tool of this Witch and she inflicted it on friend and foe alike.

These canine demons were well prepared to do severe harm with their razor sharp teeth and long, club-like tails. I remembered my father's description of the *Dungeon Dogs* he'd encountered from time to time in his travels through the outer and inner spheres of this realm. They were a fierce lot he'd said and could only be beaten if they became separated from their controller.

Though my Faerie friends had rejoined me, I couldn't use them in this situation as Ursa and these dogs were not the dumb beasts the *Trogladytes* were. My plan was to follow Ursa to where she was going to see what she planned for her Pit creature to do, or perhaps it was only her personal body guard.

The *Dungeon Dog* began making a grinding sound from deep in his throat that I took for a whine. Clearly, it had detected me even though it couldn't see me. The Faeries by now had buried themselves somewhere under my thick hair as Ursa and her Demon pet got closer. The *Dungeon Dog* began a low throaty growl and started whipping its shaggy black head from side to side, its tail thumping against the sides of the cave as it kept syncopated time with its head swings.

Ursa seemed preoccupied and yanked the leash hard to make it heel. I heard it whimper with the jolt of sharp pain it must have felt when the spikes bit into its neck. I heard a few words of her mumbling as she passed within a hair's breadth of my body where I pressed against the wall. There were clumps of loose dirt and stone dislodged as I squirmed backward even further to allow her to pass without brushing my body in the close quarters.

A few of the bigger clumps of dirt fell to the tunnel floor, sounding like a landslide in that closed environment. I froze and tried desperately to slow my heart beat and breathing so she couldn't detect my trembling presence. "You stupid creature!" Ursa screamed like a frightened little girl. "Your tail is causing dirt to become dislodged…are you trying to cause a cave in?" She gave the leash a mighty tug and I heard the Dungeon Dog choke as the collar dug again into its muscular throat. For a creature twice her size it showed complete obedience to the Black Witch. It was obvious that she was preoccupied as she hadn't sensed my presence as she hauled the Dog along like a toy poodle.

With Ursa still mumbling invectives at the creature they continued past me until they turned down a side passage. *Hey, why didn't I see that?* I thought as I watched her and her pet disappear from view. I had felt instinctively that my path to my mom was ahead of me so I ignored that newly revealed passage way and stayed the course. My Faerie companions agreed that I had chosen wisely as they shouted in my ear that Dagda's Daughter, Brighid the Beauty, as they knew her, was somewhere just ahead. They felt the warmth of her special Magic though her life force seemed to be fading.

I didn't like the sound of that and increased my pace hoping not to encounter any more surprises along the way. We ended in a fork in the tunnel passage and I asked the Faeries if they sensed my mother's Magic still. They said she was definitely to my left. I stood there for one more moment zoning in my own senses to pick up some indicators of her position. And there it was, like a tuning fork being twanged. I heard my mother's unique way of chanting.

I spoke to my tiny companions and told them there was a slight change in our direction and with that made a sharp turn to the right following the sound of my mother's lilting voice. My little riders were rather tossed about as I more or less sprinted down the new pathway

I slowed to a stop, giving myself and my fellow travelers time to regroup. That's when I heard the distinct sound of something being dragged across the floor of the tunnel. It seemed to be coming from my left, but all I could see was the crumbling dark red walls of the passage way.

"You really can't keep me here without the *Mother* knowing. And what will you do when She reaches out to punish your impudence in holding me prisoner?" It was my mother and she clearly had a visitor though I still detected no doorway to any holding area. Just then I heard a sound like grating fingernails or chalk on a black board. The hairs on my arms and neck stirred with the chilling voice that answered mom.

"I don't believe in the power of your *Mother*, Brighid. She is only a whisper in this vast universe and I rule where I want. Your continued allegiance to this *"Green Mother"* would be heartwarming, if I had a heart!" With that it burst into laughter that was a combination of howling Demons and screaming banshees. The rest of my hair stood up at this sound and I knew this was the blackest of Demons. When it was called up from the Dark Pit by Ursa, she clearly had no idea of the power she was unleashing upon herself and this realm.

After several seconds of that hideous caterwauling, I heard the Demon making threats against my mother, trying to weaken her with fear, but without any success. My mother's chanting resumed and grew stronger which enraged the Demon tormenting her. I knew my mom couldn't keep this up indefinitely and when she weakened physically her Magic would begin to dim. It was time to act.

I decided to stay close to the wall where the voices were coming through, but I had to be sure the Demon was gone. I asked the Faeries to create another diversion, but this didn't involve biting and hair pulling. Though they looked disappointed they readily agreed and began to use the wall sconces to light a fire causing the candles to melt into a large wax pool where the Faeries placed tiny bundles of explosive green sticks. They assured me these would become hot and explode into *green fire* within a Faerie's breath. And so they did, causing a flare of green fire to begin to eat at the pitted walls and creep slowly toward me as I stood fascinated with its beauty and energy.

The Faeries came back to me and poked me into action before I got myself fried. I noticed there was a slight shimmer to the wall as the fire hungrily crawled up its face, turning the red clay into a puddle of rusty looking soup.

"Keep the fire burning until I get my mother out of here, friends." With that I leapt over the spreading red puddle and into the cell where my mother was chained to the wall by her waist.

It was more than a little understated when she said, "Why hello, dear. So glad you could make it." I grabbed the first breaking spell I could think of and tried to free her, but she sighed and said, "No use with that pet, it seems immune to our Magic. As you can imagine I have tried."

I took hold of her right hand and said "Let's call on our Faerie friends to help us mom." With that the two appeared and each took an extended finger as we all joined in our own power circle. I could feel the energy of our bonding begin to bubble under the surface of my skin like a geyser. I could see my mother's reaction was the same as she seemed energized and renewed. As the surging power grew to a crescendo, the links forged in the

Demon's fire were breaking like glass beads and falling around our feet.

"Come on, mom. No time to talk. Just run." I put a cloaking spell over her and renewed mine and the two Troopers. We were out in the passage in three minutes. From what I saw of her, my mother looked pretty ragged. I assumed they tried to break her Magical strength and couldn't so they tried attacking her human frailty to defeat her spirit.

As we raced back through the tunnel to what I prayed was still an opening, I instructed the Faeries to cast *Faerie Fire* at anything that moved to slow us down. I wouldn't have time to stop and use my own spells as we needed to gain that exit! And they were quite good at flying and frying just about anything!

We saw the two *Trogladytes* where we left them near the hole. Each of our friends took turns hurling flaming green stick at them until they retreated with looks of terror and confusion in their usually dead black eyes and making chattering sounds like monkeys as they backed more deeply into the tunnel. It's always easy to frighten bullies.

With the way clear the two of us practically flew through the opening with our staunch little companions holding on like tiny cowboys at a Rodeo. When we got outside I saw the moon was gradually fading under the gaze of a new day's sun. "Mom," I said briskly so as not to lose control of the situation to her. She was slightly prone to pontification at the oddest times. We needed to put lots of space between us and Ursa and whatever she had dredged up from the Dark Pit of the Sleepless Dead.

"Let's use my cranked up version of locomotion and get us all back to the compound pronto."

With that I repeated my spell and by the last word we were riding on the wind fueled by the *Mother's* aura, toward safety and some serious questions, like what had Ursa brought up from the Dark Pit and was our Magic strong enough to send it back?

Chapter 26

It's no use trying to get my mother to listen to reason when the fires of her Irish temper have been ignited. After her experience at the hands of Ursa and her deadly companion, there was little to be gained by telling her to rest and let others do some of the planning. She has never challenged my Magical abilities, even comparing them to her This and That style--to her mind a huge compliment, to be sure. But now, she had a debt of Magical honor to restore and would not be dissuaded from joining in the fight from strategy, to spell binding and whatever else might be in our arsenal.

We were both quite certain that Ursa would be mounting a siege upon the Wiccan compound using her army of *Trogladytes, Blood Blodggets, Dungeon Dogs* and any other creatures she could drag up from that blighted Underworld.   We had the Wiccans and their special, rather gentle Magic, the Faeries that now numbered thirty-three again, and mom and I to stage a defense.

I went into the kitchen and gathered up a few things I thought I needed. Taking Joanie with me we went outside to the back of the squat house and located the well that had been original as the source of their water from the early 1940s. It was fairly deep and situated just inside the compound. We had taken two very large pails with us as well as an old ice tub I had discovered under a stack of very bald tires.

"Joanie, I need you to bring those two pails over here and put one on each side of the well head." I didn't have to remove the lid to the well as I intended to use my Magic and *Mother's* benevolence to secure what I needed.

After the pails were placed on the ground as I'd directed, I took a shovel I had found in the shed and putting a small motion spell on it, dug a deep trench around the well and began filling the large tub with dirt. With that completed I was ready to call on the *Green Mother* to provide a fountain from the still waters below.

I said my spell very softly at first and then repeated it with more and more volume. "Sciotan Tobara!" Joanie had been present for many of my Magic tricks as she so blithely named them, but I noted her eyes always betrayed the excitement and awe she was feeling. I was going to blow the lid off this well and had asked her to stand close to me for a minute. She was so nervous she was practically vibrating in place.

I repeated my spell three times, imploring the *Green Mother* to let the waters burst out from their deep vaults in the earth. We both felt a tremor under our feet which grew to a violent shaking, knocking us both to our knees. As we scrambled for some kind of footing on the shifting ground there was a sudden whooshing sound and a fountain of crystal blue water shot into the air. It forked into two gushing arcs filling the pails to over flowing. *Mother* is always generous when you ask politely.

Joanie's mouth was still open when the last drop fell back to dry earth. "I don't know what you're planning to do with all of this, but I want to help," she said in her sweet adamant way with a few drops of my precious water racing down her freckled nose.

I said, "I could definitely use your help, Joanie. Just don't get freaked out when I put this all together."

"Sweetie," she said, "nothing you do ever surprises me anymore!"

With a wave of my hands to produce some locomotion I jockeyed the pails and heavy tub back to the front of the shed, knowing it would provide a bit of shade as the day wore on. I sent

Joanie back into the kitchen to see how the others were doing, realizing we'd be out here a long time. I had her tell them we were checking the grounds so they wouldn't be worried at our long absence. When she returned a few minutes later, I saw a disappointed look on her face. My mother trailed slightly behind.

"What's wrong, Joanie?" I asked quietly, already guessing that she didn't appreciate my mother's intrusion.

"Oh, nothing, Cathleen," she answered with a weak smile. Mom approached me and without saying a word took the scene in, smiled briefly while nodding her head in unspoken approval. Still without speaking, she turned and went back inside.

"Wow! I've never seen your mom just leave you to your own devices like that, Cathleen. Amazing." I understood my mother liked what I was going to do and she didn't want to ruin Joanie's experience by horning in. She can be pretty considerate when it's most needed.

"Joanie," I said quickly so as not to lose my momentum, "I want you to start mixing the water from one of the pails into the pile of dirt that I spilled on the ground there. Just put enough water to turn the dirt to sticky mud. The paddle I've conjured will stir, but I want you to keep adding more water as needed. It's going to be dirty work. Still want to help?"

"Of course I do. If I go back inside I'll have to help with another purification of the house and if I don't smell burning sage for another lifetime that would suite me just fine."

While she was involved in her mixing process I called on the Faeries to give me a hand with my own pile of dirt. They were able to tip the pail with a unique levitation and dump charm, used by them for some mischief no doubt, while I briskly stirred the mess together by whipping my hand in stirring motions. The resulting clay was perfect as was Joanie's. "Looks good Joanie" I said with a grin. She was streaked with mud along both arms and must have been wiping her hands down the sides of her jeans as they were damp and grungy. All in all, she looked quite proud of her work.

I stood back from our handiwork to view the dark red clay and asked Joanie to stand next to me again. The Faeries were all excited with the prospect of the Magic that was about to happen. Faeries are like Magic junkies. They can't get enough of the stuff.

I extended my hands over the two piles and shouted out my father's finest spell for binding materials into forms. *"Lomadileas!"* I squeezed my eyes shut, so even the daylight couldn't distract me and using my inner eye saw the form of a giant *Trogladyte* covered in dark reddish hair and hunched over with the weight of its muscled shoulders. It was perfect in every detail right down to its lifeless beady eyes.

I opened my eyes and the creature I had created from the red clay stood before me like the good soldier would do with his commander. I gave Joanie a quick look to be sure she was still there and hadn't fainted with fear when my monster materialized.

She looked back at me and said "I saw the clay we made pulled together, and then this thing started to take shape into that!"

"I'm glad you didn't run off Joanie. It might have distorted my vision."

"Run off?" she said with a tinge of hysteria in her voice. "I couldn't even move I was so afraid. Are you sure you have control over that…thing?"

"Oh yes, indeed I do," I responded with a small hint of pride. I had worked very hard to learn to control it.

With that said, I spoke directly to Skip, my very own *Trogladyte.* I had to name him so he would respond to me when I called. He would actually be the only of his kind with a name.

The Dark forces do not bestow sweet sounding names on creatures they brought up from the muck and slime of the Dark Pit.

Skip stood at a sloped shouldered attention, with both arms stretched full length so his knuckles touched the ground and his hands formed relaxed finger cups. His eyes seemed unfocused, but I knew they were fastened on me, even though Joanie kept complaining they were staring at her. I stepped close to the beast and said, "Hello, Skip."

It turned a baleful gaze on me and then grunted. "Skip, we will soon be having others that will look like you and act like you, but they are not like you at all. They are from the Dark Pit and you, Skip, are from the Light. The *Green Mother* has allowed me to bring you forth so that you can do what is good by serving me, your mistress. Have you got all that?" Knowing I couldn't imbue Skip with extraordinary intelligence because I had limited my spell to strength and loyalty, I let Skip take a minute to process all of these facts.

He shuffled from foot to foot on those huge stump-like legs and finally grunted again. I took that for a yes and patted him on his tufted shoulder. It felt like it was padded in boulders. *Probably was come to think about it,* I realized with a shrug.

Joanie was standing a bit apart from me and my protégé by then and said from that short distance, "Uh, Cathleen, sweetie, you weren't thinking of taking Skip inside were you? I honestly think he'd put everyone into cardiac arrest."

"No, actually he needs to be hidden out here and when I need him he'll answer to my call."

With that said I dropped my cloaking charm off the Corvette and Joanie jumped back in amazement. "Where the heck did *that* come from?" she asked when she found enough air to speak. I was glad I had decided to add my own Magic to my mom's earlier, as her charm had been disrupted some time ago and the car would have just appeared from nowhere, sitting like a glossy cherry baking in the sun.

I told Skip to get into the car and sit quietly until I needed him. Because *Trogladytes* are guards by their nature, I told him he was guarding the machine until I called for him to come to me.

I made it clear that he should come to wherever I was at the time and he would follow my instructions to the letter when I gave them. He gave yet another eloquent grunt and sat behind the wheel of mom's dream machine. If I wasn't imagining it, I could swear he smiled as he grasped the wheel with two hairy hands. Guys will be guys no matter what breed.

I quickly closed the door and with that both Skip and the car vanished from the view of any human eye. Joanie blinked and missed the whole thing. Not that she really wanted to see any more of the giant I had created out of our mud.

When we were still in grade school, Joanie had the misfortune of sleeping over on the night mom decided to make some special cookies for the Faeries she expected to visit the next day. She had doubled her recipe and decided the oven was too slow in the baking process, so she added a "wee bit of Magic" and Joanie and I got to witness the kitchen turned into an industrial size oven that melted every plastic container and utensil and reduced our pots and pans to molten puddles on the bubbling heap that was once our stove. Even our cutlery was fused together in the smoking drawers.

All told, mom had to get dad to help and they had a heck of a time restoring the scorched kitchen to normal, moving all the melted objects outside of the house where they could be turned into flower pots and yard tools. Nothing went to waste naturally, but Joanie refused to share in any of the cookies that mom conjured as a quick fix to her baking efforts. Guess she was afraid they'd burst into flame or something.

It's really hard to figure out how the non-Magic user thinks.

Chapter 27

I returned to the house with Joanie trailing a few feet behind as she watched over her shoulder, looking for the Corvette. I needed to keep Skip under wraps so that if things got hairy, Skip could throw some muscle into the heavy lifting.

I was convinced that Ursa's secret confederate would not be coming to the Wiccan compound with Ursa. This Demon spawn would let Ursa take the risks and falls; then move in to take over all the Wiccans gained for its own sinister use. Ursa was pretty naïve about the hunger for freedom of the Demons from the Dark Pit. The fastest way to escape was by subverting the Magical powers of others.

We stepped inside the house and were almost overcome with coughing fits, due to the heavy amount of incense and white sage being burned. I asked Wynn why they had gone to such extremes and she answered, "We believe that Ursa will use every one of our beliefs and Magical connections to nature to find our weaknesses. When it comes to purifying our house, it makes the others feel safer when their senses are tingling with our efforts." I would not describe my wheezing and coughing as "tingling," but then I just made a monster out of dirt so who am I to ridicule others?

Joanie jumped right in and started to help Maud and Luna secure their rooms from unwanted visitors. They chanted together while lighting more incense in each bedroom. My immediate fear was that they'd burn down the place or drive us all outside because we were suffocating in a heavy fog of fragrances.

My mom was nowhere to be found and I learned from Jemma, who had been helping her find some clean jeans and a top that would fit, that she was walking the perimeter of the compound and placing wards against intruders.

Jemma added, "Your mom is so brave Cathleen. I wouldn't want to be out there by myself."

"Well, Jemma," I said with some pride poking through, "My mom is pretty resourceful and her Magic is very strong. Besides, she is one of the *Mother's* favorite Celtic Mage's." Having impressed both of us, I went in search of this fabulous woman I call mom.

I found her crawling around on the ground, in a pair of my jeans, as if she was searching for something of immeasurable value. She was so intent she hadn't noticed my approach until I knelt down beside her. "Mom, what are you looking for?" She reacted to my sudden appearance as if we had just left off a conversation.

"Well love, I am not looking for anything, but rather getting ready to put something here around the house. We can't protect the whole of the compound property, but I will fashion a wall around the house that will help slow down, if not stop any attack."

"Oh, I see," I said, totally not seeing at all.

"Cathleen, just as you can make whatever you decided to make from the sacred clay *Mother* allowed you, I will fashion my wall from natural elements. Watch dear, while mummy works a wee bit of *this and that*!"

She stood up, so I followed suit as she slowly turned to all four directions with outstretched arms and hands and called up a wind that swirled just outside the perimeter of the house, collecting every scrub brush and scraggly bush within a two mile radius and piled them at least six feet high and two feet deep, completely encompassing the low adobe building as she turned in a slow circle. While the strange wind hummed through the air she wove the whole mess into an intricate pattern, a device that would strengthened the whole structure against impact as it eliminated weak points. *And I only made a simple Trogladyte,* I thought with some envy.

When she was finished she brushed her dirty hands on my jeans saying, "I had to crawl around the whole area, so I could put the footers in place to hold my natural fence. By the way dear, I took a peek at your own handiwork. I must say I am very impressed." With that she gave me a quick kiss on the cheek and walked off before I could say thanks for making me feel better about my own Magical achievement.

I looked for small peep holes in the solid, prickly fence and saw a completely denuded dessert stretching out around us. I was hoping no planes made this their normal flight path as they'd think the aliens had landed for sure!

From my inspection of the new barrier I had to admire its imposing appearance. Since it was a work of natural elements, the Wiccans would be pleased if I suggested they come outside to call down blessings on its tenacity against the coming assault. Anything that slowed the inevitable down a tad is always good when you're basically making it up as you go along.

Mom looked very pleased when they all piled outside to admire her Magical prowess and Wynn was more than happy to do a strengthening ceremony with the others. It was after noon by then and I suggested we all get something to eat now as dinner might be a little sketchy. Neither mom nor I would hazard a guess as to when Ursa would show, but toward dark would be a Black Witch's happy hour.

Wynn and Jemma had Luna's help in the kitchen this time to prepare a lunch while the other girls set the table and placed the extra plates on the counter space made available for the over flow.

I wondered what we'd do when the other five Wiccans showed up. "Mom," I said quietly, so only she heard. "Where do you suppose the other girls are?"

"Oh tosh, Cathleen," she answered, looking somewhat embarrassed. "I forgot to tell you that I decided they might prove a bit dangerous until we could check them for any concealed Demons. So, I put them on ice for a tad, dear."

"On ice? Like real ice, mom?"

"Well lass, more like a big freezer where they are all breathing, but not mobile. It's quite safe, pet, just a little nippy I would imagine."

"Mom," I said, looking at her with real concern. "Where is this freezer you put them in? Tell me it's not back in the Scotsman Butte."

"Well that's exactly where it is, Cathleen. It was the only option at the time. I couldn't send a passel of Wiccans off to your people here until I could determine if they were clean of Dark creatures. You could never have handled them alone."

"But why did you tell me they were on their way and I was to check them for any riders?" I asked.

"Because I needed Ursa and her Dark Creature to think they were all beyond their control. So I hid them all in plain sight. Works every time," she said smugly.

My mother is the Queen of devious. "Mom," I said. "Is there any way the other Wiccans can be returned here before Ursa attacks? If they aren't contaminated we might be able to use their help."

Mom studied my face for a moment and giving my curls a soft stroke she said, "Don't be worried about this little challenge, Cathleen. I will be by your side. I promise." I did feel better knowing she'd be there with me, but as she turned away, I realized she still hadn't answered my question. I needed to speak to the Faeries.

I went back to my room which for once was empty of all, but me and the two Faeries that had been riding around in the pockets of my sweatshirt since we got back here. I roused them gently as it isn't smart to poke a Faerie that's napping.

When they were both fully awake I asked them what they knew of my mom's big freezer where she had stashed the five Wiccans like a pack of popsicles. They tried to demure at first claiming to have been elsewhere at the time in question, but that didn't last longer than a stern word of disapproval from me on their being less than honest. They hold honesty in the highest regard right up there with sneaky tricks.

By the end of my interrogation they were back in my pockets and I was ready to rejoin the group. I heard the low murmur of conversation as I approached the kitchen. The rich aroma of freshly brewed coffee nearly brought tears to my tired eyes.

I was immediately offered a seat by Alana who looked at me and said, "You probably could use a seat, Cathleen. You look pretty tired out." I thanked her and sat down and before I knew it there was a plate with a heaping scoop of macaroni and cheese, a grilled chicken salad and fresh fruit waiting on the side. I dug in and didn't speak again until it was all devoured, leaving only a barely used plate to be removed. Wynn seemed preoccupied as I complimented her on the great meal, though Jemma and the other helpers seemed pleased. I guessed she was beginning to feel tense as the clock moved toward sunset.

I looked around me at the expectant faces of the others and said, "Time to get to work, ladies."

My mother was the unofficial leader by now and she and Wynn were constantly going off to huddle and plan. That left me with the other Wiccans to finish up preparing our little surprises for our expected invaders.

Finger-like shadows were beginning to lengthen on the red grounds surrounding the adobe house, covering the fading light like a gloved hand. Everyone was warned to stay together and not get separated from the others. When Joanie walked up to mom at one point and asked out loud when they'd need to return to their circle, Mom said, "As soon as the sun retreats from the heavens, girls and not a moment later!"

They already had a dozen tapered white candles spaced around the inside of the circle to provide light as I had warned them that Ursa and her assortment of nasty creatures, prefer to operate in the dark where they felt more at home.

Looking around at them, I thought Alana seemed to be the most afraid as she kept looking around to make sure the others were nearby. I caught her peering out the window several times as the others were moving about the rooms.

I approached and asked her quietly, "Alana, are you Ok?" She burst into tears, a reaction I wasn't quite prepared for. I got a few looks from the others, wondering what I'd done to provoke that reaction I took her elbow and steered her to the front room where she sat and I hovered over the lumpy coach.

She was wiping her eyes with the ubiquitous tissue that seemed a necessary part of Wiccan life. "I'm so sorry," she was saying through a stuffy nose. "I am so scared that Ursa will come for me again. I haven't slept since she first came through my dreams. I'm terrified that I'll let my guard down and she'll find a way back inside my head."

I knew Maud and Luna were having similar anxiety and sleep was only entered into for quick snatches, more of a nap than a real rest. This state was beginning to wear them all down. I hadn't really anticipated this and now wasn't a particularly good time for breakdowns of any sort. I left her sitting there for a minute to go find my mother. I needed her to calm these girls before they unfurled like flags in a gale.

She was outside behind the shed making certain the sage brush fence was doing well by testing it against her own revved up wind. When I approached she immediately said, "I thought of driving the lovely vehicle into it, but I didn't need to have a damaged rental car on my hands."

"Mom," I said, trying to capture her fleeting attention, "would you please take care of our three rescued Wiccans before they blow apart at the seams?"

"Oh dear, that sounds ominous, my girl. What seems to be troubling them?"

"They haven't had more than a few winks of sleep because they're afraid of Ursa's power over them when they begin to dream."

"Well, that should be easy enough to fix, Cathleen. Do you want them frozen in a sleep state, or functioning, but sleeping?"

"You mean like sleep walkers?" I asked with some alarm. Putting these three Wiccans out of action or into any sort of dream state might prohibit them from helping the coven to fight against Ursa. As surely as I needed cream in my coffee, Ursa was going to hammer away to break through their sacred circle.

"Let's try a different tact," I offered. "How about you just secure them in Magical bonds that hold them even if Ursa tries to take them over through their dream state. Can you program their dreams with some sort of subliminal suggestion so they won't respond to her manipulations?"

Mom looked happy with this solution and said, "That's a splendid idea, Cathleen, but I'll need to have them unaware so their minds will not be full of fear."

"In that case," I said, "let's get the group into a positive mood."

We went back inside after mom was certain her wall would sustain a heavy onslaught at least for a short time. We hoped that by the time Ursa's forces broke through we would have our other defenses in place. Of these, the Faeries had an important part to play as did my newly minted *Trogladyte*.

They'd been wearing the same clothes for most of a day and a half so mom suggested the girls get freshened up and change into their ceremonial wardrobe. We left them to continue testing other sections of the wall which took another half hour and several lectures from my mother on engineering techniques. How did my father maintain such a sweet disposition after years of mom's micromanagement? Oh yes…love.

The Wiccans had all changed into what must be the emblematic uniform of their ancient religion. The long skirts covered in designs from nature's creations, floral displays so colorful I felt I could almost inhale their sweet fragrances, vibrant blues and greens of the seas that brought to mind the perpetual movement of the waters as the women swayed their hips entering the room, orange suns and midnight moons bringing glorious light and the promise of peaceful nights. Their colorful tops were accented with hand-made jewelry, some with strikingly colored bird feathers and polished stones. I was beginning to feel pretty frumpy standing among them in my dusty jeans and sweatshirt.

I noticed that Wynn wore a finely made silver Pentagram pendent that hung from a heavy silver chain and like the rest of the women, she had put dried flowers in her hair as a sign of devotion to the beauty of nature. Wiccans are a beautiful sight in full regalia.

I went around to the three girls recently returned to us, Maud, Luna and Alana and asked if my mother could have a quick word with them about their lack of sleep. "She has a wonderful idea of how to keep you safe while you sleep," I said briskly. I didn't want them to feel as if they were being targeted because of their previous experience with Ursa.

When she had them all sitting at the table in the kitchen with her, my mother put them at their ease by first complimenting how lovely they looked and then poured them each a cup of Brighid's Spiced Green Tea. "I thought you lasses might enjoy a wee cup with me while we visit. I do hope you'll like it as it's an old recipe of mine." That was for sure. The recipe part that is. They all took sips and sighed with contentment. I noticed the more she spoke the more they drank, until they were all holding their cups up and draining them dry. As they replaced them on their saucers each girl had a fixed look of attentiveness upon her face and my mother gave them the entire dream they would now share in common. "Go along now dears and find your beds for a wee nap. You will awaken before the sun sets."

With that they trooped out of the room looking as normal as before except they went directly to their own rooms and toward the arms of a sweeter Morpheus. None of the others took note of the three girls as they closed their bedroom doors. Most of them were in their own rooms or in the front room finishing up the laying down of sacred talismans.

"That was a great *Dream Charm,* mom," I said, sincere in my deep admiration. She had managed to subdue their fear and instill a sense of calm into their subconscious so they could sleep deeply and safely, something they desperately needed.

There was also a dream barrier in place so there could be no intrusion from outside. Mom's Magic was back on track now since her return from the deep tunnels of the Scotsman Butte. Whatever had been interfering with it seemed to have lost its potency, and she was once more the strong Celtic wizard, Brighid, feared by all enemies of the *Green Mother*.

"When they get up they'll be fit as tuned fiddles, Cathleen," Mom said as she turned to leave me in the kitchen with a quick peck on the cheek and a pat on my head.

I felt like a little girl again and I had to smile at how quickly I went from Mage to Munchkin! My mother's presence had given my Magic and my spirits a real boost. Who needed sleep?

Chapter 28

After washing what seemed like a small dune's worth of red dust and sand from my hair, I had to admit that I felt invigorated. Luckily I had packed a third pair of jeans, since my second pair was snuggly secured to my mother's posterior. I put on a long sleeve cotton shirt in a pale sky-blue, topping it all with the Harvard sweatshirt as it kept me warmer than my thin jacket and reminded me of my fellow Magic lover. *The world needs more of his ilk,* I thought smiling. It can get pretty lonely in this realm.

By the time I reemerged from my bedroom the group was taking a walk around the now enclosed grounds with my mother. It was still a good two hours until sundown and she had told me this would provide everyone a needed respite from the anxiousness of the preparations. I welcomed the peace it provided me as I hadn't had a minute to myself and wanted to call Jason.

It was only Thursday so I got him at the office. "Hello, Sheriff," I said when he answered.

I could feel his smile across the miles as he said, "Well, hello yourself, Magic Girl." This was his favorite tag for me and always put me in a good mood.

"How are my favorite Sheriff and my hairy son making out in that winter storm?"

"We're doing just fine, Cathleen, and thanks for putting me first just now." He chuckled and told me about local doings around town and how Ollie had recently endeared himself to the folks at the Evergreen Nursing Home and proved himself a fine Deputy in the process.

The Vet's office had closed early due to the heavy snow storm, leaving only the Vet to tend to Ollie, their lone boarder. When the Vet got an emergency call from a local farmer about a cow having difficulties birthing, he called Jason to come and get Ollie until further notice. Ollie was tucked under his desk when Jason got a call about a disturbance at the Nursing Home. Jason grabbed the dog and off they went to investigate.

"What on earth sort of disturbance among all those sweet old folks?" I asked.

"It seems two of the ladies were vying for the attention of one of the older gentleman and it came to a food fight with biscuits flying and oatmeal sticking. Not very pretty." He was laughing at recounting the scene and said "That's when Ollie stepped in and took over. He ate the biscuits, lapped up the oatmeal, and then licked the old folks on their hands to thank them. They were so charmed by your boy that they forgot to be angry with each other. When I left they were watching a game show together."

"Nice to know I raised Ollie to be a peace maker," I laughed. "And how about you, Sheriff Tate? Have you been busy with other altercations …maybe at the pre-school?" I joked.

He hesitated and said, "Not much happening on the law front, but I do miss my Magic Girl being around. By the way, there was a registered letter that came for you, so I had Mildred at the Post Office hold it with the other mail after I signed for it."

"Hm," I said. "Who'd be sending me a registered letter?"

"Actually, the post mark indicated it was from San Francisco. Maybe that means another possible investigation."

"Well, I'm curious that's for sure. But I wouldn't relish another extended time away from home …and you."

Just as Jason began to say something more intimate back to me the front door opened and the whole gang piled into the front room and stomped on my peace and quiet. "Gotta go, Jason. Please take care of yourself and Ollie. Love you both." I said this so quickly I don't know if he even registered my spontaneous comment. *Probably just as well I* sighed, and switched mental gears from sweet thoughts, to Demons run amok!

Wynn was coming toward me and asked about the sleeping girls left in my care. "They're fine Wynn. I checked on them before I came in here. All three had very peaceful looks on their faces, so no bad dreams either." I shot my mother a quick confirming look. She nodded and moved into the kitchen to put on the kettle.

"The air has turned decidedly chilly," she told me in passing. But there was something unsaid in her glance.

Hmm, wonder what's up, I thought, with a look she totally ignored.

I figured the sleeping girls had another half hour of sweet slumber before my mother's built in alarm clocks would rouse them. By then the circle would need to be prepared with the incense and a few extra candles placed in the center with Wynn. Wynn seemed somewhat preoccupied and I figured she was anticipating the coming showdown with Ursa.

The sky began to shift in nearly imperceptible phases. From the occasional puffy clouds that scudded like fat rocks thrown across a deep blue pond, to the slant of the sun rays as they stroked the earth in smaller and smaller numbers. We all began to stiffen our relaxed bodies in preparation for a dreaded darkening of the world around us.

In the stillness that seemed to envelop the kitchen and the women sitting and standing sipping cups of strong green tea, we heard the rattle and creaks of old doors being opened. My mother's cheery Irish brogue cut through the thick apprehension that gripped the others. "Oh, that'll be the darlins' from their naps won't it!" There was an audible sigh of relief like air moving through a bellows. The girls all watched expectantly through the arched opening into the kitchen waiting for their friends to appear.

The three Wiccans under this surveillance were padding through the front room on bare feet, sporting smiles and swinging their sandals as they walked into the kitchen to join us. "Hey guys," Maud was saying over the greetings from Luna and Alana.

"How are you girls feeling after your rest?" mom asked, looking at each girl as she spoke. They seemed rather surprised at the question as if they had forgotten just why they had been napping in the first place.

Luna was the first to respond. "I guess we all got zapped by your special tea, Brighid. I know it really helped *me* relax." Maud and Alana were quick to agree.

"If you three are ready then, we need to finish our circle preparations," said Wynn with a brisk resolve in her voice.

Mom came over to where I stood by the stuffed couch. I'd sprawled out there during my phone visit with Jason and only jumped up when everyone came trooping in. "So dear, how's that Sheriff fellow of yours doing on his own?"

"Just fine, mom," I said, looking distractedly at my boots. I really hated personal questions of this nature because my mother was always trying to help me to snare the perfect man, using her special recipes. It made me feel a bit too plain to get the job done myself, something a shy person doesn't need for their ego. Mom loved me and loved to meddle; a bad combination.

By the time the Wiccans had completed their individual preparations for what they feared would be a long siege we were mere minutes away from sundown. A palpable feeling of anxiety started to fill the room like a bad odor. I searched the faces of the

Wiccans. They were all standing around the area as if transfixed by rising fear.

I said in a firm, but quiet voice, "It's time to form your circle, friends, and may the *Green Mother* be with you."

My mother added, "And may your *Mother*, the Goddess, fill your hearts with courage and hold your circle inviolable until the dark forces are vanquished."

The Wiccans were settling into their places inside the circle. I noticed they had brought some of the special water I had saved back from the fountain the *Mother* had provided. They would use it now to drink and if needed, to spray the sacred waters onto any Demons that came within reach. It would act like holy water on a Vampire; not a welcome event for the wet Demon.

Their circle was tight, as they sat holding hands, knee to knee, elbow to elbow. Wynn sat in the center, legs crossed, back stiff. I had learned that Wynn had Navajo and Shoshone Indian blood running through her veins, which explained her high cheek bones and maybe her attachment to this area. I tried to read her face to gauge how she was dealing with the pressure. She had closed her eyes and was softly chanting, probably trying to prepare herself for their rites.

I turned away in time to see mom grab the jacket Luna had lent to her as she passed through the back door of the kitchen. She had been placing more wards in that area of the compound.

Mom hesitated for a minute as we passed the circle of women and seemed to be listening to Wynn's chanting. We exited the house as quietly as possible, not wanting to draw attention to our leaving.

The dark quickly swallowed us as we got further away from the glow of candles and fireplace, coming from the adobe house. Speaking in hushed tones, as if she feared awakening something sleeping in the purple shadows, mom came close and said "Cathleen, I think you can handle Ursa on your own love, with the help of the Wiccans of course and your new friend Skip."

I was going to protest, but she went on, "I need to go back to the Scotsman Butte to deal with the Demon from the Pit. There can be no real victory here if we don't destroy that monster." I knew she was right on all counts, but that was no comfort when I thought of her facing the terror that still held sway over the sleeping night.

I leaned forward and said "What *is* that thing, mom? You never said."

"She is the *Black Scaborious Rose Eater*, but you'd remember your da' calling her the Queen of Rot. She was a Geilt, a shaman or witch called so in the old Druid language, known many centuries ago for her powers. She was a recluse like others of her kind and shunned her people. But when the villagers fell under the influence of a rouge Wizard, she turned to Dark Magic to strengthen herself. That's when she reached out to the Black Arts of the Pit and became addicted to the Black Scaborious Rose.

After centuries of consuming the petals, her addiction transformed her in spirit and being. Her human form was changed into part human female, part lizard. Not terribly attractive, dear." That was one of mom's better understatements. Mom continued, "I tried to remind her of her once human life, but it was useless. Her spirit is forever lost to the hold of Dark Magic."

"Are you sure you don't need me to go with you, mom?" I said, almost pleading for her to say she did. "She won't be alone down there, but you will."

She only smiled, shaking her head from side to side and putting her hand on my cheek said, "May the *Mother* keep you, my Cathleen. The Faeries I've left will do your bidding, pet, so have no fear." With that she turned on a *Wind Charm* and sped off into the darkened Valley of the Gods. The small group of Faeries accompanied her, clinging like berries on a holly bush.

Chapter 29

I quickly returned to the coven to be sure they were calm and prepared. I found them softly chanting and paying homage to their Goddess. They seemed well focused so I quietly exited back outside and went to the cloaked car parked in the shadows of the shed.

I illuminated it briefly with a spark from my hand and saw my *Trogladyte* sitting as I had left it, with hairy knuckles wrapped around the steering wheel and a rather contented look on its homely face.

Looking at my own soldier I was reminded that my mother would be doing battle on her own against the Queen of Rot. Dad had told me of this Queen's legend, saying she was especially feared by the Magic world because of the awful powers she could wield after consuming the dark petals. In actuality, he told me, the Queen had turned herself into a slave to that twisted flower.

This tainted bloom only grew in the sludge and corruption of the Pit of the Sleepless Dead. It drew its life and sinister powers from the life force of the damned that populated the Pit; those who have perverted, tortured, or destroyed what was natural and beautiful in creation. This Pit was their special punishment.

As I was thinking about what might lie in wait for mom, I decided it was time to extract my *Trogladyte* minion from his hiding place to keep him close at hand. I knew the clock was ticking down toward a major assault on this compound and I needed to muster my forces as few as they might be.

The desert always held a special beauty in the night hours. Nocturnal animal calls and mewling wind sounds were carried from far distances, as if from another world. Now, it was as still as a dead heart out there. Its pulse of life silenced as if holding its breath before some calamitous event about to unfold.

Skip seemed reluctant to leave the comfort of the sports car, but obeyed my order to stay behind me at all times until I called his name. Then he was to stand at my side and await my next commands.

I stayed to the shadows cast down by the house as much as possible. When I was close to the back door, I knelt down and oddly enough, so did Skip. He was casting his own inky outline and I was glad I didn't have to look back at him too often to know he followed along. Even though I was his pseudo mother, he was assuredly an unsettling sight.

Kneeling on the cooling ground, I leaned forward and pressed my hands against the earth, calling to the *Green Mother*. I hadn't realized that a few of the Faerie Troop had reattached themselves to me as I had on my heavy sweatshirt, but as I knelt there making my entreaties to the *Mother*, they all swooped down and mimicked my gestures. I'm sure we created an odd scene, with one human female, ten green, pink, purple and orange Faeries and one very hairy *Trogladyte* imploring the *Mother's* aid in the coming battle.

As I shut my eyes to the distraction of the little visitors, I started a chant to create another soldier to fight alongside me in the expected time of need. I began to feel a tickling sensation under my knees. This grew into a tremble that one might associate with the passing of a speeding train. Then the tremble became a slight tremor and I heard rattling from the nearby shed. Just as I was beginning to chant louder, the earth rolled under me and opened with a tearing sound like a giant bandage being ripped from an enormous wound.

A dark arm reached out not three feet away from where I knelt, and I heard the faint cries of my Faerie friends as they immediately leapt to my head and buried themselves in the curly mess of my hair and in what space was left in my pockets. Normally that would have annoyed me, but at that moment I was too mesmerized to speak or move.

The hand attached to the heavily muscled arm looked like it could crush the life out of any living being. Its long fingers were tipped with curved nails like dragon talons. This seemed an unusual response by the *Green Mother* to our pleas for help, but then who was I to question *Her* wisdom?

I forced myself to stay where I was and luckily, Skip did likewise and only grunted once when the arm was joined by a second, both pointed straight up like a diver ready to take the plunge. Within a heartbeat, an entire being shot up out of the ground and loomed over my tiny group like a behemoth swimming in a tiny pond. I felt like the frog on the Lilly pad watching the circling crane overhead.

If my eyes weren't deceiving me, I thought I saw a rather pleasant face looking down on us and then a deep voice shattered the silence like a hammer on a pane of glass. "Greetings from the *Mother,* Cathleen O'Brien, Sworn Protector of the Green Guild of Wizards, Daughter of Liam and Brighid, Mages of our Celtic Lore and Magic, Master Protectors of the Guild. I am of the Elements. You may call me Scythe, for I am the Dealer of Death to all who escape the Dark Pit." That was a mouthful and my own mouth was still unhinged in awe.

I had to speak, as Scythe stood patiently looking down on me in an expectant manner. I finally found my voice. "I'm grateful to our *Mother* for sending you, Scythe, as I'll need all the help I can get to defeat the coming Demons and their leader, the Black

Witch." I heard Skip grunt and shift behind me so I thought an introduction might be in order.

Scythe, this is my *Trogladyte*, Skip. He is also from the *Mother* and will aid us in our battle. Please don't hurt him as he's working with me." I felt a tug on my ear to remind me of the hidden Faeries and added, "And also, I have a Troop of Faeries that are part of our defense team." Scythe looked like he almost smiled and said, "Faeries are most beloved of the *Mother*." There was muffled tittering, as the little folk loved compliments.

"Good, it's settled then. We have our *A Team!* I said with some confidence as I stood once more. I asked Scythe to patrol the perimeter and destroy any Dark ones trying to infiltrate our compound through my mother's spiky fence. He marched off like a giant Sequoia among saplings, casting a murky shadow to conceal himself. *Woe to any bad guy that steps into his path* I thought with a grim smile.

"Skip," I said in my most commanding voice "you will follow me into the house, but you must allow me to conceal you, or the Wiccans will all freak out." With that said I cast the cloaking charm over his hunched body bringing it down to the ground to cover his dragging knuckles and said "Stay close to me Skip, and let's kick some Demon butt!" He grunted twice. Guess he was feeling chatty.

Inside I could hear one voice chanting and others responding. All was peaceful. I shouldn't have had that thought I guess, as all the windows blew inward at that instant, blasting shards of glass and wood around the front room and onto the chanting Wiccans. They were screaming in fear and clutching each other with looks of terror on their faces. I yelled for them to stay in a tight circle and I would cover them over with a protective spell.

Having said that I quickly conjured a *Sphere of Safety*. A soft green luminescence glowed within an earth shaped dome, covering the terrified women and sealing itself against invasion. I wished I had done this earlier, but discounted using spells that might be alarming to the already terrified girls and I thought they'd be more frightened being enclosed so dramatically.

They stood griping hands and reforming their circle. They seemed very relieved after my Dome was immediately tested by a dirty wind that came roaring into the room; especially as it transformed itself into five *Dungeon Dogs*.

Along with the other debris, I noticed lots of tumble weed and other scrub that had once been part of mom's fence. *So much for that barrier* I thought glumly.

As they stood arrayed like battle ships, the *Dungeon Dogs* fiery red eyes and lethal clubbed tails were almost more intimidating than their gigantic size. But they were the least of my immediate concerns as they stood in a scrimmage line formation awaiting commands from their mistress, Ursa.

I have to separate her from them I thought frantically, knowing they couldn't act independently. I spoke to Ursa like an old buddy, "Hey there! You're just in time for tea and scones." She didn't look amused, but raised her hand to give some kind of attack order to her dogs. *That won't do* I thought with just a touch of smugness.

Before she could speak I threw a *gag spell* over her mouth and secured it tightly around her mass of wiry black hair. She immediately started to tug at it with her ten inch nails, but it was impervious to her blackened claws. She was already lacking in any human aura I noted as I watched her struggling while making garbled animal-like sounds through the gag.

She wore a dark violet tunic over a long tiered black lace skirt. There were gobs of greenish slime that trailed off her like a snail wherever she moved. Her eyes were wild with frenzy as she tore at the gag; her fury growing as it resisted.

I said, "Ursa, you are going to release these dogs back to the Pit, or I shall have to destroy them right now." She looked at me through dead, red rimmed eyes, her pupils dilated with blind rage. I took that as a "no" and turned to Skip who stood invisible under his cloaking spell. I said, "Destroy all of them, Skip."

Like a moving tree stump grinder, Skip went into action grabbing dog after dog and destroying their physical beings and releasing their spirits back to the Dark Pit. The only thing left of them was an inky shadow left where they had stood, gape-mouthed and growling. While the Wiccans could witness the destruction of the monsters, they couldn't see how that was being accomplished. I thought the Dogs were scary enough for them without adding Skip into the mix.

I heard Ursa try to shout through the gag and almost didn't catch the imperceptible movement she had made with her hands. Suddenly she was screaming, somehow releasing the gag and charging me like an enraged bull.

I barely had time to tell Skip to deal with her, when I heard her say something that stopped my Trogladyte as he made a grab for her throat, while simultaneously dropping my cloaking charm like a stone. Up until then, it looked like a weird pantomime and the Wiccans had no clue about Skip's existence. Now I was certain Ursa had access to some very powerful Magic and her threat tripled for all of us.

I quickly retreated to the kitchen backing up all the way to keep her in my sight. *What the heck happened to Skip?* I was thinking frantically. *One minute he's my Mr. Destructo and the next he's standing like a hairy slag heap.*

With only a blink of time to conjure up something to stop her from turning me into some kind of Celtic centerpiece for her den, I raised another *Sphere*.   It wasn't nearly as nice as the one surrounding the Wiccans, but when she lunged for me, she got a nasty bump on her matted head for her efforts.

While I was secure, I needed to somehow reactivate Skip and this would be a good time to do that while her attention was still on me. I quickly reversed my original spell making him my personal body guard and replaced it with one that would blur his allegiance to either Ursa or me. Since I was quite safe inside the Sphere that she was beating on, Ursa was the target of the re-programmed Skip's immediate attention.

Chapter 30

I had my nose pressed against the opaque curve of my Sphere and began smirking which had the desired effect of enraging Ursa to new heights. She was too far gone in her crazed behavior and high pitched screaming to notice that Skip had come up behind her. When he reached his long arms around her and started to squeeze her like an orange, I intervened and brought him back to my control.

I really didn't want to destroy her here in the Wiccan compound. It seemed sacrilegious and could get messy. She needed to be driven back to the Dark Pit of the Sleepless Dead where she could be contained for a bleak eternity.

Skip kept his iron grip around her and I slapped her with a *Word Muzzle* so she couldn't conjure any other buddies from the Pit to join her, or change Skip's mind about who was in charge.

I went over to the girls still clutching each other's hands and staring wide-eyed at the scene unfolding with their ex -sister and Skip. They didn't realize Skip was formed by me with *Mother's* blessing and I only lost control because I had forgotten to ward against the Magical manipulations Ursa had used on my *Trogladyte*. That's a mistake a rookie makes and I could hear my dad saying just that.

"Girls," I said, "you'll be safe in there until I get back. I have to go check out our other defenses, but I'll drop the Sphere as soon as I return." I knew they could hear me, but from the petrified looks distorting their faces, I figured I'd better have Skip and Ursa go along with me. I told them that and they seemed relieved not to have to endure looking at them in the same room.

"Skip, pick Ursa up and follow me." With that ungraceful command, Ursa was hauled off like a sack of onions. Great for the stew she'd found herself in.

I headed to the place by the shed that I had left Scythe and when I couldn't find him, just followed the piles of sludge, bone and gristle strewn over the hard-packed earth and in various stages of turning to ash. As I rounded the corner on the far side of the house I saw him dispatching a *Pitted Choker* with one hand while spinning a *Bleak Phantom* into a knotted mess with the other. *Very impressive* I thought admiringly.

Scythe dropped the two Demons he'd just dispatched and turned a baleful eye on Skip who grunted as if anticipating a knock on the head. I quickly intervened before something unpleasant occurred and asked Scythe, "How many Demons have you dispatched back to the Pit?"

He seemed to puff up a bit and replied, "I no longer calculate such chores among my important feats, but you will now have fifty-seven less Demon spawn to deal with. *So much for not counting* I thought.

I had almost forgotten that Skip was half dragging, half carrying Ursa and asked Scythe if he could unburden us so I could go to my mother. He took Ursa after a very short tug of war as I told Skip to let go. Scythe said he would confer with the *Mother* as how to safely contain Ursa and her Black Magic.

I was content to leave her in his huge hands and taking Skip back to the Corvette, told him to sit like before. He was behind the wheel before I finished talking. I left the cloaking spell in place and told him to wait quietly until I returned.

After removing the Sphere and giving the Wiccans a brief description of what was happening, I had them unwind for a few necessary minutes outside the circle. "I never thought I could be so afraid, Cathleen." Joanie had quietly come up beside me and I put my arm around her shoulder to try to comfort her. I let all the girls know that we had Ursa under control, but there was still a threat out there in the desert.

"What kind of threat?" Jemma asked. The look on all their faces said, "I can't take much more," so I tried to down play the scenario a tad, so as not to scare the living day lights out of them.

I began, "It seems that Ursa was very busy at the Scotsman Butte, dredging up an assortment of Demons from the Dark Pit of the Sleepless Dead." There was a general intake of breath at this and more clutching of hands and whispered prayers to their goddess. I hadn't heard this much praying since my foray into the monasteries of Tibet to ferret out a soul eating Demon posing as a monk. But that's another story.

"Ursa has unleashed her Demons on this compound, but they are being dispatched as we speak so you'll be safe when I leave."

"LEAVE?" they all screamed out like a team of cheerleaders.

"Oh, you can't go, Cathleen," said Joanie, looking at me like I was pulling away in the only life raft.

"I won't be leaving you for long and I won't be leaving you alone girls. I will station two of my own trusted servants to watch over you. I have to go back to the Scotsman Butte as quickly as possible because that's where my mother is trying to defeat the Demon that Ursa hadn't counted on dragging up from the Pit." I gave them a minute to process this new character's existence.

"My dad named this Demon the Queen of Rot. She's a powerful Witch addicted to the Black Scaborious Rose, the same rose that Ursa wanted to force on you three girls." I looked at Maude, Alana and Luna and saw them shudder and go pale. "Those who eat the petals of this corrupt flower are given great powers, but they are condemned to join the other lost souls to an eternity without healing dreams, in a sleepless state forever. Their only hope in that bleak existence is to find a way out using their powers to re-enter the realm of the living."

Wynn had been uncharacteristically quiet up until then. She said in a subdued voice "Cathleen must help her mother, girls. If this Demon is even half as dangerous as she is described, she has to be sent back to the Hades she came from." No one argued with that statement.

I told them I would see to the guards I was leaving and they all returned to resume their circle. They were lighting new candles and incense and doing stretching exercises to keep from stiffening up as I gave Joanie a quick wave and left through the kitchen door.

Scythe was standing with his feet spread wide apart and looked annoyingly fresh and calm. Unfortunately, I was beginning to smell like a gym locker stuffed with old workout clothes. My nerves were as jangled as sleigh bells. "Scythe, I want you to stay out here and patrol the perimeter. If you encounter any threat from the Dark Pit, you are to destroy it. Do you understand?"

"I am here to serve these needs as you have described them, Mistress." He was wordy, but I liked him anyway. Ursa was lying in a heap on the ground near his huge feet and seemed thoroughly subdued. *One less problem* I thought, turning away.

I went to the shed and uncloaked the car, once more illuminating Skip's bloodcurdling presence with the small flame conjured in my now grimy hand. I had a hard time learning to control the fire I could produce this way. Consequently there were several scorched shrubs at home to demonstrate my learning curve. Jason called it a neat parlor trick, but I'd never be dumb enough to do this indoors!

"Skip," I said, "You will be cloaked so that I can leave you inside the house." He grunted eloquently. "You are NOT to take commands from any other being, living or dead, except me. Is that understood?" Again a grunt, but this time accompanied with eye rolling. "I can't have you seen by the Wiccans so you will be hidden from human eyes, but you will protect the Wiccans from any Demons, or other creatures that might harm them." No grunt and no eye rolling. He just loped off and entered the house by the kitchen door, opening and closing it like the phantom he had become.

I sighed deeply and not just to get fresh air into my lungs. I had some serious doubts about the two big oafs I was leaving in charge of security, as I'd never had minions before this. But I had no choice if I was to help my mom destroy the Queen.   All my instincts were telling me she needed my help and quickly.

My mother was a superior Wizard and few other Magic users would dare challenge her Magic, but this Queen from the Dark realm would have access to as much Dark Magic power as she wanted; drawing it off the countless supply of the undead from the Pit. She was capable of overwhelming an unwary Mage with an array of torturously evil spells, but then I thought with a tight grin, *she'd never crossed Magical swords with my mom.*

Chapter 31

It's no easy matter getting from here to there, especially when the "there" is a few miles away and underneath several hundred thousand tons of ancient rock and dirt. The Scotsman Butte was magnificent in its structure and grandeur, but the Dark forces had used it as an unwitting servant to their own evil ends. This perversion of the natural beauty of the *Mother* would not go unpunished and I felt I was an instrument to carry out the sentence.

Once again I used the *Wind and Aura* charm to speed my progress toward the Butte and when I got there I did a quick reconnoiter to see if Ursa had left any of her own *Trogladytes* around the base. Luckily, she was vain enough to think she'd simply smash through our defenses (she did cave in my mom's nifty wall) with her overwhelming number of Demons. Bet she never counted on running into the likes of Scythe. And Skip must have given her something to think about while being hauled around like a battered suitcase.

The opening I'd made earlier was still there, but I knew it wasn't as safe as it was inviting. I had to accomplish two things now and couldn't take unnecessary chances. I had to help mom defeat the *Queen of Rot* and I had to help find and rescue the five Wiccans taken captive from the coven several days ago. That presented a dilemma of its own. What if they had already become tainted and turned by forcing them to eat the petals of the Black Scaborious Rose? Maybe instead of finding five young women, I'd be confronting five lizard ladies in the making.

Since I didn't want to enter the tunnel by using the hole I had initially made, I decided to form another and this time I would make it more carefully, taking the time to broaden it to accommodate at least two people across. I located my new entry at a site farthest away from the original because I reasoned guards would be stationed closer to that one. Not a very sophisticated subterfuge, but I was playing this out by the grubby seat of my pants.

I made a complete circuit of the Butte on the Aura charm, riding as silently as the stars before I decided on a prime spot. It was in the deepest shadow of the looming obelisk. With the moon suspended almost over head of the first hole, I believed the guards would assume I'd use that light and easy entry point, counting on their lack of imagination.

The air was clean and soft on my face and as I knelt in the silky darkness, I felt a complete calm enter my being. I knew the *Mother* was near and sensed that my mom was still safe. She had escaped this place of evil once before and I was determined she would be leaving with me again soon.

Placing my hands upon the cool earth I spoke softly in the old tongue. *"Baisleac, Mother, please touch my Magic with your power. Help Brighid, your favored daughter and I to destroy the blight that has entered this realm."*

The new entryway I saw in my mind's eye was forming as I concentrated on its shape and when I raised my hands, a force drilled into the side of the Butte like a great, but silent boring machine.

All seemed to be going well until I felt a presence looming near me. I stayed on my knees and didn't react to the sharp change in the air and temperature. The softness of the night atmosphere had shifted suddenly into a bone-chilling cold. I felt as if I'd been transported into the heart of an iceberg.

I opened my inner eye wider, scanning the area around me like a barn owl on its perch. Standing nearby in a rough semi-circle were five young women, their eyes unblinking, bodies as rigid as marble figures and just as white. All were wearing the clothing and jewelry that screamed, *We Be Wiccans.*

It seems my new bore-hole led directly to the freezer my mom had conjured to hold the five captured girls until they could be safely tested for Demons and reunited with the coven. *One less thing I have to locate,* I thought with some relief. That left only my mother and her whereabouts which were still a mystery. The labyrinth of tunnels that Ursa had created down there would present the biggest challenge to my search.

I stood up and approached the Wiccans carefully. I wasn't sure how aware they were of my presence, but I needed to check them for tag-along Demons before I tried to penetrate their frozen condition. As I began to step forward to investigate further, the two Faeries that had come with me on this search and rescue mission popped their heads out of my sweatshirt pockets, making high shrill noises of alarm.

I backed up a foot and focused my inner eye on each girl; scanning her like a bar code so I could read any signs of a dark being. The first two were clean and so was the third and I started to relax and wonder why the little guys were still in their high-pitched alarm mode. I was beginning to feel like I was at a school fire drill and the whole scare was a false alarm.

The fourth girl scanned Demon free and harmless. I sighed and asked the Faeries to pipe down while I checked out the last girl. She was very pretty, with blond hair cut into a short, un-Wiccan pixie style and big green eyes that now were so unfocused, it seemed they'd start flashing Vacancy at any moment.

As I walked slowly around her I noticed she had a very notable hump protruding from her left shoulder and partially down her back. I knew Wiccans accepted any of good faith and physical imperfections were merely facts of nature. But this particular protrusion seemed to be throbbing with a life independent of pixie girl.

I started to back away from her and the hump as it began to crawl toward her right shoulder. Stirring the fabric of her green blouse it looked like shifting grass being moved by something slithery. I carefully took another step backward and was now a mere three feet away from the shifting hump.

I reached down and holding my hands flat, palms up, the Faeries each took a hand and watched the moving hump along with me. While we all faced the unknown hitch hiker, I spoke quietly in the old tongue so that only they could understand. "Friends, I need each of you to get ready to throw a *Net of Nettles* at whatever is squirming under there. I will follow with *green fire* as soon as you have it secured and it's away from the girl. "

Just as I finished my last words of instructions, a dark, anvil shaped head poked out from the rounded neck of the blouse. As it slowly crawled from its hiding place, I saw what appeared to be a lizard-like creature, constantly darting its forked tongue, as if licking the frigid air. Its stout, grayish body was covered in black scales glistening like grease slicks on a mud puddle. Its hooded yellow eyes revealed the stare of a predator on the hunt.

It slithered out from under the unfortunate girl's shirt and wrapped a muscled tale around her stiff neck as if she was some kind of hitching post, while draping most of its body, parrot fashion on her narrow shoulder. I flinched when I saw it flex its feet, exposing sharp claws that it pressed through the soft fabric of the blouse and into the poor girl's shoulder where the green material soaked up drops of her blood like a sea sponge, making me flinch yet again.

While this Demon was not an impressive size as Demons go, it more than made up for that in sheer nastiness. When it hissed at me and my Faerie friends, it shot out a long vile smelling stream of acid that luckily fell a foot short of where we stood. I quickly backed up a few more paces as I watched several holes appear in the dirt floor where the acid ate away at it. I quickly spoke a protective ward to shield us from any other foul spitting by the ugly runt.

The Faeries asked if I was ready for them to throw their *Net of Nettles* to secure this rascal and I told them to be careful of the acid and throw quickly. The sooner we could zap this creature, the sooner I could search for my mother.

Each of the Faeries had conjured a net created from the prickly nettle plants they so loved. They were a natural protective devise for their kind to employ when threatened with capture or discovery. Not many folks will willingly go plunging into a heavy growth of nettles unless they relish the agony of a million stinging barbs from the fine hairs that cover these unique wild plants.

As they held the nets in their tiny hands the Faeries began to twirl them around their heads like rodeo lassos. As they gained momentum the nets spread out wider and wider until each was several feet across creating a blur of movement with their incredible speed. At the last minute before the nets threatened to take off like helicopters, they were thrown in perfect unison at the hissing lizard.

They landed with a quiet plop around the Demon's body with the exception of its tail, which still remained coiled, tightened now like a noose around the girl's throat. I couldn't exactly tear it off her as its claws dug deeper into her skin and she seemed to be bleeding more profusely. Now I was worried about losing her to the poison it was likely injecting into her and destroying her arm if I just yanked the little devil off her shoulder. I decided to put the darn thing to sleep so I could remove it with less fuss and no muss. I knew I could heal her arm and neutralize any poison, but I had to get closer to do anything.

The Demon was using its front claws and lots of sharp looking teeth to try to tear away the restraining netting, but they held fast, sticking their lovely little barbs anywhere on its body that wasn't covered in scales. The more it struggled, the more of the nettle's barbs were pushed into its body.

I moved us a bit closer as the lizard thing was pretty involved in trying to escape the netting and took advantage of its lack of attention on me, to quietly cast a really great *Babysitting Charm* on its ugly head. It was asleep in a blink of its dead, yellow eyes.

I twirled my hands slowly to unwind the long tail from around the blond Wiccan's neck. Letting that hang down her back, I waved my hands over her shoulder to carefully remove the claws one at a time. The skin was deeply perforated and turning an ugly shade of blue-black. I could see black streaks where the poison slowly moved from the shoulder down into her arm. Though she was in an unanimated state, I wasn't sure of the lasting consequences of the poison. After dispatching the sleeping Demon back to the Pit, I said in old Druid, "Farcbain thu," to speed healing, and watched the black fade and disappear from her arm and wounds, returning the skin to a healthy but pale color.

The Faeries were quite happy with themselves for their part in vanquishing the slithery thing and I praised them and said they were truly *Mother's* champions. That bit of ego stroking done, I asked if they would start one of their special fires so that we could exit this freezer. I had goose bumps on my goose bumps and now that all five Wiccans were safe to transport back to the compound, I wanted to do that before they slipped out of our grasp again.

The little people were wonderful for starting fires when needed, but pretty iffy about the control issue. I saw a blaze eating away at the walls and melting the ice away, but it seemed to be escalating as it spread to the floor we were standing on, beginning to reduce the dirt and sand to a red slush. If they kept up the intense heat, the dirt floor would eventually turn to glass. Very pretty, but not what we needed at that moment. I quickly extinguished the flames which seem to irritate my little helpers, but I assured them they had done splendidly and I needed them to help get these girls back to their Wiccan sisters safely.

They began chattering, as they buzzed around my ears, asking how best to accomplish that particular task. I'd decided to keep them in the frozen state mom placed them in and attach a note explaining they were all clean of Demons and safe to have at the compound. They would need to be put somewhere out of the sun and I remembered the Meditation room, and figured they could all just stand in there until we got back to wake them.

I warned the other Wiccans not to try to waken them as I needed to do that slowly and carefully lest they become too terrified and disoriented. As a precaution I decided to send one of the Faeries along with the speeding bundle of girls so Scythe knew they were allowed to enter the house and to keep an eye out for any further invaders, though with Ursa out of commission that looked unlikely.

I constructed one of my mom's favorite means of communications and sent a hologram along with the girls, explaining things briefly. It wasn't inter-active, but they would at least have the important information.

To avoid any tampering, I used the Old Tongue to conjure a snug fitting capsule for the Wiccans and attached my small hologram to the Faerie accompanying the group. It would be activated when they were safely inside with the coven. This unique bundle was launched like a low flying rocket, back to the adobe house. Hopefully they would awaken later healthy in body and spirit. Never having dealt with this particular situation, I wasn't at all sure. But for now, it was enough that they were free.

Chapter 32

With the five girls out of harm's way and down to only one Trooper, I now had to concentrate my energies on locating my mother, somewhere within the maze of tunnels. I tried to focus on what I knew about the Queen; she definitely had her own agenda and Ursa had unwittingly become her servant instead of her master. Dad had spoken of the Queen as a *predator*, saying she was, "capable of devouring lost souls that came within her reach by using their weaknesses to tempt them to evil deeds." Ursa's weakness was her hunger for power and now she'd lost her humanity and soon her spirit would dwell in the Dark Pit of the Sleepless Dead where her loss of her humanity would only be part of her suffering.

Ursa had probably lost control of lizard woman soon after she brought her up from the Pit. There was no way a Demon that powerful would subject her own will to that of a mere mortal, but Ursa was so blinded by her jealousy of Wynn and her hunger for control that she never saw the writing on the tunnel wall. If we hadn't already captured her, it was very likely she would have been dragged down to the Pit by the very creature she conjured to help her take over the coven.

After all my ruminating I needed to get into action. I asked my lone Faerie to scout ahead for me and alert me to any Demon activity and if my mother was located, to please get back to me immediately. You always have remember your "please and thank you manners" when it came to dealing with the Faeries as they abhor rudeness and have very long memories.

It flew off down the mutely lit passageway while I used my inner eye to detect anything coming up behind me to catch me unawares. I felt a ripple of temperature change on my face and hands and knew there was another presence following behind me, hidden in the oppressively dim tunnel. Rather than turning around and making them aware that they'd been detected, I kept my pace steady and tried to act nonchalant as possible without whistling. I didn't have time to use my concealing spell and knew I'd already been spotted, so why bother.

Walking down one tunnel after another in a seemingly endless network had my nerves on edge. When I came to a fork in the path I took it so quickly, the creature following must have gone forward for a few steps without realizing I wasn't still ahead. I wanted to confront this mystery stalker. I was certain my mother was somewhere nearby and wanted no interruptions while searching for her.

That's when I heard the distinct sound of something being dragged, something heavy and long. *Couldn't be mom,* I was thinking. She's not heavy and certainly at five feet two, she wasn't dragging any extra appendage.

The tunnel was murkier down this new pathway, as the wall sconces held candles that had already burned down to black stubs, or guttered out completely. In the feeble lighting I detected a fine red dust lifted into the clammy air every time I moved a foot and I thought I heard the distant drip of water cascading down a rock face somewhere ahead. This might have been a newly excavated portion of the tunnel system. Guess Ursa still had work to finish for her mistress. She proved herself a better mole than a Wiccan.

While I heard the thing coming up behind me, it still kept a discrete distance as if it only wanted to observe my movements; not interfere with them. In the confines of the tunnel the sound of an object being dragged along the corridor was quite distinct. I tried to visualize the creature shadowing me and kept coming back to the Queen herself, as half woman, half lizard, and that meant a tail. I decided to test my theory and as soon as I ran into another cross path I darted to the left again only this time I had cloaked myself and was pressed against the packed dirt of the tunnel.

The distinctive sound of my stalker came to an abrupt stop at the cross path and I still had no view of it. I hoped it was the Queen as she'd likely lead me to wherever my mother was stashed. Or was she actually hiding from the Queen and I was being used to search her out?

Before I could reason out the answer, my pursuer paused as it came to the sharp corner, but instead of turning left to follow me, it jagged right and I never got to see it. *Darn!* I thought disappointed by this change of positions. Now I would have to become the hunter and that didn't always end well.

I retraced my steps to the turn-off point and proceeded straight ahead only this time it was me who was being cautious in my speed so as not to overcome my prey. There was one good outcome of the turning of the tables. I clearly saw the drag marks on the tunnel floor and that would make the hunt much easier.

I maintained my cloaking charm and crept along, following the revealing markings of what I suspected was the Queen's lizard half. *I'd sure hate lugging that thing around,* I thought distractedly. I didn't look forward to meeting up with her, but I believed my mom was at the end of this parade.

I was aware of a strong fishy odor as I followed the trail. Upon closer study of the markings, I discovered green phosphorescence faintly coloring the channels of the markings. The Queen's lizard parts had a glow-in-the-dark quality to them, likely very helpful in the Dark Pit. *Hm,* I thought, *evolution even for the Dead.*

The tunnel was better lighted in the area I now entered as the candles looked newly placed and lit. *This must be where her "majesty" does most of her scheming* I thought with a sour expression. I couldn't even begin to imagine giving up my humanity for a lizard bottom. I already had a hard time finding jeans that fit right.

As I was getting into a rhythm of movement in this game of chase, a sudden pinch on my ear lobe reminded me of my little Trooper. The Faerie had returned and was saying something about mom, but talking so rapidly I only made out every other word. It was clearly agitated as it jumped up and down on my head like it wanted to pound the information into me. It darted close to my ear where it hovered like a bumble bee drunk on nectar, repeating its message. "Brighid has gone to the Dark Pit. Brighid is with Trembler, speaking of the return of his Queen."

Huh? "What did you just say? Trembler, The King of the Dark Pit of the Sleepless Dead is negotiating with my mom?" I whispered frantically. My Faerie friend was moving its head up and down like a well pump being primed. I stood still and tried to collect myself. If my mother was down in the Dark Pit, how did she manage to do that and still be alive? I couldn't even contemplate an alternative.

I knew I couldn't just grow roots in my current position so I moved ahead and kept following the markings left in the dirt. As I came to another fork in the tunnel path, I looked to the right and saw a much brighter light coming from somewhere further down that tunnel. *Beats being in this semi dark* I thought as I moved in that direction. My mom's safety was paramount in my mind, but I had to try to find and subdue the lizard woman, or she'd have to be dealt with in future. If my mom wasn't by my side I wasn't sure how, or if I could accomplish that Magical feat.

Another buzzing in my ear from my Faerie buddy brought me to a halt. The Queen or one of her minions was just ahead to the right. I checked my cloaking charm for any impurity and found it whole and securely in place.

Stepping as lightly as a ballet dancer can while wearing heavy boots, I came to the opening of a large, carved out room. Its ceiling was very high as it was impossible to see to the top.

Scanning the room carefully before entering I saw what looked like a small assembly line of human looking creatures. I counted ten of them standing in a staggered row near the back wall. There was something even more unsettling about the beings than just their humanness. *They look like the Wiccans in Joanie's coven! I thought with rising alarm.* I recognized all the faces even the five newly returned Wiccans were represented in this weird sorority.

I studied the familiar faces. They had no expression in their eyes as they looked straight ahead, yet I felt they were alive and waiting for orders. When I had discovered that Ursa had taken blood from her recent hostages including Jemma and most likely from Wynn while she was in her zombie state, I thought it was only used in drawing the deadly circles. There had been one on the coven floor and I saw one clearly marking the scaly leg of Rain while she was transformed into that annoying, giant eagle. The blood was used to control, but now I believed it was used also to produce these fake Wiccans. But to what end?

My dad said I tended to overlook the obvious while searching frantically for the hidden meaning or message. So I slowed down my conclusion gathering process and just let the answer float over to me from the fake Coven members themselves.

Destroy the other coven and these ladies can move right into their places to do the bidding of the Queen of Rot; stealing the spirits of the unsuspecting to help populate the Dark Pit with other subjects for her and her King, Trembler. Corruption and consumption of the dreams of the innocent was the ultimate goal starting with the Wiccans, whose beliefs were based on the purity and sanctity of the natural world. And what better subjects then nurses who cared for those who were at their most vulnerable.

I moved further into the room to study each individual more closely. I noticed that Ursa was not represented, but then she already was a servant to the Queen. It was a relief to see Joanie wasn't there, and since Rain was destroyed, she wasn't to be found among her phony sisters.

I had counted correctly, but had put Rain on the minus side of this crazy equation. While I was recounting on my fingers and mumbling names to myself my tiny companion was nearly inside my ear canal trying to tell me we had company. I moved as quickly as I could without stepping out of my cloaking charm and hugged a wall in the narrow chamber. Faster than I could say *Wow,* Rain walked into the room.

I'd never met her outside her feathery freak persona, but I knew who it was immediately. Of course I was helped with this deduction when one of the stony-faced bogus Wiccans spoke up. "Rain, someone is here for you." *Uh Oh! This could prove rather dicey. I thought frantically.* Sometimes I remind myself of my mother - scary really.

I guessed the ten copies were more aware than I realized. They had seemed totally unconscious of the world around them *and* of my presence. I knew they couldn't see me, but suspected they had highly developed senses thanks to the manipulations of the Queen. The girl that had just sounded like Sally Secretary spoke up again and this time I saw it was the phony Wynn.

Chapter 33

It was just plain wrong to see this version of Wynn trying to warn one of the bad guys about my presence. But maybe it wasn't my presence she had noted in her trance like state. I shouldn't ever assume things. As my father would say "If you assume you are correct you'll never take the extra step to *prove* you are correct."

Directly behind the line of the newly minted Wiccans I spotted the slightest movement within the shadows. It was so subtle I only sensed it at first, before my inner eye was drawn to some kind of flow and ebb to the air current. *There it is again* I thought and I focused my full attention on an inky smudge absorbed into the dark of the far wall.

While my attention was somewhat diverted, Rain had stepped into the room and approached the nasty Wynn clone. "There is someone here. We all can feel a presence," she said to Rain. "The Mistress wants you to remove whoever has infiltrated, as she is nearly ready to move on the compound." I wondered if the delay in her plans was due to a certain Celtic Mage.

Rain was very tall and rather stocky in her build; sort of like a shot put champion you'd see in the Olympics. Her arms looked very well developed and strong. She didn't have that soft look of the other Wiccans, and the sneer on her hard mouth reminded me of a slash rather than softly curved lips. The only thing "Wiccan" about her was the long dress she had on that was covered with splashes of deep reds and ochre flames. She was just big enough to look like a walking campfire.

I didn't like the sound of the warning from fake Wynn, but at least I knew what was happening with the Queen. I just needed to deal with her new servants quickly. Right now Rain seemed the biggest threat so I'd need to incapacitate her immediately before I tackled the others.

After a quick whispered conference with my Faerie companion, we decided my best bet was to throw one of the Faerie's handy *Nets of Nettle* over her and because she wore very human skin, that was bound to smart and keep her still. The only drawback to this plan was that I had to drop my cloaking charm so we could act. Nothing was ever easy in Magic.

With little fanfare I was standing quite noticeably by the entrance and just as nonchalantly called out "Hey Rain! You looked better in eagle feathers." She turned around and seeing me standing made a high pitched screeching sound like the bird of prey she used as her familiar. Her body shot forward to grab me with incredibly long black nails. At the last second before she ripped my throat out, the Faerie threw the Net of Nettles over her and pulled it down, stretching it to her black, two inch toe nails. *She could hurt somebody with those things,* I thought with a small shudder as I took an automatic step backward.

Our new prisoner struggled for less than a minute when she decided any more movement on her part would only inflict more pain on her already nettled self. I quickly looked over at the line of Wiccan doubles and saw they hadn't moved an inch to try to help their wicked sister. I had an, Ah-Ha moment when I realized that since they weren't animated yet they had all their senses in hyper drive, but no mobility to act. That was very good for me, but definitely not for them. I approached the group cautiously and noticed that each had been leveling their dead eyes on me and I was beginning to feel like a blip on their radar. Only their eyes moved as they followed my steps as I got closer. I spoke softly in the Old Druid tongue so that whatever else was in the chamber in the guise of that shadowy spot, wouldn't easily over hear.

"*Oidhe amhailt*... Doomed phantoms... You are an abomination, a construct of the Dark Queen. Your spirits are from the Dark Pit, brought into this realm to torment the innocent and rob them of their dreams. As a sworn *Protector of the Guild of Green Wizards*, I condemn you all back to the Dark where you will live your eternity among the filth and degradation of the Sleepless Dead."

With that long speech, I raised both my hands and slammed my best Deconstruction Charm into each of them and stood silently by until there was nothing left of them but their evil shadows. These were quickly caught up in a whirlpool of black sludge and sucked back down to the Dark Pit for they no longer had a place in the living realm.

It was good to stand in the now empty room and no longer feel the power of the Dark presence there. The real Wiccans were safe from the imposters and the mortal realm was no longer threatened at least for the time being.

I looked over to where I left Rain standing uncomfortably under her personal net of pain. She too had vanished leaving only the net behind which the Faerie was gathering up into the size of a water pearl. Those little folk are pretty remarkable and I owed this friend a huge donut when we got back to the compound.

I was congratulating myself on the tidy Magic I'd just performed when I felt the stirrings of another energy force in the chamber with me. *Oh yeah,* I thought with a mental snap of my fingers, the murky shadow along the back wall. For some reason I knew this was not the threat I feared it was earlier. Now that I focused on it I could tell it was not just one being, but several...*Faeries!*

As soon as they knew I had identified them they broke their single body formation and swarmed me like a caressing rainbow; their iridescent wings shimmering in the glow of the candles. These little guys had been with my mother and finding them here without her was unsettling.

I said "It's wonderful to see you my friends, but where is Brighid?" Before they could all start in at once, I pointed to a pink Faerie and holding out my hand palm up, it stepped onto this platform to speak. I could see it was very fond of "Dagda's Daughter, Brighid the Beauty," as they all knew my mother and I had to interrupt the beginning of a long list of praise being heaped upon her name and that of our family.

"Please friend, speak quickly," I said. "My mother may be in need of our help." That seemed to staunch the flow of adulation and I was told that my mom was with the Dark Queen and her King as we spoke. "When you say *with them* do you mean she's visiting them, having tea? How do you mean?" I heard a tiny "tut-tut," coming from this pink fellow and then as if on cue, they all came back together into a flying wedge and left me standing alone with my sole Faerie nestled into the pocket of my sweatshirt yet again.

I knew there was no way I could follow the racing Troop, but they had thoughtfully left a trail of luminous crystals that I easily picked out in the flickering of the wall sconces. I gently prodded the outside of my pocket to get my passenger's attention. It poked its head out and I asked it to check the tunnel ahead and to let me know if there were any demons, creatures, or unlikable critters waiting to surprise me. The Faerie did a wonderful impression of an indifferent yawn, but zoomed off anyway in pursuit of a new adventure. Faeries love to be scared witless because nothing really scares them.

If I could have found someone to bet with down there, I would have bet that the Dark Queen and Trembler knew exactly what happened to their little team of Wiccan imposters and I'd also venture to guess they knew who was responsible. It was reasonable to figure that they might be more than a bit ticked off at me, so I needed a plan.

Looking down the shadowy tunnel I was following, I decided it would be safer to wait where I was until my tiny scout returned which it did almost as soon as I'd stopped moving. It landed on my shoulder and spoke into my right ear, relating that there were no scary things up ahead, just a very unattractive lizard woman and a grey man covered in warts and green slime.

With that alarming description, the Faerie dove back into my still warm pocket leaving me with my heart racing and my thoughts tumbling over in my mind like water barrels down Niagara Falls. I began to wonder what exactly would constitute a *real* threat to my pocket pal.

Chapter 34

It's no use kidding yourself about the kind of trouble you find yourself in. You can't rationalize it away, or diminish it as not being *that* bad. You just have to face it when you are outgunned, outnumbered, out of luck, or out of your mind. So I did the only sane thing I could think of, I threw myself onto the dirt floor of the passageway and begged the *Green Mother* for two things, my mom and another friendly creature just like Scythe. In fact I really wanted Scythe as he was already expecting me to boss him around. But I had left him to safeguard the Wiccans from any other intruders, so he wasn't available.

I closed my eyes to make my most sincere plea for help and when I opened them again I saw my mother standing in front of my prone body. I wanted to shout out to her, but knew that wouldn't be too smart with the Mistress of Demons just up ahead. It's just as well as mom was again in her favorite form, but still as warm and loving as a hologram could ever be.

The first time I saw my mother take this shimmery appearance of life was when I was three. Not an extremely stable age when it came to emotions and sudden outbursts of energy. She visited me over several nights to help tuck me in for bed, as I insisted to my father there was no way I'd go to sleep without her goodnight blessing.

Mom had been called back to Ireland by the Majordomo of the *Protectors*. He was in charge of any business regarding the Guild's status in the Magic Community and my mother's use of a particular spell had been called into question. Like doctors, the Celtic Mages' promised to *Do No Harm* unless it was to destroy a

Demon from the Dark Pit, or to restore order to any chaos caused by an evil doer such as a Black Witch.

It seems my mother had to return to Ireland to stand before the Guild and defend her use of *This and That Magic* because her charm had caused the sprouting of a second head on an odious man named Paddy McFrackland.

He had secretly been forcing parents to send the young boys from her village to work in the deep and dangerous coal pits around the area, threatening their families with loss of jobs if they didn't comply. These young boys were built perfectly to fit into tight and narrow spaces and could be used to fill coal cars with any lose coal left behind. A normal size man couldn't reach it.

This child labor went on unreported until one of the adult miners sought out my mother to intervene. When she heard of the terrible practice being perpetrated upon the boys and their parents, she flew into one of her more famous Irish rages and went directly to the mine. When she found the mine's unapologetic owner, she told him that if he couldn't make good decisions with one head she'd give him a second. It was reported she left quite abruptly after that.

Subsequent to her hearing, the Guild found that she needed to restore the man to his single, greed-driven head, as he hadn't been able to leave his house in weeks. She went to him and swore that if he ever used this odious practice again, she'd give him the tail of a jackass. He complied and all was restored to order.

She was returned to me and the careful symmetry of our home life was also restored to its customary routines and comfortable sameness, but I did keep poking her to be sure she was real which did prove rather annoying to her after several days.

As I looked up at this newest projection, I felt the same reassurance. "Hello dear," she said, "I knew you would be here, lass. Our Faerie friends have that wonderful mind-merge to share news, don't you know."

"Mom," I tried to whisper, "Where are you right now? Are you being held again?"

"Nothing so dramatic, pet. Just down the path a bit more. Oh, and the Queen and her King, Trembler are probably right between us now in their chambers, I expect."

Well at least that was something that could help me strategize my approach to catching them off guard. "Mom," I said. Watching the hologram shimmer and shake was giving me a headache and I blinked to help clear my head.

"Mom, could you come up with something from *This and That* to secure the pair of them in place?"

"Why certainly, dear, just give me a minute to get closer to them and we'll use the old Roman Pincer movement on the unsightly pair."

With that said, she winked out and I resumed my brisk walk down the passageway. I prodded my pocket and brought the now grumpy Faerie into focus again. After I asked it to reconnoiter ahead and return to let me know of the Demons exact location, it shot off like a tiny comet. I was not about to go into their lair without some strong Magical armor so I brought out my specialty, the sturdy, inviolable, not very fancy, *Sphere of Safety.* It doesn't have lots of bells and whistles, but it will hold up under serious bad guy assaults. Just to make it a bit more sophisticated and perhaps impress my mother a tad, I added the frosted glass look I'd used earlier for the Wiccans. Why reinvent the wheel if the one you're using is turning just fine?

I situated myself snugly into my newly conjured armament and proceeded slowly down the faintly lit tunnel. The black candles here were shivering like they had caught a chill so I figured my mother was somewhere close at hand. I stopped for a moment to listen and thought I heard sounds coming from my left. As I studied the passageway, I realized that it curved off in that direction so I had to make a decision whether to continue toward the right, or to turn the corner and be surprised. Since I loved surprises, I was about to turn left when my Faerie companion finally decided to return with some scouting intelligence. I was learning that the little folk do not make good spies as they like to dawdle too much.

My small friend dive-bombed me from the tunnel ceiling and perching on my shoulder, making my ear into an echo chamber while recounting important findings in a high pitched voice. The Old Language had piercing tones and my ear was tingling with the vibration as I tried to listen to information that could be critical to survival, and resist swatting at my head in irritation. The Faerie must have sensed my twitchiness and was quick to talk and retreat to my cozy pocket.

It seemed the Queen and King could be found together in a chamber that appeared very inhospitable to any living being. When I asked how that conclusion was drawn from the Faerie's observations, I was told it had something to do with the two *Dungeon Dogs* guarding the doorway to the chamber and perhaps also to the presence of their favorite pet, *Cringe*.

I had only ever heard of *Cringe* from dad. Mom said it was a fabled Demon created by parents wanting to frighten little kids to good behavior. Dad always looked at mom sadly when she denied *Cringe* existed in the Dark realm, shaking his head like she was a few electrons short of a lightning bolt. They were both adamant about what their version of the truth was and now I was about to face it.

I was beginning to feel like I was inside one of those snow globes you shake to watch the small blizzard of white crystals fall on the tiny church inside. I loved my globe until I had to know just how it worked and smacked it sharply with Dad's hammer for a closer look. My current frosted dome wasn't made for wide-eyed children and I sure hoped it would sustain more than a whack with a hammer.

Looking ahead I easily made out the forms of the two *Dungeon Dogs* and they certainly spotted me. They began a chorus of guttural growling that even in my Sphere, made the curly hairs on my neck go straight and stand up. They were chained to the entrance of a chamber where I was sure I'd find their Demon masters. I wasn't sure of the length of their restraints, so testing them seemed the logical approach.

I moved directly under the splotch of light cast by wall sconces set on either side of the entry way. As if on cue they both made a lunge for me, smacking heads, paws and long toothy snouts on the side of my frosted fort. It would have been amusing if they hadn't had that salivating killer look in their fiery eyes. I instinctively jumped back from the onslaught and heard my Faerie companion give a high pitched chuckle at my reflex for self-preservation. Saving face wasn't as important to me as saving butt…mine to be precise.

As the two Demon canines nearly strangled themselves trying to make good their attack on me, I heard a deep rumbling voice ordering them to desist. Even inside my contained environment, my ears felt like something sharp and pointy had slammed into them.

It had to be King Trembler as he was famous in the Magic world for a voice that was forged from the sounds of misery and pain. His guttural words made my enclosure vibrate like a sheet of tin in a tornado. He had the kind of malevolent tones that could melt every figure in a wax museum, or send a flock of birds plummeting from the sky. He rasped out a command to the beasties and they immediately turned on their splayed black paws, tucking their clubbed tails between their legs and lumbered into the chamber.

Obviously, the chains they were secured with were long enough for the two canine mutants to return to their master's side.

I could hear the clank of the irons as they fell to the chamber floor, so I guessed Trembler had unfasten them to set them free to maul whatever was disturbing the peace. That would have been me, except for the dome's durability I would have been so much puppy chow. The *Dungeon Dogs* I had dealt with earlier were just as large as these two and they all have that club-like tail, but these two must have been hybrids as they also sported spikes on the ridge of their tails which could likely inflict a lot of damage at treat time. I was fascinated by the size of their teeth as they began to circle me slowly all the while dripping yellowish gobs of saliva from their gaping jaws. I pulled my attention away from their armament and decided I better to get the job done soon.

I needed to send these Demon dogs back where they belonged and be quick about it as my mother was likely waiting on me to clean up the area for her big entrance. I thought I'd pull something from the dust bin of the Golden Age of Magic, and because he had long ceased to exist on this plane, I knew Merlin would have no objections.

I recalled how this Master of Masters had used a certain spell to declaw, defang and in general destabilize a particularly nasty Demon from the Dark Pit designed to hunt down and destroy any wizards within the natural realm, along with their beloved Dragons. I had studied the old Celtic verse from a tablet with ancient Runes that found its way to my father's clan. I could recite it flawlessly.

Holding my hands palms down, I made a repetitive circle with each like I was polishing a table top. Slowly, I repeated Merlin's formula and watched as the *Dungeon Dogs* each stopped in their tracks and began to quiver. It started like a sharp spasm, but soon escalated until they literally shook themselves into two large pools of gunk on the floor of the tunnel. It was very impressive Magic, even to me. When Trembler screeched out for them to return to him, he must have been surprised at their lack of response. I heard something scraping the dirt floor like the heavy shuffle of very large feet.

Trembler's resemblance to his Queen was about the same as mine. Zilch! He poked his hairless melon-shaped head out of the chamber and I immediately thought of a newly hatched baby gargoyle. Not many people outside of the Magic community knew those things were just waiting to be re-animated by some renegade wizard, but that's another story.

Trembler's face was like a mask that someone had stepped on in the dark. His ashy grey skin hung down in deeply trenched jowls that shook as he moved his head from side to side. As if the slackness of his flesh wasn't revolting enough, what I could see of his upper torso as he leaned forward was heavily covered with dark, bristly hair. Where his skin showed through this coarse matting, he was covered in warts seeping a thick greenish fluid.

As he stepped cautiously into the corridor and presented me with a clearer view, I nearly gagged at the unwholesome aura he exuded from his every pore. I noted the rest of his body bristled with a heavy covering of blackish grey hair that made him look like a body double for a Silver Back mountain gorilla, but Trembler was nowhere as good looking.

My Fairy hadn't told me about another feature of this regent from the Dark. His arms were heavily muscled and even through a heavy coat of spiky looking hair, his brute strength was obvious. He was stooped over rather like the *Trogladytes*. His gnarled hands had thick ropey veins that seemed glutted with too much blood. They ended in long curving talons that still had strings of some kind of meat hanging from them, as if his dinner had been interrupted.

As he was trying to peer into my opaque Sphere I was able to note his eyes were hooded by folds of grey warty skin and held the same clotted blood sheen of the other Pit dwellers I'd encountered.

Trembler moved slowly toward me and I wondered why he didn't just lunge. That's when I noticed he was impeded from any quick moves because of a heavy looking chain fastened to his left leg. I was shocked to see him in similar shackles to those that held the *Dungeon Dogs* in check, after all he was supposed to be King of the Dark Pit. Not the best of jobs I guessed.

His own chains were much longer though, I quickly realized, and he easily reached me where I stood to the left of the chamber door. While I was puzzling over his restraints he tried to tear open my frosted fortress. His claws and teeth were quickly rewarded with a numbing cold, but no Magic girl.

He then attempted to get all the way around my cone, but the shackles stopped him from circumventing me completely. I turned to watch his progress, or lack thereof, and saw that his temper had risen to a fairly demented pitch as he was frothing at the mouth in frustration.

I knew I was still safe, but I also needed to neutralize this hairy highness so that I could tackle the real power from the Dark Pit, the Queen of Rot herself. *I have to find out her real name,* I was thinking rather abstractedly.

269

Chapter 35

Thinking of eradicating Trembler reminded me that my mom was still nowhere in sight. I thought perhaps she was just waiting in the wings until I had sent him back to the Pit. It would appear being a King didn't amount to much when it came to who wore the Magic pants in the family. Trembler clearly took his orders from the Queen and that meant she was more powerful than we anticipated if this warty King was doing her bidding.

I was giving my attention over to choosing a really good spell that would remove Trembler from this realm completely, not leaving a single hair, when I noticed that my dome was starting to lose some of its own constitution. *What's going on?* I thought frantically as the frosted structure began to shimmer along the bottom like a rocket ready to blast off. I knew then that the Queen was interfering with my defenses, helping her Consort out without having to expose herself to any danger.

The warty King also noticed my shaky fortress as his bruised purple lips began to curl back into a sneer, showing teeth the color of rotten green tomatoes, worms and all.

My Magic was sorely tested as I willed my shield to hold firm while some other power was pulling it up so that I would be exposed to Trembler's gnarly hands. I spoke to my lone Faerie and told it to fly off at the first sign of the King reaching me. Instead my intrepid friend told me it had its own plan if the cone raised high enough for it to exit. I was too busy trying to hold my Magic in place to question the little Trooper so went back to throwing another ward over myself, making in effect, a dome within a dome. I felt like one of those enticing nesting boxes, one fitting within another, each exposed until the last tiny box is revealed and opened. Nothing good could come of that!

My first Sphere was beginning to shatter. I saw small fractures appear at the bottom and move upward at a slow, but determined pace. I couldn't stop the tears in the fabric of the first Sphere and decided to concentrate my Magical energies on preserving my secondary shield. My muscles seemed to strain with the effort of maintaining the integrity of my second line of defense when, with a cracking noise like ice being broken by a falling body, my first shattered and fell around me.

Trembler had put on what I assumed was his happy face as he leered with bloodlust at my small form inside what now felt like an insufficient defense system. Getting his hands on a trained Wizard and a sworn Protector to boot would be a real coup for him and earn him some points with his Queen no doubt.

It took me another minute to conjure some nasty spikes to arm my dome this time. As I was busy trying to stay alive, the Faerie had managed to squeeze itself out the backside of my unstable safe place undetected by the King who was focused entirely on destroying me. I didn't have time to consider just why my stalwart scout took off, but self-preservation made perfect sense.

Being so engrossed in defending against Trembler, I hadn't seen the Faerie move off to an undetected distance preparing one of those nifty *Nets of Nettles*. Out of the corner of my eye I saw a blur of motion and then the little Trooper must have cast the net over Trembler because he gave out a bellow that brought large clogs of dirt falling from the ceiling. *Oh great* I thought *all I need is a tunnel collapse.*

Not to seem ungrateful, I gave a big thumbs up to my tiny helper who immediately interpreted that to mean I wanted it to conjure yet another net which it did immediately. The King was still struggling with the first net when he was hit with a second and then a third and a fourth, until all he could do was topple over under their weight.

This was the best possible outcome and I praised the Faerie for its brave and effective methods. I decided I would exit my dome to cast the last spell Trembler would ever hear in the realm of the living as he lay thrashing about on the dirt floor. His screams of fury were bouncing off the narrow passage ways and seemed to be gaining in volume as they traveled the length of the tunnel and circled back to where he lay thrashing about on the dirt floor.

The Sphere of Safety evaporated as I raised both my arms and shot green fire at Trembler's wart covered body. His arm and one hand had already succeeded in escaping the nets and he was tearing them away from his face and head when the fire exploded around him consuming his form completely until just a tell-tale smudge was left upon the dirt floor.

I stood very still trying to catch my breath when my little pal landed on a shoulder and when I smiled back at it I saw that one wing was dangling at an odd angle. "You're hurt," I said alarmed. I opened my hand and it rolled carefully into it while I spoke a soft spell of healing. I knelt down on the cool earthen floor and felt the Mother's warmth surging up through me and into my hand to where the Faerie had curled up in obvious pain. The heat pulsed around the tiny form and before my chant was complete I could see the Mother's healing had mended the broken wing. I was relieved and pleased when my little champion popped back into my sweatshirt pocket for some well-deserved rest.

With the King destroyed and safely sent back in the Dark Pit there was the last challenge of the Queen of Rot to be faced. She was obviously not going to be too pleased that Trembler was removed from her service so abruptly and I was sure that displeasure would be focused on me.

Since she hadn't joined the King in his last foray into evil doings, I assumed she was elsewhere in the tunnel complex. I hadn't considered other possibilities as yet. I'd soon find out that there was much more to this desert obelisk than its deep endless tunnels.

Chapter 36

I shivered with a premonition of bad things coming my way and mentally tried to prepare myself for the battle that loomed ahead. What I *didn't* know was where my mother was in that dreary labyrinth as she went off earlier to do her thing…whatever that was.

She had said she would help me destroy the Dungeon Dogs, but oddly hadn't made an appearance. Guess she trusted me to handle the pooches, but that didn't answer the question of just where she'd gotten to in the meantime. With the Queen unaccounted for, I was beginning to wonder if mom was in trouble again.

Sometimes, it takes a while for facts to catch up with my brain and I just realized standing in the shadows of the deep terrain below, that this Butte had more than these tunnels and chambers to be investigated. When we found Jemma in a blood circle on the top of the Butte, mom and I both noted it would make a perfect launch pad. I couldn't feel any other life force in the tunnel complex and knew it was time to go top-side.

Surely by now the lizard woman knew her King had been returned to the Pit and eager to avoid the same fate, she would transfer herself to another hideout. The Valley of the Gods was filled with other Buttes and moving into the adjacent, Monument Valley she would have even more to choose from as her new warren.

I had to get to the top of the Scotsman and quickly. I concentrated my energies on locating my mother first as I didn't relish facing the Queen alone if I could help it. I poked the resting

Faerie and pleaded with it for one more mission. "Find Brighid, little friend. We need her help now!" Upon hearing my mother's name the little Trooper snapped out of its drowsy state and was soon swallowed up by the shadowy maw of the tunnels.

I decided it was time to investigate the Queen's abandoned chamber before I went up to give the Trooper time to search out my mother. I needed to see if the lizard Queen had left any surprises in the form of other Demons behind to guard her retreat.

I brought my hands up in case I needed my *Green Fire* and entered a cavernous chamber filled with two long rows of flickering black candles in various stages of consuming their wicks. They were spaced far apart as they retreated back into the chambers depth. The scene put me in mind of an airfield landing site. There was a high-backed chair set between two floor plinths holding candles the size of small tree trunks. Next to this, a large open cage was set close to a bowl shaped pit, filled to the top with soft looking yellow sand. There was an ebony plate set to one side of a depression the size of a *Dungeon Dog* or King, piled with chunks of red, bloody meat from some unknown being. A dish the size of a baby pool with enough water to swim in was close by the questionable delicacies.

The Queen and her King had made themselves quite comfortable in our realm with all the creature comforts of the creatures they were. But then there were those annoying shackles attached to the one leg of the throne chair. I supposed the King was only a few hairs better than the *Dungeon Dogs* in his Queen's eyes.

I began a soft chant to bring a small amount of *Green Fire* to my hands as I moved further into the room. That's when I was hit with an odor that stung my nose and brought tears to my eyes. In fact, the burning sensation caused me to cover my mouth and nose with my elbow so that I could breathe without gagging. I had dosed the *Fire* from my left hand so I could keep my sweatshirt over my lower face without singing the cloth, but I raised the volume of the flame in my right hand to make up for the loss. The room brightened considerably with that, though there was no way to illuminate the depths of what appeared to be a colossal-sized chamber, leaving me to wonder what lurked within the jittering shadows.

I poked my nose out of the crook of my arm to test the air as I passed the sand bowl and throne. It was still rank with the stench I recognized as death. The sickeningly sweet, cloying smell of decay seemed to saturate every molecule of air and dirt. I felt it leaching into my very pores. I had to get out of there before I was overpowered by this feeling of eternal damnation, the end of all life and hope. The only thing I'd find further into that cairn of blighted stone was going to be dead and I knew that my mother wasn't going to be among those lost souls.

I quickly retraced my steps out of the fetid chamber and immediately used a cleansing charm to rid myself and my clothing of any trace still clinging to me. As I emerged, my Faerie friend made a timely appearance and seemed very agitated with whatever news it had to share. I slowed down the flow of words, gathering that my mother was indeed in the sky…translation, on the roof of the Scotsman Butte and that she was, "preparing to do battle with the Queen who reigned among the Sleepless Dead."

Having achieved somewhat of an understanding of the situation she faced, I raced back to the hole I had made on my first visit here and using the *Wind and Aura charm*, propelled myself upward to hang like a Blimp above the Butte. I scanned the flat expanse below and saw two figures facing each other from several yards away, each with arms raised. It wasn't hard to determine which one was my mother. She'd be the one *without* the stout body and tail. The Queen's lower body looked very much like the back half of a Gila Monster.

Thankfully, I made a soft landing, my heavy boots taking the brunt of the impact and stood at my mom's side like I'd been there all along. In her typical nonplused fashion she merely turned to me momentarily and gave me a nod and a tight smile.

I could see she was getting tired and I suggested she step back and renew her energies with the *Mother* while I took over. I had already armed myself with *Green Fire* and threw in a *Knotted Hand* charm so I could send some good whacks over to the Queen when she couldn't see them coming.

Mom was more than happy to comply and immediately knelt down to regain her strength while I wailed away on lizard lady and threw my Fire into her really unattractive face. She had that same grey sagging skin of her late King, except that while his hung in gross, warty folds, her skin was rippling with scarab beetles, yellow maggots and other unnamable things that feast upon the dead. She sure must have hit every branch of the Ugly Tree on the way down to the Pit!

I was able to keep the Queen occupied while shielding us from the long threads of venom she shot across the distance between us. Everywhere it landed sizzled like steak on a grill, chewing holes into the dirt beneath. She had conjured a *Bleak Phantom* that rose up behind us. It was reaching for mom when she threw fire at it and placed a *Guardian ward* to guard our rear. If anything came at us from behind, the ward would zap it like a fly catcher.

Mom was fully recovered by then and I heard her say in the Old tongue, "Let's finish this beast, shall we pet?" With that we both turned up the heat and threw some serious *Green Fire* her way, the whole time walking forward to inflict more damage. Her skin began to make loud popping noises as it boiled up. Beetles burst under the assault of the flames. All the while my *Knotted Hands* were still slapping her around the head to keep her off balance.

She must have done some harm to my mother before I arrived as I noticed mom was limping slightly and had a tight grimace on her face. Mom transmitted her desire to move by nodding in the forward direction.

As we closed in, the Queen tried to sweep us off our feet with her long, heavy tail. We saw the muscles in her heavy scaled legs bunch and were prepared to jump back out of range. The Queen had been screaming her own spells the whole time our fire flew at her, but mom had neatly woven our fire into a flaming shield that held fast under the black curses.

The Queen had been slowly moving backward as we advanced, swinging her thick tail back and forth and creating a ground fog of red dust and particles masking her movements. She neared the edge of the Butte's roof.

"We can't let her escape, Cathleen. It's time for your Da's spell." We both hit her with my dad's unique *Iron Bands* spell which takes two Wizards to carry out successfully. She was immediately as tightly bound as a wine barrel within an iron hoop. For our own protection my mom also placed a *Restraining Dome* over her so she couldn't spit her venom into our faces.

My mother turned to me and asked, "Do you want to do the honors, dear?" and with that I sent the Queen of Rot back to the Dark Pit to rejoin the other Sleepless Dead. She left only a stain where she had cast her sick shadow; this was quickly dispatched as the contaminated earth opened and absorbed all the Demon had touched in her final battle.

"Mom," I said, "What about the Black Scaborious Rose that she was going to harvest and feed to the captured Wiccans?"

"Why, I had our Faerie friends destroy them all earlier, Cathleen. They told me they smelled them long before they found them, so putrid they were. I had them save one petal for me which I used to prepare an antidote if we needed such a remedy for the girls we released."

"Do you think they may be infected?" I asked, clearly concerned since I'd sent them flying back to the compound earlier.

"Perhaps dear, but we can handle that problem when we return. For now, I think we'd best cleanse this horrid place and return it to the *Mother* as healthy as She made it."

The Faerie Troop that had accompanied us were scattered throughout the tunneling beneath Scotsman Butte, doing my mom's bidding in the cleansing process. The ones I spotted flitting about seemed content in this happier work of restoring back to nature what belonged to nature. There was much *Faerie Fire* being employed in the process as anything that wasn't of the *Mother* was sent back to the Dark where it belonged.

I was grateful to them as I wouldn't have to re-enter the royal couple's chamber. The smell of rot and decay was still in my mind if not in my nose and I didn't want to face that filth again if I could avoid it. As always, the little folk were happy in destroying all sign of the Dark and I was happy to let them.

I finally got to ask my mother the question that had been bugging me. "Dad always called her the Queen of Rot, but I've been wondering what her real name was."

Mom took a moment to consider her answer, looking back into some opaque past only a few living Wizards recalled. "When she was still of this natural realm, Cathleen, she was called Morgayne of Rossmoor, a renowned Wizard of the time before the Great

Dark fell upon the world and Magic was still a sacred tool of the *Mother's* followers. Her life in this realm was recorded in the History of Wizardry in the Middle Times, a book your own da' studied closely over his own lifetime. She was quite beautiful it was said, before she became entranced by the Dark Powers and taken down to the Dark Pit where she became a slave to the Black Scaborious Rose petals. Your da' called her the Queen of Rot because that's what she reigned over; sadly, that's what she traded her human spirit for."

We were both quiet for a minute and mom started to move toward the opening we had made earlier and I noticed she still favored her right leg. "Mom," I said, "I saw you limp while we were fighting the Queen and it looks like you might still be having problems. Are you hurt?"

"Her tail connected a bit dear, but there's no real harm done."

"When we get back let's have Joanie check it for you."

Mom grew quiet for a moment and with a look that seemed mixed with relief and a weary foreboding, said "Let's return to the Wiccan compound, pet. It's time."

Chapter 37

Traveling with the wind is always very exciting as you are caught up in the upward or downward drafts and eddies of air currents that can toss you about like the fuzz off a dandelion. Our trip back to the compound was pretty tame by most wind travel standards, as it was a very calm day, with only the occasional uphill surges of wind. After our battle with the Dark forces, I welcomed the calming effect of our quiet glide.

We were gently deposited near my mother's concealed rental car and when I lit the interior and mom saw Skip I had to talk fast to explain that he was the same Trogladyte she'd seen me making and that he had proved a great help in ridding the compound of the Demons sent by Ursa. "Ursa! " I cried out, finally remembering the state I'd left her in.

"Where is the Black Witch dear?" mom asked, with a skeptical look as if anticipating some bizarre charm being used to secure her. She was close. I had left Ursa with Scythe and now I had to explain his presence here just as I had with Skip.

"She's under control Mom. I have Scythe on the job and he's very good at crowd control, so I'm sure he's doing a great job."

"Ahem," mom cleared her throat and I had to clear her doubts.

"Mom," I said, "I had to ask the Mother's intervention in a big way because there was just so much going on here that I felt I needed a little helper." With that said, Scythe was rounding the corner of the house dragging what looked like a bundle of old rags behind him. Mom's eyes traveled from his big feet up to his boulder-sized head.

Mom stepped closer to the prisoner and said, "Cathleen, as you know, Scythe is the Dealer of Death and while he sends the twisted Magic user to the Dark Pit, he may not have been the best choice as a guard for Ursa. After all, we may be able to save her yet." As if on cue, the bundle of rags came alive and with straining arms and hands made a lunge at my mother.

Ursa had the blood red eyes of her old Mistress and flecks of foam covered her mouth as she tried to puncture my mother's larynx with her long, corroded nails. Fortunately mom was a tad faster than Ursa. Scythe pulled up on the rope secured around her waist and let her dangle in midair like a broken puppet on a string.

That was enough to prove my mom's good intentions misplaced as far as the Black Witch was concerned. I told Scythe to deliver her to the Dark Pit immediately as she was lost to this realm. The packed red dirt began to tremble and opened beneath him as he clung to the screaming and biting Ursa and they were swallowed up by the gapping darkness.

It's always rather disconcerting when the earth just opens up like a clam shell and gulps down whatever, or whoever, happens to be standing there, but I was even more chilled by the residue left behind by Ursa. It looked like a black tar pit had formed where the Black Witch had stood when she attacked mom.

As I peered down at the smelly, thick sludge my mother came over to me and said "Don't fret dear, it's just the after effect of consuming the Black Scaborious Rose. Ursa must have been addicted to the petals for some time to leave this much residue behind. I fear she was lost to this land of life for many a day."

Having said that she stepped back and allowed the earth to claim the last vestige of Ursa's existence on this plane.

With that done she walked toward the car and Skip. *Oh yeah I have to do something with him, don't I.* I kind of enjoyed having my own *Trogladyte* around to be my minion, but Wizards are not supposed to get that comfortable in their work.

Mom removed my cloaking charm quite easily, which rather annoyed me, but then she had the original recipe and without any more interference from the Queen, her Magic was restored to its full power.

Skip was still gripping the steering wheel for all he was worth. I said "Skip this is Brighid and she is a Master. You need to do as she instructs."

Mom looked quizzically at me and asked, "Why do you want *me* to send him back to the Pit, Cathleen? " I must have looked a bit saddened by the prospect and she simply said "Oh, I'll do it then."

She had raised her hands and was about to send Skip on a one way trip down when I stopped her and asked if it was possible for her to conjure the same car he'd grown so attached to so that he might take it with him. Mom smiled and looked at me for a minute before saying, "So much like your da' you are." Before I blinked twice, Skip was off in his own red Corvette and probably would sit contentedly on its soft leather seat for whatever eternity his kind enjoyed.

We turned toward the squat house. Looking at it, I was reminded of a frail outpost on the edge of a wild frontier as it seemed to hunker down even lower on the cracked red earth. Feeling ahead with our senses we encountered only one source of energy from outside of this realm, but there was something else that caused a ripple in our sensor probe.

Mom said casually, "Shall we have a wee spot of tea, pet. I'm fairly parched with all the dust and such. "

"Sounds good to me," I answered, but I would reserve my full enthusiasm until I knew what else was going on.

We headed for the kitchen door as there was a light on and we knew the Wiccans all liked assembling there for its warmer atmosphere. Mom had communicated earlier with the Faeries we'd left at the compound to restore the returned Wiccans from their frozen state since all checked out as free of Demon riders. When I opened the door, eleven Wiccans froze like a small herd of deer in the lights of an oncoming semi. Their paralysis lasted only a heartbeat, and then we were under an avalanche of arms hugging, patting, touching our faces to see if we were the real McCoy.

The Sphere I'd left the group under had dissolved with the destruction of Ursa and they were happy for their freedom. The five returned sisters were standing bunched-up like the strangers they must have felt like as they quietly watching the happy reunion. They hadn't been animated long and it would take a bit for the others to let their guards down with them.

Through this barrage of attention and the sense of relief they exuded, there was a pin prick of darkness somewhere in the group. It was masked by the warmth of our reception, but my mother and I exchanged a brief look that said we both knew it was present; the petals must have been consumed by one of the returned five girls

"We need a strong cup of your delightful green tea, Wynn, if you'd be so good," mom said, with a big smile on her face and her eyes on me. Everyone was scurrying about trying to put together a quick tea party with slamming cupboard doors and the gathering of mismatched cups. There was even a newly baked coffee cake. Jemma seemed very pleased with offering it, so she must have been the baker. I looked at each of the girls as they bustled about and only one smiling face looked back at me with empty eyes.

*Oh boy! I thought we were home free…*That thought I kept to myself.

I asked Joanie to check my mom's leg for any sign of skin laceration as that would surely mean she'd have poison in her system. After a careful check of her lower leg, they returned from mom's room and she was declared merely bruised. I was relieved at this news as I knew mom would be needed in the near future to ferret out the petal eater before she could strike at the heart of the Wiccan coven.

Chapter 38

We were all sitting on chairs, or the counter tops in the cozy kitchen, a soft light from the fireplace in the front room enhancing a subdued mood. They had only switched on the small light over the sink, as if no one wanted to see their friend's faces too clearly. Mom was presiding over the group in her usual take-charge fashion. The Wiccans were all entranced at her retelling the highlight of the events of the past night, while the sun was beginning to tinge the last of the deepest shadows with a bit of hopeful light. We had drunk several cups of tea and demolished the cake when mom said, "Cathleen, would you be a dear girl and bring me my jacket? There's a bit of a chill in the air."

Because I knew she didn't have a jacket and already had on her only sweater, I figured she wanted me out of the room for some reason. *She wants me as bait,* I thought with a tiny chill of my own.

The idea was to divide and conquer in the mind of my devious mother. If we were separated even for a minute or two, the fallen Wiccan would have to take advantage of the time lapse. I got up to supposedly retrieve the nonexistent jacket, smiling back at my mom as I left the room. I went directly to the Meditation room, standing just inside the door I waited for the girl to show herself.

She came into view as I pretended to look for the non-existent jacket hanging from the hook on the back of the door. Our eyes met for a split second as I said, "Hey, Wynn. I guess you aren't here to search for a jacket, are you?"

Wynn's eyes shone brightly with a hint of deep red around the dark brown of the iris.

"I'm so sorry it's you who ate the black petals, Wynn," I said with real sadness in my voice.

"Not as sorry as I plan to make you, Cathleen." She moved steadily but cautiously closer. I backed an inch or two, knowing I'd meet with the resistance of the bed soon enough.

"First you and then your meddling mother. I know you have sent Morgayne and Trembler back to the Dark Pit and you conveniently destroyed Ursa for me too. That leaves *me* as the new Queen of the Dark Arts in this realm and I intend to start with this coven…a ready-made following of servants to my will."

I needed to keep her talking to give myself and hopefully my mother, a chance to subdue her. "Wynn," I said, "You were corrupted by Ursa when she put you inside her blood circle and into a zombie state. She must have forced you to eat some of the petals from the Black Rose to enslave your spirit."

Wynn looked at me like I was some kind of delicious dessert and she clearly had me boxed in as there was no way out but past her. I had been preparing for this moment since I entered the small room, calling up my ward of protection so I wasn't too concerned. Something about Wynn's hesitancy in making her attack on me seemed like a good sign. Perhaps she wasn't totally lost to the Black Arts and clung yet to some thread of humanity.

Wynn hadn't moved any closer or I'd be on my mom's bed as the back of my legs had already made contact. Instead she began to shake her head like she was trying to dislodge something from her ears. After a few seconds of that, I heard a low animal-like growl come from her throat and braced myself for the charge, bringing my ward forward to create a solid wall of thickly condensed atmospheric vapor. It was raining.

Mom had told me on the way back to the compound that those who have been seduced by the Black Scaborious Rose couldn't bear to be touched by the clean waters of the *Mother*. I used the least lethal method I could think of to stop this possessed Wynn from reaching me.

The rain was coming down in a solid sheet and seemed almost iridescent as it shimmered in the soft glow coming from the fireplace, located directly across from the Meditation room. The Wiccans had kept the fire going since I destroyed the *Budgie Phantom*. They didn't want any other Demons trying to gain entry through that medium, so kept fresh sage and other scented herbs burning along with the essence of *Faerie Crystals* that the Troop slyly contributed toward their fire rituals. It was still only early dawn so the light from the flames still lent an air of warmth to the rooms.

I stood very still behind the sparkling waterfall as it splattered across the floor and began to edge quickly toward Wynn and across the darkening wood floor. There was a look of alarm on her face as she began to back away from the oncoming water. I moved again, bringing the torrent with me which propelled her to an even quicker retreat.

I realized belatedly that this was all happening within earshot of the others, but they had given no sign of being aware of my situation. I was certain this was my mother's plan, luring the wicked Wiccan out of the group. I wasn't too keen on acting like the sacrificial goat pegged out and waiting for Godzilla, but we needed to keep it simple. Mom wanted to use the old Roman Pincer method, her old favorite standby and get the Dark Wiccan between us where we would in theory be able to coral her and remove her as a further threat. That was the theory.

As I inched forward, shielded behind a continuous cascade, I began to feel a tad uncomfortable in the deadly quiet of the house.

Where the heck is everyone, I thought, getting a little twitchy. *And more importantly, where is my mom?*

As these disturbing questions meandered their way through my brain, I heard Wynn mumble something. It sounded like, "No Kelp for you," but it might have been, "No *help* for you." Guess the sound of my waterfall blurred her words.

I had to throw my voice using breath control so that she couldn't misunderstand me. "Wynn, we have a way to save you from the Dark Pit. Brighid knows the secret of releasing you from your addiction to the Black petals."

She snorted and began to laugh manically.

For some reason, as I studied her face more closely through the downpour, she seemed to have aged and withered in the short time she'd exposed herself to me as the fallen Wiccan. Even her snow white hair had taken on a dull, yellow tint, like the nicotine stain on a heavy smoker's fingers.

She said, "You have no idea of the power of the Black Scaborious Rose, Wizard. Your Magic is nothing in comparison to what I'll be able to achieve. With this coven serving me I will reign as Queen of this puny realm." She seemed to be gazing into a future that was predetermined. Then she added ominously, "All will bow before my power." That sounded pretty final to me and I had to accept we'd lost Wynn forever.

We were now in the front room with the fireplace painting shadows across the floor and illuminating my water works with a bright shower of colors. I took a quick look through the kitchen doorway and what I saw didn't give me much comfort, but it did confirm my suspicions.

A whole gang of Wiccans standing around in different poses, leaning against the counter, washings cups at the sink. I saw that Joanie still sat at the table with Luna and sticking out slightly beyond the door frame was my mom's arm, resting comfortably on the table. They had all been put into a sleep state of some sort and I knew how. "Wynn, you put something into your wonderful green tea didn't you?"

She responded with that same mirthless laughter I'd heard before with Ursa. Then she said, "Take down your ward, Cathleen, and I will make you invincible like I am."

I couldn't see myself as invincible since I really enjoyed my human foibles. I didn't think she should be invincible either, just not a good idea to have two Titans working the same territory. Besides, if I could never be beaten. I would be proclaiming my superiority to the *Green Mother* and that was about as likely as me sprouting wings and a hallo.

Realizing we were at a *Mexican Standoff* I changed things up a bit. I dropped my water works and instead threw a Quick Freeze Wave at her, but she was pretty wily and threw up a hasty wall of air deflecting my Popsicle maker.

I took a step backward and using my own breath I called up a *Windmill of Air* to capture her and reduce her to a spinning blur. Guess she was on her Magical toes as she turned that around toward me and I nearly got sucked into the churning vortex of the wind like a rubber ducky in a draining bathtub.

This wasn't going to be easy. The power from the *Scaborious Rose* was stronger than I first imagined. Now I needed to meet fire with fire; and that's what I hit her with. Instead of turning her to ashes, I used my hands to weave a wall of green fire so she would be contained and unable to respond with another dandy spell of her own. Unfortunately, Wynn seemed ready for that ploy. Before I could smirk with pride at my Wizardry, she had turned the fire away from herself and I was the one surrounded by a green pillar of flame.

Hey, this is what Joanie dreamed about, I thought with some alarm. *Wonder how that ended?* I had to act and act fast as Wynn was moving back toward the kitchen and her helpless prey. I could hear her begin to conjure a charm as she moved forward, the sway of her long skirt like the ticking of a clock as she swept in an unhurried, self-assured fashion closer to the drugged girls and mom.

Now sometimes I am just a tad obtuse as I proved to be at that moment of hemming and hawing about what to do next. Then it occurred to me this was still the *Mother's* own *Green Fire* and I could still use it as I needed.

I held out my hands and made a cutting downward stroke creating a seam within the wall of flame. Stepping through, I grabbed the cold flame and hurled it at the retreating back of the would-be Queen. It hit her like a ton of bricks fresh from the kiln and she was driven to her knees with the weight. I quickly secured the wall around her and for good measure added a dome to cover the whole thing. The fire would burn as long as I wished and the dome was just added insurance as Wynn had proven pretty crafty.

I rushed into the kitchen, all the while hearing the muffled sounds of screaming from the fairly mental witch. I went straight to my mother and called out to the Faerie Troop that I knew would linger here as long as their beloved Brighid needed. They all materialized in that rather jarring manner of buzzing and poking and pulling of hair.

I politely told them of the situation and they immediately spun off me to my mother where there was much concern and fretting. I had to refocus them so that they would produce a solution rather than a funeral dirge. They stopped wailing and coming together like a colorful congress, I could see they were arguing about the best course of action to take. Meanwhile Wynn kept up her caterwauling and I had enough of the noise and indecision. I spoke sternly to the one Faerie that seemed to be the head honcho. "My friend, we must act with haste as much depends on you releasing Brighid and the others from the effects of the drug used to paralyze them."

That seemed to do the trick as the Troop broke apart, each of the Wiccans and my mother had several tiny folk land on heads and shoulders. A high pitched song was humming through the air like an electric current turned lose in the room. Suddenly, like a switch was thrown, everyone became animated as if they hadn't just been motionless.

Mom had been in a conversation with Joanie and Luna it seems as she immediately laughed at something one of them must have said twenty minutes ago. I left Wynn sheathed in fire and the dome in the front room and entered the gaggle of talking and relaxed women.

"Hey mom," I said, "can I see you for a minute?"

"Why certainly, Cathleen. Excuse me, girls."

When she saw Wynn smoldering with anger inside my dome, she looked over at me with her eyebrows raised in genuine surprise. "Cathleen, was it Wynn then, pet?"

I said, "Mom she spiked the tea and put you all into a frozen state. The Faerie Troop brought you all back."

"Oh dear," she said, shaking her head side to side in resignation. She looked genuinely sad about this turn of events. "I really hoped I was wrong about Wynn, Cathleen, but I've suspected all was not quite right with her almost since I arrived. She had begun to slip some obscure verse into the Wiccan chants that I overheard and recognized as of the Dark Arts. Her coven sisters wouldn't have guessed at them as she wove them in so intricately with their own prayers. She was preparing herself all along for the right moment to take over their dreams and spirits."

This was news to me and news I wished she had shared, but my mother did things in her time, in her way. "What should we do now, Mom?"

I was looking for some Magical cure, but mom only offered a terse, "She has to go."

Without another word she raised her arms and hands palm outward, removed the dome and instilled the green fire with a spell that almost instantly consumed the newest Black Witch, reducing her to a pile of gritty black ash. This she swirled into a small dust devil and opening the front door with a flick of her wrist, dropped the unholy pile onto the red earth where it was absorbed and vanished from the plane of natural life.

We both stood silently for a moment, a moment to consider the extent of the loss to this coven and the impact upon their lives as Wiccans. Wynn was an admired and charismatic leader. Her ending would be traumatic and unreal to the group she was about to betray.

"Now pet, we need to go back in there and tell the girls what's happened. I suspect this coven may not sustain itself after all it's been through."

Mom sighed deeply and we returned to what was left of the Wiccan sisters. No leader, little trust and no hope had bound their fate in cold iron links.

Chapter 39

The group stopped, talking and fussing with dishes the minute we stepped into the kitchen. It must have been the looks on our faces that wouldn't be hard to read as they reflected the distress we both felt. Joanie was the first to speak. "Cathleen, what's wrong sweetie? You and your mom look like you've seen a ghost." Everyone's eyes were fastened on us, studying our expressions.

I was almost relieved when Mom said, "Actually dear, we didn't see a ghost… we made one."

There was a stunned silence as everyone was trying to decipher that response. I continued my mother's report trying to avoid alarming them with ghost stories. My mother is a bit dramatic at times like these. I'd learned a lot from Jason's police work, such as that the hardest part of solving cases was telling the story without the embellishment of fear, or accomplishment.

"Girls," I said, looking at each of them and picking up where my mom had left them dangling. "While Wynn was under the Zombie spell within the circle of blood, we discovered she had been fed the petals from the Black Scaborious Rose." Over the intake of breath and soft murmurings, I continued, "She became a willing servant of the Black Arts, and was planning to replace Morgayne, better known as the Queen of Rot, as the new Dark Queen in this realm." By this point in my statement of facts, the Wiccans began making moaning sounds like a dessert wind shifting through a starless night.

Mom took up the thread of the story line once more. She looked determined as if she might meet with some resistance to her recital from the agitated group. "We could not save Wynn from her addiction, though we wanted to very much, but she was too far under the influence of the Dark and had come to crave the seductive Dark Powers of the Rose." The tight knot of girls seemed to spasm with those words. "She had turned her spirit from your Goddess. Her only desire was to dominate this coven…making all of you her unwitting slaves. She had utterly committed herself to Black Magic."

There was a low sound like the groan of the newly bereaved, rising from the astonished girls as the realization sank in that they had been so close to Wynn and the whole time she had embraced the Dark. The fact that they had all unknowingly been in grave danger before we exposed and destroyed Wynn, was beginning to seep through the initial shock.

Maude was standing by the sink and as the oldest of the group she seemed to rise to the position of leader. "We've all been touched by the Dark in one way or another since we arrived here," she said. "If I hadn't been saved by Cathleen and her mother, I would have been lost in that Darkness forever. I for one am not going to let fear rule me. It's time for us to come together and seek out the Goddess for Her guidance and to remember the sisters we've lost in a better light than we see them now."

With that she walked out of the kitchen toward the front room. The rest of the girls stirred themselves and began to follow. A wobbly line of Wiccans moved out the door, long skirts stirring the air in their silent retreat while the innocent flames of the fireplace cast their shadows like a second coven walking with them to pray.

I turned to mom in the now empty kitchen, grateful for a few minutes alone so I could speak with her further about the fate of the remaining Wiccans. "Mom," I began, "are these girls safe now?"

It was disconcerting to remember how I always saw Wynn as sweet-natured and content with her place in the natural world of her Goddess. I admitted to my mother that I felt I was easily duped.

Mom was looking down at her hands, folded on the kitchen table, her long braided hair shinning a rich silky auburn under the single kitchen light. We both were quiet for a moment and then she looked up and answered, "There is only one thing this family of Wiccans can do dear, to truly be safe from the influence of the Black Magic that moved freely in their midst." I looked searchingly at her, afraid of where she was leading.

"My darling, Cathleen, they must burn this house to the ground and cleanse the earth it stood upon. They must never return to this compound as it will forever be a portal to the Dark Pit of the Sleepless Dead and its minions." She looked down once more as if reaching out with her senses and continued, "Although I don't feel any other Black Arts users among them, I fear their individual curiosities might have been enflamed by the prospect of so much power and the thought of an eternal life of feeding their appetites for more power. Even the most stalwart soul would be mightily tested."

"You're saying they must disband so they don't carry some sort of "taint" within the group, mom?"

"Most assuredly, my girl, most assuredly," she said with a sad, but deliberate force. I knew she was never wrong about her strong intuitions. Giving her shoulder a quick squeeze, I walked out into the front room where the Wiccans were chanting softly within the sky-blue circle. How could Wynn have betrayed everything she believed in and all these girls that believed in her to lead them? She used her newly found Black powers to look like the leader they all loved and respected. I knew she had been forced at first to eat the petals from the Black Scaborious Rose, but by the time I brought her back from the zombie state it had already darkened her heart with a hunger for more power, a hunger that might have been there all along, just waiting like a spider until something touched its web.

I was deep into my thoughts when I realized a silence had replaced the chanting voices. Looking up I saw all the girls watching me expectantly, standing like good little soldiers awaiting their next orders. Now I understood that being that unquestioning, that easily led, must have made Wynne's masquerade much easier.

"It's good to ask why," my dad always told me. "Never accept something as a truth just because it sounds plausible, Cathleen. There could be a wee lie hiding behind the other fellow's accuracy." I took a breath and moved closer to the circle.

"Girls, would you mind returning to the kitchen? I believe Brighid has some important insights to share with you." I delivered this message as calmly as I could so as not to cause undue anxiety about what was to transpire. They exited the circle as they had entered it, one girl following behind the other. The fire seemed to snap to attention. Orange and red flames sprang up as they passed, shadowing their retreating forms.

My mother had been busy in my brief absence as there was hot tea and the assorted cups set out around the much-scared oak table. This was some of my mother's special brew of that I was certain. She must have had a webbed hand from her adoring Faeries to have pulled this all together in just the few minutes she was alone.

"I thought we could all use some calming tea so I brewed up a pot for us," she said addressing the returning girls. Somehow she had managed to add a few folding chairs that I remembered from the shed. They were placed around the table which was now centered in the room, giving easier access for seating. The few girls left standing used the counter tops and we made a nice cozy grouping. The fragrant tea worked its intended Magic as everyone sipped it and contented sighs filled the quiet spaces in the room.

Mom looked around and when she was certain everyone had finished a full cup or was sipping a refill, she said softly, "We need to discuss our plans girls." They had all riveted their attention on her and she continued. "There has been much troubling this coven of late and Cathleen and I suspect that Ursa's influence went far beyond even the recent events."

There was an uncomfortable shifting of eyes among the girls as they looked at one another with veiled suspicion. It was always the what if's and maybe's that undermined the cohesiveness of a group trying to act with a single purpose.

My mom continued on to the hardest part of her speech. "The Wiccans of this coven must face the fact that both Ursa and Wynn had worked to undermine the Wiccan beliefs and pervert the purity of your faith. That has made for an unfortunate but necessary conclusion. This house must be burned to the ground." There was a small sound which swelled to cascading voices raining down questions and objections and renewed fears. I raised my hands to quiet the tumult and looked directly at Joanie for help in quieting the group.

"Sisters," Joanie called firmly, "Please, let's allow Brighid and Cathleen to finish so we'll understand their concerns. I know they have our best interest at heart." That little speech seemed to pacify the girls and mom continued after smiling her thanks to Joanie.

"We believe that this house will carry the taint of the Black Magic practiced here. It will always be a doorway that the dwellers of the Dark Pit can use to penetrate this realm. It must be destroyed and the grounds cleansed and sanctified by the *Mother* once more."

"Where will we go?" asked Jemma with a tremor in her small voice.

"You will not be able to sustain yourselves as a viable coven," I said. You will never have that wholeness of spirit and oneness of faith that you once shared."

I continued to look at each girl closely, trying to gauge responses and added, "Your coven must dissolve girls. Each of you must search for another coven with strong beliefs and a fertile environment for you to grow again in Wicca."

Mom looked at me intently and I could read the approval in her eyes and the small smile that touched the corners of her mouth. "Thank you, Cathleen dear. Well put. Do you girls understand the importance of this sad act we must perform?"

As one, they answered yes, some mumbling their response, others more firmly. "I can assure you all that Cathleen and I appreciate the deep sense of loss you must all be experiencing, but if you each have the resolve and the faith to go forward, you will find new covens, or form your own."

With this I stepped over to where mom was sitting at the table and said, "It's time to pack your belongings, girls, and prepare the house and grounds for final purification. We'll put everything in our cars and move them away from the house to the far perimeter of the grounds to the north. I think we need to notify the Tribal Police that we are going to be performing a ritual cleansing that involves fire so as not to alarm them unnecessarily. If you have no objection I think we should also invite their shaman to attend and perhaps even assist in the ceremony as this land is as sacred to them as it is to us."

There was much bobbing of heads in agreement and even a few good idea comments that proved to me the Wiccans were ready to move past their shared nightmare. Mom stood and placing her arm around my shoulder gave me a quick squeeze saying, "Very smart, pet. I like your plans very much."

Since that seemed the consensus, we all moved out of the kitchen and went our own ways, packing up personal items and clothing and searching out garbage bags for items that could be saved and donated. The pace was slow but constant and by early afternoon we were ready for a break and to regroup.

"Mom," I said, coming into the Meditation room where her own bag was open on top of the narrow bed. "What do you think about having a lunch break? I've already got the others fixing up our last meal here.

"Of course dear, I'll just close this bag and be right along." As I turned to leave the room I heard Mom snap the case shut and then I heard her begin a soft chant.

Hmm…Wonder what that's about I thought.

Chapter 40

I entered the kitchen, grateful for the normalcy of the scene. The girls were bustling about fixing lunch for the large group, engaged in quiet conversation. The soft swish of long gauzy skirts moving the warming air was soothing until I felt the presence of an unseen observer.

I scanned the large kitchen for anything or anyone that shouldn't have been there and realized my senses were still jittery with the expectation of discovery. I returned to the front room where we still had the fire well stoked and merrily jumping about behind the screen. Again I used my senses to probe the area, to no avail. I decided I needed to get mom for a quick recon inside the house.

She wasn't in her room, but I heard her voice coming from just outside the open front door as I passed it. I found her smiling up at what could have been the Native American poster boy for handsome, rugged, and noble and by some strange coincidence he wore the uniform of the Tribal Police.

I walked up to the two of them, deep in an animated conversation. Mom seemed unaware of my approach, but had the uncanny skill of knowing I was near before turning to me and saying, "Cathleen dear, this is Thomas Little Bear of the Ute Tribal Police."

I had noted the insignia on his uniform and greeted him. "Nice to meet you, Captain. You must have good hearing. We were just saying we needed to contact your office."

He had removed his hat while speaking with my mom, holding the baseball style cap with its tribal insignia. When he cocked his head a bit to look into my face, his hair shone a deep black in the new sun of the day, with just a hint of grey around the temples. He wore it in military fashion, giving him an even more authoritative look. His eyes were a rich dark brown under a pair of thick black brows and the intensity of their scrutiny would certainly give anyone with criminal intent a moment's hesitation. The deep creases on his dark face added to a ruggedness found in people who lived in challenging environments and were like marks of honor for their survival.

He was very tall, perhaps as tall as Jason, and built like a boxer, a well-tailored tan uniform showing off his heavily muscled arms and legs. Personally, I preferred Jason's strong, lanky build to the Captain's, but he was certainly impressive.

I remembered from earlier reading on the area that in historic times there were about 11 different bands of Ute in Utah, but they often intermarried and had good relations within the clans. If they were all this good looking, it was easy to understand the inter-marriages!

"I guess I could tell you I was in the neighborhood, but I've already told, Brighid (he gave her a rather admiring look. H*m.)* that the medicine man of our tribe had spoken to me of the Wiccans a few weeks ago, and last night he came to me and was very disturbed." My mother picked up his story from there.

"Thomas (*Thomas? Hm.*) told me their holy man saw evil surrounding this house and coming from the smoke in our fireplace. I was just going to explain our situation. Perhaps you'd be so good as to do so, pet."

"Why certainly, but the girls have been preparing lunch so perhaps the Captain would like to join us." I knew there was no way he'd want to be with a bunch of witches so when he gracefully declined, claiming pressing police business, I was ready with my counter offer.

"How about meeting here at three this afternoon, Captain? Then we can give you a complete run down of the affairs here. I also think it would be a good idea to invite your Shaman as he may be able to aid us in a cleansing ceremony we're planning before dark."

He seemed pleased with the invitation and said that would give him an hour and a half to round up their Medicine Man and bring him back with him. He was sure their Shaman, as he referred to their holy man, would welcome an opportunity to visit the compound.

We said goodbye and he started walking back toward the distant driveway that led into the compound. I wondered aloud if he walked all the way here from the main roadway. "Of course not, dear. He merely parked his vehicle and circled around until he could come onto the grounds as if he'd walked in. Very crafty of him. He was doing his own reconnoitering, I expect." She was still smiling brightly as if having been spied on by the local law enforcer hadn't fazed her in the least. And he was awfully good looking. *Hm.*

When we got back inside the girls had everything ready for us to eat a late lunch. Since we would be evacuating the building and grounds around four, it was just as well that we ate while we still had an opportunity. Mom led the way into the kitchen with me in tow. Smelling the fragrance of fresh brewed coffee, I realized that this homey feeling would pass all too quickly.

As we all gathered around the buffet style spread to fill our plates, mom asked if the girls had finished packing. Some were still in the process, but nearly done. "I think," she said to them, "that we should all bring our suitcases and bags into the front room and from there walk together to our vehicles to pack up. That way, we can give one another a bit of help to stay organized." Mumbling their general agreement through mouthfuls of buttery turkey croissant sandwiches, they ate this last meal like hungry convicts, waiting for some alarm to ring before returning to cells.

The luncheon finished, all food stuffs were packed into a large cooler to be given to the Captain upon his return for the local food pantry. We headed back to our rooms. Twenty minutes later we were gathered in the front room, bags and belongings in hand. Like a mother goose, we all followed mom as she carried her own small suitcase and led the way to the parking area adjacent to the house. It took another twenty minutes to get everything stored in individual cars. Mom's Corvette had been explained earlier as her speedy transport. With only a few looks of surprise, no one questioned its sudden appearance. Joanie just chuckled like a fellow conspirator.

We were standing in loose groups when we saw the dust of what turned out to be an old Jeep Wrangler. A minute later, Captain Little Bear came to a stop next to the newly exposed sports car. He was giving it a closer scrutiny while he walked around to open the door for his elderly passenger. He spotted mom and after a quick nod and smile he reached into the Jeep and offered his strong arm.

The Shaman was stooped over and very frail in appearance. He looked to be into his advanced nineties, with a wizened face darkened from many years in the sun and winds that swept across the red wasteland of his reservation.

He leaned upon a knotty wood cane that immediately brought to mind dad's own Shillelagh, handed down to him through the generations of O'Brien men. Guess they feared a woman might use the famous cudgel on one of them so it was safer not to provide the opportunity. Ironically, he had it with him on the boat when it went down. He called it his tomorrow stick, saying when he held it he could sense what the next day would bring. A bit of Magic that likely warned him he didn't have many tomorrows left. Mom said, "He was probably holding the darn thing instead of paddling!"

The old Shaman wore a beautifully beaded vest over a faded yellow denim shirt. It looked freshly pressed. Its long sleeves practically covered his spotted, boney hands. I could almost see through the prominent veins carrying his ancient blood through his fragile body.

His pants had been washed so often they lacked any discernible color and hung around his narrow hips with a length of braided leather; probably cut to his small size. I noticed he was wearing a pair of old moccasin slippers on bare feet as he climbed down from the police car with the help of the Captain and the gnarled wooden cane.

I thought the lovely vest was likely a sign of his high place within the tribe's hierarchy; a place he most likely held for many years. I felt immediately drawn to him as he gave me a warm smile on catching my eye as I studied him. When he nodded to me like an old friend, I felt the tiny chill I always experienced when first meeting another Magic user. I felt my mother quiver as the same response must have alerted her senses.

Mom only had eyes for the handsome Thomas Little Bear after she had looked over his Shaman. He almost looked as if he'd grown bigger and taller since we saw him less than two hours ago. He was still very friendly and charming my jeans off mom, as she beamed up at him like they were just crowned King and Queen of the Prom.

The lawman presented his Shaman to the assembled women as Jonathan Sky Hunter. Up close he appeared even more brittle as a wind had come up and he seemed to be struggling to stand in place. He was looking down like he was concentrating on keeping his footing when I addressed him. "You are most welcome here among us, revered one," I said solemnly, just as my mother had instructed me. I then turned my attention back to the Captain.

"We have just packed our things, Captain," I said, bringing Little Bear's attention back to me from my mom's annoyingly coy glances. *I just have to get her back to Ireland,* I was thinking as I raised my voice a bit over the sound of the racing wind. "The house is now empty of our belongings and we were getting ready for the purification ceremony."

With that my mom turned to the Holy Man and said, "On behalf of the Wiccans you are most welcome, Jonathan Sky Hunter," with all the respect and deference she'd have given any Royalty.

He looked up at her even though she is short like me, but forced to do so by his stooped posture. With a content look on his weathered face he said, "My eyes are happy to behold you, child of the *Mother.* I have been told of your coming in my quiet dreams and have seen you are a favorite of the *Great Mother.*"

"I am honored that the *Mother* has chosen me to help in *Her* work here," mom replied.

We all stood quietly impressed and in awe of the deep respect these two people afforded one another. In fact, I felt like that third thumb and wished I could quietly slip off so I wouldn't intrude on this meeting of Magical spirits. I needn't have been concerned as mom turned quickly to me and taking my hand in hers introduced me as if this was entirely my show.

The Shaman turned his full gaze on me. That's when I realized his eyes were nearly white with encroaching cataracts. *They are nearly the same color as my creamy coffee,* I thought in a bizarre observation even for me.

He was probably close to being completely blind, but there were no signs of being handicap as he radiated strength and independence. I had the distinct feeling his milky eyes were not needed as he looked around himself at the gathering of Wiccans, nodding his head, as if affirming each face looking back at him.

Little Bear stood respectfully to the side so as not to disturb this slow surveillance by his Holy Man. It was easy to see the pride he took in their relationship as he looked on, his thumbs tucked behind his gun belt and a small smile on his face.

My mother broke the spell of this silent introduction to the Wiccans saying, "Venerable one, will you sit with us at the table we have placed in the shade of this house, so we can tell the story of what has befallen these young women in the past days? You would do us great honor with your presence."

He turned, facing my mother and said clearly, "I will open my eyes and ears to see and hear what you share." With that invitational ceremony completed, we all moved around to the side of a somewhat somber looking structure to where the worn oak table from the kitchen sat in the last shadow cast by the doomed adobe house.

This coven was to become a memory, perhaps a bad dream for these girls, haunting their lives, but I was hoping the coming ceremony would release some of their fears and anxieties into the night; mixed with the ashes of what had been their sacred gathering place.

Chapter 41

The girls had taken the four kitchen chairs and placed them around the table and spread several of the blankets from their beds on the hard ground. After everyone was settled it looked like a church picnic was taking place, but felt more like the luncheon after the funeral.

The members left in this coven all knew the drastic measures we had proposed and all were sadden by the finality of our plans for the compound and for them. They understood that there was no viable way this coven could move forward; the darkness had just penetrated too deeply into their center.

My mother sat on the Shaman's right side and I indicated that Captain Little Bear should take the chair at his left as I thought he might be more comfortable taking that protective seat near his Shaman. He moved his chair slightly to the back of the table and indicated his thanks to me with a nod and dazzling smile. *Wow! No wonder mom is infatuated* I thought as I quickly refocused my attention. I stood slightly to mom's right and waited for the story to unfold.

My mother and the Shaman looked every bit like sitting judges from the Inquisition on a witch hunt. And here, sprawled out in front of them were eleven of them. In a sense they were deciding the best and final solution to purify all that was touched by the Black Magic and dangerous dreaming that nearly destroyed these young women and did destroy their friend, Rain and leader.

As his nearly colorless eyes scanned the attentive faces of those sitting in front of him, the Shaman spoke in a surprisingly strong voice. "I have seen much evil and darkness coming from this place as I lay dreaming in my wikiup these many days past. And as I walked with my spirit brothers under the woven blanket of stars in the great stillness of night, there, we felt the evil again; only now, it lived in one of the red giants that stand on this land, messengers from the *Great Mother*." Every eye was riveted to the old man as he continued.

"My dreams have been full of this same darkness and the evil that dwells within the dream mist. The smoke of your fires has been lifted by my brother spirits and sent to me so that I might know the source of this evil that would destroy the spirit of the *Great Mother* upon the land. I have said many prayers and chanted and sung many songs to prepare for this day. I have brought strong medicine to cleanse this earth where evil has walked. I am ready."

After the Shaman finished, I realized there was no need for further explanations of the events of the past weeks; he already had seen it all.

Captain Little Bear stood up and gave his hand to the Medicine Man to help him rise stiffly but solidly to his feet. We all stood when he did as if we had rehearsed this scene from some dark play. My mother turned to the Holy Man and spoke in soft whispers close to his ear. He nodded and said, "As you will daughter." Mom turned back to the expectant faces of the group and motioned them to follow and to me, she put out her hand. We walked hand in hand back to the front of the house.

The Shaman using only his twisted cane for support began to chant while holding his free, knobby hand toward the front door. From somewhere unseen by us, he had produced a long bone carved with mystical symbols and held it out as if he's throw it at the darkened house.

We stood several paces apart when Mom began a quiet chant of her own. I recognized her summons of *Green Fire* to her hands. She nodded to me and I did the same until we both stood with the cold green flames dancing from our finger tips. The quiet that had descended upon the group was so profound I felt like we had slipped into a pocket of space only we occupied.

At a look from the now silent Holy Man, my mother and I both moved forward as he retreated as quickly as he could, this time accepting the strong arm of the Captain.

The *Green Fire* became like a living thing, shooting from my hands and finger like taffy drawn through a pulling machine; it lengthened and widened until it finally touched the low adobe walls. I glanced quickly at my mother standing several feet away from me now and saw her flames licking furiously at the weathered face of the old structure.

There was a sudden whooshing sound as the whole building became engulfed in the hungry green inferno. If Little Bear had any fears of witches they would be confirmed at the sight of our destructive powers. The adobe house seemed to shudder into an unresolved terror and within a few minutes it collapsed inward as the fire continued to burn downward into the very ground the house had stood upon. It was all over in less than four minutes; the house and the ground under it were reduced to grayish black ash.

I closed my eyes and began a different chant and cast a spell of healing, invoking the *Green Mother* to bring new life to this wound upon her face. I was vaguely aware that my mother was doing the same spell. We sounded like chanting monks in the gathering dusk as the sun was doing its own Magic, sinking behind the tall red Buttes of the Valley of the Gods.

It was only after my mother came to my side and put her arm around my shoulders that I became aware of the sobbing behind us.

The once nature loving and spiritual Wiccans had become a tight cluster of weeping and sniffling girls. The finality of our actions hit home and hit hard.

The Shaman retook his seat by the table as the effort seemed draining to his feeble body. The Captain stood close behind his chair watching us all. He had an unreadable look on his handsome face and I couldn't tell if he was in awe, or too stunned to register a reaction, but it seemed likely he had witnessed his Shaman's own magic and ours would not be too shattering to his comfort zone.

The smoke drifted upward to a sky growing darker and closing itself off with heavy cloud cover. *What's next* I thought as my mind was pulled along with the rising gray blotch as it hung over the burnt remains. *What's next for this broken coven?*

Mom steered me over to the tight knot of sobbing, nose blowing girls and using her calming voice told them to pick up the blankets and place them on the table. They immediately did as asked and then stood like soldiers awaiting their next order. "Girls," my mother said still using that quieting tone, "you all need to journey back to your own homes soon, but first we must complete this purification ceremony to return harmony and order to this sacred land."

"What can we do, Brighid?" It was Maud whose voice sounded composed in spite of the tears she wiped with the back of her hand.

"Well friends, I believe you need to have one last circle as a coven to help relieve the pain inflicted upon your group," Mom answered.

After exchanging many desperate looks within the group they all moved off following Maud and joined hands in a tight circle of eleven young women. This time, no one stood in the center of this last circle as a coven. Standing erect in the last blossom of light, their hair and skirts rippling in a fragrant desert wind, their chanting was both beautiful and haunting. The Shaman had risen to his feet as if to acknowledge the power and holiness of this prayer of healing. My mother and I moved off to one side of the newly formed ash pit, to plan our final restoration of the polluted land.

We needed to reduce the shed and its contents to ash as well, so we walked over to that dilapidated structure next. Mom said, "You take care of this task, pet, and I'll make the rounds of the perimeter." Nodding to her, I turned my attention back to the leaning pile of gray wood and shingles dappled in the last of hint of light. Before I began my disposal chore I glanced in the direction mom had taken and saw the handsome Captain moving toward her like a dark panther on the hunt. *Hm,* I thought with a smirk.

It took less than a minute to bring the shed to a state of smoldering ash and even less to open the ground and ask *Mother* to reclaim it as Hers. With that done I hurried after my mom more out of curiosity than out of an urge to help her out. I trailed behind the two figures that seemed to be enjoying the slow tour around the immediate compound grounds, but I knew mom was casting her inner eye for anything left of the Dark.

I followed at a polite distance until my mother called out to me "Cathleen, the Captain and I will start making a wider circle around the compound. Would you be a lamb and finish up this perimeter for me dear?"

Hm. "Lamb and dear in the same sentence, I thought, smothering a chuckle. At least my mother still had romance in her heart. My dad wasn't really what you could call a romantic type. He once gave her a box of frozen chocolates for her birthday. She nearly melted him and them on the spot!

I waived back my compliance with her request and moved quickly to where they had been circling so as not to lose the thread of coverage. I scanned the grounds with my inner eye carefully, seeing nothing out of the ordinary and was nearing completion as I approached the group of Wiccans.

They had all retrieved the blankets and were sitting quietly close to one another like school kids on an outing. I wondered if it was still ok for girls to hold hands like we did when we were in first and second grades. Sometimes I feel sad at the sweet openness that is lost with the coming of age.

As I moved over to the group, Maude made a point to scrunch over a tad so I could sit beside her. "Cathleen," she said in a soft voice though all present could certainly hear, "We all wanted to thank you and your mom for doing what we weren't prepared to do."

"You mean destroy your coven and your compound?" I asked with a tinge of sarcasm in my voice. I couldn't help feeling guilty about pushing this drastic change down their throats, but truth often precludes alternatives to actions.

Maude looked steadily at me and answered, "Yes. We have all suffered because of the corruption that invaded our coven like a virus we couldn't fight. You and your mom have saved us from the Dark Magic of Ursa and Wynn, but we still mourn their loss." She said this last while looking down at the ground, and I saw a tear rolling down her tanned face.

"Maude," I said, "I think you and the girls should all start heading back to your homes and put this all behind you so you can heal, just like these sacred grounds."

Standing up, I looked around me at the upturned faces and knew that they must have felt leaderless and disoriented. "You should all begin your trips back home now, girls. It's no good waiting until my mother gets back here. She'll be awhile with her cleansing ceremony. You can get rooms at the local motel in town and make whatever reservation changes you need until then for your trips back home."

Jemma called out, "I want to stay at that Youth Hostile near Monument Valley. Anyone interested?" A few of the girls raised their hands.

"I'll drive us," said Luna, who had decided to join Jemma's group.

"What about going into Colorado for a while, until our scheduled times to fly back... then we won't have to change reservations." That was Joanie speaking up and she had two takers on that proposition, girls without cars of their own, who had likely come with Wynn originally.

Some renewed enthusiasm and excitement was taking hold of the group. They could part under happier conditions. Their goodbyes would be easier on their terms and not dictated by the sad circumstances of the last few weeks.

I wandered off into the background, leaving the more animated girls to sort out driving and destination arrangements. I had nearly forgotten about the Shaman sitting like a garden gnome on the kitchen chair watching the group as if viewing a live play production.

When I approached I saw he had one hand gripping his knotted walking stick while the other held a beautiful feather by its spine. It was a minute before he acknowledged my presence, but when he did the smile that creased his already deeply creased face, somehow seemed warmest within his clouded black eyes. He gestured for me to sit in the empty chair to his left.

"You are wise beyond your short years, daughter, like your mother was before you I expect." He chuckled and it sounded like the burble of a clean flowing brook. He said, "Give me your hand daughter," and when I extended my right hand to him he unerringly placed the feather onto my palm. I took it up by the quill, not wanting to lose it to the restless winds.

Under the soft glow of the new moon I believed I was holding a feather from a hawk. We had seen many of them coasting along the temperate air currents, or diving to pick up a slower moving rodent or reptile off the desert floor. It was many shades of brown and yet its coloring was cohesive and deliberate as only nature can dictate, perfect camouflage for an arid environment. It was soft as I gently brushed it across my palm and for some primal reason I just had to smell it. I held it close to my nose and sniffed. It was resonant with the odors of sand, hot earth, basalt rocks, and strangely, its own death. It had come from a bird that was vanquished by some enemy, or fell to the waiting earth like a meteorite in the throes of a natural demise.

When I looked up again the old Indian was studying my face closely. He said, "You will have many challenges, daughter, in the years ahead of you as you walk with the *Great Mother*, but you possess a deep and true well, where Magic flows and is renewed by *Her*. And when the sun does not rise hot and round in the skies above your home and the moon turns her back upon your face, have no fear. The *Great Mother* holds your feet close and warm near her beating heart."

He rose effortlessly like the strong warrior I felt him to be. Just as he did, my mother and Little Bear came into sight as they passed the scattering ashes of the old shack and came toward us, holding a quiet and seemingly private conversation.

Little Bear spoke first. "Revered Father, are you ready to leave this place for your bed?"

It was getting close to ten o'clock and full dark. All the girls had left for their scattered destinations, except Joanie's car full. She was waiting to say goodbye to me and my mom saying, "I don't know when I'll get to see you again this year Cathleen, unless you get to Pittsburgh this fall for Thanksgiving with my family. You know Jason would be more than welcome too."

I knew these past few days had been pretty harrowing for my sensitive friend and wanted to reassure her that normalcy prevailed once more.

"Joanie," I said, holding her hands, "I'll check my schedule when I get back to Iron Mountain and see about taking a more relaxing vacation around spring. I have a letter waiting for me from San Francisco, according to Jason, and I'm wondering if it's an invitation for some detective work. At least that's what I'm hoping for. If it turns out to be something like that, maybe I can convince you to take a trip with me out there."

It was something of a mystery, but I had received several requests from far flung locals over the past few years, wanting to engage my unique detective skills. I relished any opportunity to solve a conundrum and using my Magic kept me on top of my skills. As a sworn *Protector of the Green Guild* these assignments were a natural part of my duty as I saw it.

We had moved off to have this private conversation. I have always been careful about keeping my life pretty much under the radar. Growing up in a household with two highly trained Wizards tends to put a damper on having many close friends. Joanie was the only exception to my rules about letting others inside my world of spells, wards, Demons and Faeries. I always treasured our close friendship; even with the few years difference in our ages, Joanie was still very young or I was overly grown-up, probably a little of both.

When Joanie left the area to go to nursing school I was just getting out of high school. Her leaving probably encouraged me to take the scholarships I was awarded and helped me earn my Degree in Communications. We've always encouraged one another to bigger and better things in life. That was our motto. I was never quite clear on what constituted bigger and better, but I was very content in my life so that seemed like success to me.

Right now I could see tears forming in my friend's eyes as she broke off her hug and said "Let's make plans for sure, sweetie, and San Francisco sounds great! All I need is a few weeks' notice so I can arrange being off."

I wiped a tear that had slid down her freckled check and said, "I'll call as soon as I have any plans, Joanie. Let's do our face time so we don't forget what we look like until we can share some fun time together."

After one last hug she went back to her old El Camino, squeezing the girls into its narrow front seat. I was glad I listened to a hunch and had not loaded my bags in her car. I watched as Joanie and her soon-to-be-ex-Wiccan sisters left in a cloud of red dust that sparkled like crystallized blood in the moon light.

Chapter 42

It dawned on me as I watched Joanie's tail lights disappearing in the distance, that I now had no ride back to the airport in Durango. My own flight wasn't due to leave until late the next day. I had planned to sleep in late at a motel near the airport and then just hang out until a couple of hours prior to take off at ten that evening. I heard my name being called and turned to see my mother and the Captain approaching.

"Cathleen," she said, "I think I need your help, dear, and I think you might be in need of mine."

"Actually, I just realized I have no way back to the airport, mom. Guess you figured that out, huh?"

She said, "I think that Captain Little Bear and I have found a solution pet. You will drive the Corvette back to the car rental agency and then take their shuttle to the airport to catch your flight." I stood there trying to decide what was wrong with this plan when it occurred to me.

"But mom, how will you get yourself back to the airport? Don't you think we should go together?"

"Why, Thomas is going to drive me to Durango, dear, as he has business in the area with the local constabulary so it won't be any trouble to him. " She looked up at the hulking Captain and I could swear he looked like he'd been placed under a spell. But she was still a beautiful woman and I didn't suppose she'd need to resort to those sorts of shenanigans.

"Well, is it going to cause any problems that you aren't returning the car yourself?" I asked timidly, knowing she'd probably already made the arrangements for the switch in drop-off drivers.

"It will be fine, dear, but I think we need to get ourselves out of here now. I will go back to the station with the Captain and Jonathon Sky Hunter and make changes to my ticket as needed. So, let's get your things packed into the car and you can follow us out of here until we reach the highway that goes to your airport and the Rental Agency."

I had placed my suitcase and tote bag near the kitchen table that now looked more aged and forlorn under the creamy yellow caress of a full moon. It seemed so odd that we had all gathered around the table in a kitchen that no longer existed, in the stumpy adobe house that had provided a spiritual refuge and comfort to so many girls. Now it and they were gone, its ashes dispersed by the grasping winds. The girls had blown back into a world they understood better, but that didn't offer the shelter and warmth of their coven.

I grabbed my things, or at least tried to as the handsome Indian snatched the heavy suitcase from me and put it into the trunk. I kept my carry-on as my cell phone and other essentials needed to be close at hand for the long drive to Durango.

The car seemed so empty without Skip sitting behind the wheel with that look of contentment on his hairy face. I sniffed the air as I leaned into the front seat to place my canvas bag on the passenger seat. No odor of a *Trogladyte* driver, just the crisp smell of good leather.

When I straightened up my mother was there beside me. She looked very sad and happy at the same time; sad to see me go and happy to be staying a bit longer with her new friend. That was fine with me. I was ready to tear out of there and put Black Witches, Rotten Queens and assorted Demons in my rear view.

While I felt sorry that we had to shatter the Wiccan coven, I knew in my Mage's bones, it had too many tiny fractures not to collapse in the days and months to come if they had tried to remain a unit. It made it easier to know each girl wanted to continue their study of Wicca and eventually they might find the right coven to call their spiritual home.

Mom put her hands on either side of my face and brushing the ever present stray curl out of my eyes she gave me a kiss and a huge hug and whispered for my ears only, "You are my treasure, Cathleen. I am so proud of you and the way you honor the *Green Mother* with your Magic. Keep safe and I will see you soon. I love you, my darling girl."

With that she turned on her tiny feet and got into the police vehicle where the old Medicine man already sat in the back seat. As I got into the car I glanced over at the holy man and saw a peacefulness suffuse his dark face. It was good to know that kind of harmony could still be found in this place after all the chaos and darkness.

The Captain had gotten behind the wheel with my mom sitting beside him. He edged his car into a tight turn around and started down the long driveway that now led away from a blackened ground where once a house squatted beneath the pure light of an unforgiving moon. Now, only the solitary oak table and kitchen chairs sat abandoned under that light. Little Bear said they would be broken down into fire wood and burned when he returned from Durango so no trace of the coven would survive. He'd already stowed the cooler full of food items into his vehicle.

I watched for any sign of life near the blackened earth we left behind, and was startled when a sage brush was swept along near the spot once occupied by the old shed. It was as if the *Green*

Mother was tidying up a bit after less-than thoughtful company departed.

With that thought I turned my eyes ahead like my dear old dad would have advised me. "Don't look back, lass, unless you intend to wave."

The black earth had no witness now as I drove into a peaceful night, driving slowly over the long driveway toward the lonesome highway.

Chapter 43

I turned onto the highway ramp leading onto the exit for Durango and began my long trip back toward the airport and home. I had one last wave from my mother and winking of headlights to say goodbye from the Captain, then the powerful Corvette engine launched me onto the empty, dark road.

I had noticed on the drive here with Joanie and Jemma, a lifetime ago, how deserted this major interstate seemed. We had driven for hours and passed maybe a handful of cars on the way here and now it seemed totally devoid of any other vehicles.

I spied an occasional roadside honky-tonk, its back to the dessert. Busted up old trucks and off-road vehicles were scattered about like so many patiently grazing horses. Off in the distance, small ranches and homesteads spotted the darkened horizon and seemed to blink off and on like fireflies on a summer night.

I thought I could almost catch a few twangs of some muted country song butting up against the heavy desert air, but even with that spindly light drifting onto the blacktopped road, an unrelenting darkness ruled the night.

The radio offered some possible relief from the monotony of the highway, but it seemed I was too far away from any station for their transmitters to reach out to me in my lonely car. It was easy to see how my mother nearly got a speeding ticket in the gorgeous red beast. I was driving close to 100mph and only realized it when I noticed the highway signs were just a blur as I passed them with no hope of deciphering their messages. *Geez* I thought *time to slow this baby down before I blow by a cop!* It was really a shame as I was thrilled with the speed, but it still didn't compare to the *Wind and Aura* spell.

I wondered when I'd get to do real Magic again after I returned to Iron Mountain. My radio station hardly needed me, let alone *Magic!* Actually as I thought about it, that was a good thing. My staff was more than up to the task of running our small station, but I went in every day anyway out of a need to keep my hand in the game. And the donuts were good too.

Reminiscing about the three years I'd spent living and working in the mystical and solemn beauty of Iron Mountain, brought thoughts of a certain man to mind. Jason Tate, the youngest man ever elected Sheriff in any of the six counties in the area was that man. Well over six-feet-four with a mysterious, rugged handsomeness that only a man wearing a patch over one eye can carry off; Jason was my boyfriend and comrade in arms. When it came to fighting Demons and occasional Dark Ones that occasionally roam in the most beautiful and unlikely places, Jason never let his fear block his natural courage or call to action. And more importantly, he viewed my training as a Celtic Mage to be an asset that was to be valued and utilized to protect life.

Jason got me. That made him one in a million. Outside of his physical attributes, his intellect was sharp and inquisitive and his loyalty, unquestionable.

I sighed, wondering why we couldn't seem to get past the dating phase of our relationship and move onto the total commitment stage. I knew he wasn't a diehard bachelor as we actually discussed a future together, but still, no engagement ring.

Sometimes I can be impetuous. Not often as I'm a control freak and don't like to jump before I study something carefully. But I took a chance and pulling to the side of the road I got out my cell phone and called Jason's number at his office.

He usually took the night shift because his deputy had a young family and Jason believed his place was with them after dark. Guess he learned from me just what could be lurking in the night.

He picked up after the second ring and I heard his deep voice, tinged with professional concern for whoever was calling at this late hour. It was about three o'clock there and the whole town closed its doors when the street lights went on. "Hello, Jason? It's me, Cathleen."

"Of course it is," he said, "I'd know your voice if you were talking under water, Cathleen." We both laughed and I had a picture of him sitting there, his long legs comfortably crossed on top of his much scarred desk. His boots were the mountain hiking kind so that piece of furniture bore some hard usage on long winter nights.

I knew he'd have a book in his hands as he was an avid reader and always surprised me with the variety of interests he had from Twain to Asimov and anything by Robert Parker.

"What are you reading?" I asked.

"You know me pretty well, but then you're my "Magic girl" he said. I thought with a smile, how I liked his nick name for me

"I'm reading a book of poetry by Wendell Berry and finding myself very happy to be living this simple life here in the mountains."

"And what makes it so simple, Jason" I asked.

"No big corporations to deal with, no environmental challenges except the natural weather and well…I guess I feel pretty blessed by Mother Nature."

"Wow," I said, "You are quite the poet yourself, Sheriff. How are things there at home?"

"Without giving you too big a head, pretty boring and lonely without you" He gave a laugh and continued in his deep voice "Seriously Cathleen, when are you coming home to me.

I was smiling like the "Cheshire Cat," just thinking of my answer, "I'll be home late tomorrow. I'm on my way to an airport motel now." I remembered I faced another three hour drive back to Iron Mountain from Pittsburgh. "Why don't you get Ollie and just wait at my place?"

He said that plan would work for him too and to call when I landed in Pittsburgh International so he could gauge my arrival time. He'd have a warm fire going in my fireplace he said and I had a visual in my head of sitting close to him wrapped in his strong arms.

I was stumbling around, trying to tell him that I was anxious to see him and just hangout like we enjoyed doing. I never missed the fancy restaurants or night clubs I used to frequent with other guys. That all seemed pretty lame to me when I looked back at my life before Jason came into it.

Jason and I loved hiking together and sitting in my cozy loft where I stashed my TV, wrapped in an old quilt, watching crazy zombie movies (nothing compared to the real thing) or playing Scrabble on long snowy Sundays in my bright yellow kitchen over mugs of hot chocolate. Sometimes I ride along with him when he makes his rounds of the town. We never run out of conversation and if we're quiet, it's a shared oasis of silence where I feel comfortable and happy.

We said our goodbyes with some reluctance on both sides to be the first to hang up. After a few false starts I finally said, "I'd better get back on the road, Jason. You stay safe and I'll see you tomorrow." He was quiet for a moment and I thought I'd lost the connection. "Jason? Are you there?"

"I'll always be here for you Cathleen. I will be waiting for you, Magic Lady."

I pushed the off button on my phone and held it close to my heart as if I could impress his last words there forever.

"Gee, I think we've made some progress!" I said out loud, with a huge sigh of contentment.

As I pulled back onto the empty road I began to reflect back to a conversation my dad had with me when I was about thirteen. I was toying with the idea of having a serious crush on a boy at school and had asked him what I should know about *real love.*

He never hesitated when he smiled and replied, *"Well lass, Love is scary and powerful and wonderful...just like Magic!"*

About the Author

Francesca, pictured above with Ollie who more times than not sneaks his way into her stories, is part of a large Italian family where she discovered early on, that a love of reading was as much a part of her DNA as her mother's skill at baking. Growing up in a house filled with laughter, screaming, banging pots, fighting and loving family bonds, shaped her life and heart.

Having moved from the east coast where she was raised between New York and New Jersey, Francesca left for the mid-west where she spent several years outside the Chicago area raising a family of three children, completing her college degrees and writing introspective poetry like other young mothers.

Francesca has worked in local television, a small city zoo, founded a non-profit tutoring agency for an inner-city neighborhood which eventually served local school districts, worked for an International

Evangelical Television and Radio Station and for a non-profit organization serving challenged adults.

Francesca Quarto resides in a small town outside of Indianapolis, Indiana with her husband Patrick. She still has a great love of the written word and while she enjoys her E-Reader immensely, she still treasures the excitement of turning the next page.

Tell-Tale Publishing would like to thank you for your purchase. If you would like to read more by Francesca or another fine TT author, please visit our website:

www.tell-talepublishing.com